THE HONEY
LOCUST

Book Lovers Ball V   Feb 11 /10

John ~ great to meet you.
Glad to know you salvage friends
when you get dumped ☺

THE HONEY LOCUST

(And I wish you better luck next time)

A Novel

JEFFREY ROUND

Cormorant Books

Canada Council   Conseil des Arts
for the Arts   du Canada

The publisher gratefully acknowledges the support of the Canada Council for the Arts and
the Ontario Arts Council for its publishing program. We acknowledge the
financial support of the Government of Canada through the Book Publishing
Industry Development Program (BPIDP) for our publishing activities.

Printed and bound in Canada

Library and Archives Canada Cataloguing in Publication

Round, Jeffrey
The honey locust / Jeffrey Round.

ISBN 978-1-897151-38-9

1. Yugoslav War, 1991–1995 — Bosnia and
Hercegovina — Fiction. 1. Title.

PS8635.O8625H65 2009   C813'.54   C2009-903864-1

Cover image and design: Angel Guerra/Archetype
Text design: Tannice Goddard/Soul Oasis Networking
Printer: Friesens

CORMORANT BOOKS INC.
215 SPADINA AVENUE, STUDIO 230, TORONTO, ON CANADA M5T 2C7
www.cormorantbooks.com

Mixed Sources
Cert no. SW-COC-001271
© 1996 FSC
FSC

To my family, who have endured and loved me,
and for my friends, who are a part of me.

I have had doubts for a long time about even trying to speak about this war to people who haven't lived it themselves. And not because it would be impossible to describe it, but because any war in which we are not involved is always pushed to the margins for our private everyday "wars" which, although they may not be bloody, are nevertheless laborious struggles ...

— ELMA SOFTIĆ, *Sarajevo Days, Sarajevo Nights*
TRANSLATED BY NADA CONIĆ

CONTENTS

PROLOGUE

THE FORMER YUGOSLAVIA, JUNE 1995.

She blows out her candle and peers through the broken slats down to where the street unfurls in beaded rolls of cobblestone. Empty. She's waited long enough. She shoulders a knapsack that holds a few essentials — an extra sweater, three tins of kasha. Her Leica nestles at the bottom, near the rolls of film hidden inside socks. She checks her watch and heads downstairs.

A wedge opens in the blackness of the doorway. She slips out and darkness eclipses her solitary figure. Feet carry her softly across the broken earth and concrete uprooted by recent shelling. The road is pitted like the moon. In the morning the women sweep what they can, leaving the larger pieces for the men to remove. By afternoon, it's business as usual — or at least as much as it can be in this hell. Every evening, the dark slips down again and the constellation of lights wink out before they can be targeted. It begins all over as bombs light up and pierce the sky. It's impossible to imagine life amid the ruins, but it's here.

FOR WEEKS, SHE'D RESIGNED HERSELF to the waiting. Finally the messenger arrived, a black-shawled crone tapping her cane through the destruction. She'd offered to read tea leaves for a small sum, but stopped at only one door. Who wanted her fortune read in times like these?

They ushered the old woman in, past the brace of sandbags piled before the window. The visitor smiled, set her stick aside, and sat. The sitting room was comfortable: family portraits, knitted armchair covers, and lace curtains kept up a pleasant appearance, despite the boarded-over windows. The important work was done downstairs, hidden from casual view, though not surprisingly, word had got out: help was available to anyone seeking it.

The visitor nodded at the two women. Jasna set a teapot on the table. The old woman had known Jasna before the war. She was one of the God-given few who'd stayed behind when she could have left. So many doctors were gone and the hospitals had become difficult to reach. The other — the North American — she'd seen once or twice in the town square disguised as a villager. The North American arrived as a patient, but quickly became Jasna's helper in the *apoteka* — one of the war's many illegal pharmacies.

Tea was poured. They drank and turned over the cups on their saucers, as the old woman instructed. It was like a game, except lives depended on it. They waited as she peered into the cup. Her dark eyes looked up at the North American briefly before splintering away like mercury. She spoke quietly: *Listen carefully, but write nothing down. You will take a trip to the coast. From there, a ferry will take you to Italy. I will tell you precisely where and when. You must be prepared to leave in two days*. Cities and towns were mentioned, a contact name passed along. The Oracle dreamed her map among the leaves scattered on the cup bottom and stuck to its sides. Done, she pushed the porcelain back into anxious hands.

A palm curled around the head of her walking stick. She reached for the North American's hand. *One other thing — your ring finger is too long.* She showed them, splaying the fingers and holding the hand beside her own for comparison. *You see? You are too independent. You will never be happy with any man who tries to hold you.* She shook her head. A timid smile. *I really am a tea reader, you see.*

The stick drew up. Coins exchanged hands. A brief smile concluded this matter of freedom, and she was gone.

IT WAS ALL TO HAVE run smoothly from there — rivers forded, landscapes crossed, history poured over blank pages. But the dark streets are a no man's land now, shapes shifting to become potential rapists, snipers looking for target practice. The scavengers and looters have retired for the night, but armed thugs and drunken soldiers can spell trouble for a woman on these streets. Anyone who spots her will know she's up to something, because she isn't in a safe place at 4 A.M. Where are the people who love her?

The alley opens onto a public square where she stopped for coffee once or twice. Tonight the cafés are deserted, the chairs upturned on tables. At the far end, a church casts a churlish eye over everything. The tea reader's careful phrases come to mind as she skirts the open space, watching for shadows that might turn into men, enemies of her body.

She steps onto the square, reciting her escape route, a giant game of hopscotch: from Bihać to Drvar, past Strmica, and down the coast to Šibenik, where the boat will be waiting. Stepping stones across a sea of fire.

She's halfway across the cobblestones when she hears the hiss of tires. She turns, looks quickly over her shoulder. Headlights twitch and scatter over a wall; the car lurches into view. Panic rushes in, lifting her heels. She's a blur against dark walls. The first shot goes wide and tears into a tree as she scrabbles over stone. The second shot is closer, the car right behind her. If she turns, she'll see their faces.

I'm a fucking journalist! A Canadian!

It comes out an angry cry as she trips and lands hard on her cheekbone. The fall knocks the breath from her lungs, fear from her mind. Through the knapsack, the camera digs into her breast beside the rolls of film with their lost worlds, the tail end to many stories. She's carried them with her all this way, like a dead foetus, these faces she never knew.

Another shot. Someone is firing wildly into the square.

She pushes herself up as the car closes in. At least let me face them, she thinks. Don't let them come from behind!

She listens for the whine of brakes, doors to open, hurried footsteps. She'll make them kill her before she gives up. The roar grows and then retreats with a trickle of drunken laughter. Tires slither across the square.

She looks up. Stars above. The firmament. Night.

BOOK I
PALAEOGRAPHY

ONE

CALGARY, AUGUST 1994.

The plane landed at the airport and she disembarked without incident. A cab brought her directly to the address on the letterhead. The building appeared empty; the only sound was her voice asking directions at the security desk. Afternoon light filled the halls, gilding the passageways as she navigated the corridors. She found her name on a list posted beside the door under the heading "Bosnia — Private Hearing." One more of these endless briefings and she would be there.

None of the six people seated inside looked up when she entered.

"Is this the Thomas Commission?" she asked.

Heads nodded.

"I'm Thomas," she said.

She sat as they scrutinized her across the table, a jury of peers who couldn't have been more unlike her. She endured their questions, gave them the answers she knew they wanted. The whole time she was conscious of being at odds with the verticality of the room — the maps and charts, floor-to-ceiling windows, the shelves lined with boxes of files and videotapes.

Her casual sprawl in the executive chair contradicted the room's top-to-bottom hierarchy.

The room had grown stuffy. Someone stood to open a window. The commission head reminded her that the experiences she faced in the coming months could be brutal beyond anything she had known.

"I can tell you've never fought with my mother," she said. It was her one attempt at levity.

She believed she'd already earned her Girl Guide badges during stints in Africa and Central America. There, she'd encountered villages where entire wars were waged over the theft of a single cow. Scores were settled with hand grenades lobbed into filled churches. The day she'd arrived in Namibia, a British journalist had been hacked to death. One moment he was recording the scene, and the next he'd become part of it. A machete swiped, oozed away red, swiped again. His body twitched its final moments in the dusty street as a fellow cameraman kept recording in the interests of — what? National security? The evening news? Or just lining his own pockets? It wasn't the first time she'd been disgusted by one of her own.

She had few worries about Bosnia.

At the end of the session, a single nod seemed to confer agreement. Around the room gazes met. Someone smiled. She thanked the commission and shook hands as they told her how pleased they were to be sending her over. She would be on her way in weeks.

"Good luck, Angela," they said, old friends seeing her off.

For months she'd studied maps and books, military reports and attaché briefings, absorbing the country's current political state, its intricate history. It was a region built upon continuous waves of migration, the silt of trade routes and wars. Exile was a constant theme. For more than seven hundred years, leaders had shepherded their people like Moses on the way to a Promised Land. Wars shifted boundaries and populations back and forth. Nationalities overlapped and borders were carved out, again and again, in the hands of politicians, until finally no one could say for sure who or what had been where. Up close or at a distance, things still looked the same. It was a land defined not by what it was or might become, but solely by what it had been: the *Former* Yugoslavia.

It was a world where things were constantly erased: people, buildings, and entire towns disappeared overnight. Newspapers advised Croats how to rid their speech of Serb expressions, the better to distinguish themselves from former friends and neighbours. *Cleanse.* The word was new, but the practice old.

All of this was native territory to Angela. The months of preparation would help her close in on what she was seeking — the aura of events, the minute seismic tremors as they transpired. She scrutinized her subjects, decoding clues and ferreting out hints to unravel their secrets. Tiny traces, shards of history fell away before her eyes as she watched for the glow that sparked the instant they vanished. In Scully Hall she'd spent hundreds of hours absorbing the science of her chosen medium. While other students caroused in Grad House, she'd memorized development processes and fixing solutions. She could recite the chemistry of light, the crystalline compounds dispersed and embedded in gelatine coating that captured moments in time. Later, under her hands in the dark, she released them. Eventually she came to understand photography not as a technical science, not an ornamental sidebar to someone's morning reading, but as prophecy with a backward glance.

Photography helped her to decipher the captured moment and to uncover what lay beneath it — the invisible worlds buried under the routes of history. She fell in love the first time she heard the word *palaeography* — the decoding of archaic writing and ancient manuscripts. Photographs were her ancient manuscripts. She began to think of them as doorways in time, as if she could enter their finished worlds and be with those people.

She learned to see beyond the surface of a photograph: to turn the corners in a room and slip past its walls, follow a woman home from the lake where she is vacationing, discover whom she will meet and marry, the children she will bear.

TWO

Her camera was a ten-year-old Leica. Simple, elegant, and easily the most beautiful camera she owned. She liked the heft of it in her palm as she cleaned the body or meticulously dusted the lenses before strapping them into their case. Other cameras might be bigger or have more features, but compared to this they felt awkward. Her partner would have the video equipment, but her Leica would be the heart and soul of any personal work she did.

During her first week in Sarajevo she appropriated a closet and organized it into a developing lab. She lined the cracks with tin foil to keep out light, built shelves where she could reach for and find anything in the dark. Dark of night, dark of history. She barely took time to meet the other journalists who congregated at the neighbourhood bars and cafés. There'd be time later for making acquaintances.

She quickly got used to the nightly shelling. The city had been under siege for more than two years. The surrounding mountains, once among its prized scenic elements, were now the problem. They housed the Serb-backed troops holding the city hostage. Yugoslavia had shown the world the glories of Sarajevo, hosting the Olympics in 1984. A decade later, it retracted those welcoming images and replaced them with footage of unrelenting violence, streets filled with the dead and dying. The city averaged more than three hundred missile hits a day. One hot July night, a record of more than three thousand rounds was recorded.

When the fighting began, hastily constructed humanitarian convoys left the city daily, but the retreat turned ugly, and children had been taken hostage. Those who stayed — the stubborn, poor, optimistic, or just unlucky — were stuck there until the siege would end, whenever that might be.

Angela's neighbourhood had once been a fashionable enclave of cafés, boutiques, and bookstores. Live guitar music was popular and people had roamed the streets at night. No one wandered at night anymore. Trips for water and food were hazardous because of random sniper fire. Some neighbourhoods paid for protection from the shells and bullets, one of many heinous ways the military made a profit. Angela's wasn't one of them.

Her daytimes were filled with excursions to danger zones, learning where the action was and digging out the story, while avoiding becoming a target. How close was too close? It was a question journalists often asked.

In the evenings she filed her stories and helped her partner, a man named Allan, as he pieced together the video footage. The documentaries were shipped out by cargo flights, eventually showing up on the evening news. The fascination for watching a nation disembowelling itself was a hunger that required constant feeding.

Angela dug in. Her work provided her a relief of sorts. It kept her from thinking of her own failures. A recent separation had spelled the end of her one attempt at domesticity. Marriage: the word sparked resentment more than anything that might reasonably be called joy or pleasure. As for family, that was a war of its own — or so she thought in her cynical moments. She kept in touch with two younger sisters through an occasional postcard or phone call. Contact with her mother required great effort and greater care. Sometimes a phone call sufficed, but the conversations became an exercise in what couldn't be said as much as what could. Keeping a healthy distance from her mother without being labelled "neglectful" had been her real aim since high school.

Angela's father had died at the end of the summer. She missed him more than anything — his warmth, his humour, his honesty. He was her rock. She'd never hidden anything from him. She was at a loss for how to conduct herself in his absence, having become an outsider whose life was a mystery to her family. Her separation had capped her mother's frustration with her personal life — a life that must have seemed reckless, inconsiderate, and constantly vexing for anyone concerned about her safety.

After the funeral, her mother asked Angela to reconsider her work arrangements and stay in Canada for a while. Uncharacteristically, she'd bared her soul to Angela. She wasn't sure how she would cope without her husband of thirty-plus years and the added worry of Angela's assignment weighed heavily on her, she said. Angela considered staying but, with the divorce looming, she simply wanted to get on with her life — as far away as possible. She couldn't afford to entertain her mother's fears.

A month later she found herself in Sarajevo, a city even more under siege than she'd felt herself to be prior to leaving.

During her second week in Sarajevo, Allan came down with acute appendicitis and was shipped back to Canada. He'd been a hard worker, co-operative if a trifle conservative in his approach to life during wartime. Angela wasn't sad to see him leave and was thrilled at the thought of being on her own. It didn't last.

Allan's replacement was another story altogether. She watched him enter the compound and glance around, letting his pack slip from his shoulders to the floor. He set his camera — one of the new Sony Digital Betacams — on the table right on top of her work. Big toys for little boys, she thought. When he finally turned to acknowledge her, he seemed shell-shocked. She disliked him instantly, the vacant, hungry look of him. His leanness, as though he threatened to devour the world.

But the world had already been devoured. Hardly a single building had escaped the devastation. Wood planks replaced the glass of windows; sandbags substituted for doors — everything fell away to become something else. Landmarks stood in ruins around the city. A giant mosque burned, and its stones were carted away and buried in different locations. The perpetrators seemed to be defying anyone to resurrect it, or to say it had once stood there. Many of the trees had been felled for fuel in the gruelling winters since the war started. The rest would go soon. Furniture, books, even clothes were on the list of things to burn. History had become a tabula rasa in reverse, a stone tablet from which all traces of the people who had lived side by side for centuries were disappearing. There were so many disparate nationalities it seemed the only bond was the land itself, and that had been torn apart.

Angela watched as this kid from Quebec — she could hardly call him a man — walked into the midst of it. His appearance disturbed her — green khakis, a scarlet headband, and a gold hoop in his left ear. He looked like a tropical bird. God help them both if this was his idea of professionalism. He turned from his gear and looked her up and down as though it were she and not he who might be judged unfit for duty. He smiled and said his name — *André Riel*. He corrected her pronunciation, emphasising the nasal syllables.

Typical Quebecer, she thought — whimsical and maddeningly arrogant. She purposely flattened her accent, making it more *anglais*. His smile didn't disguise his annoyance.

"Is my name so difficult?" he asked in barely accented English.

"How about plain old 'Hey you'? I'm not here for French lessons. We've got work to do."

In that regard there was nothing she'd neglected. After Allan left, she spent time making the small, necessary incursions into the city's fractured substratum. She'd learned which connections could help and which would desert her at the last minute. She knew the checkpoint guards who could be bought with small kindnesses — a few chocolate bars, an extra pair of gloves — and the ones who'd take whatever she had, including her papers, and leave her stranded in hell without an exit visa.

Her new partner knew little of the war he'd landed in. He had no practical knowledge of life during conflict and spoke neither of the country's two dialects. She tossed her dictionary at him and told him to study it, then pointed to a cramped room down the hall. "And don't leave that stuff there," she said, indicating his camera gear.

He picked up the book and his knapsack, returning after a minute. "It has a window," he said. "Thank you."

"Makes it easier for the snipers to get you."

He laughed half-heartedly. "Is there a shower?"

"Yes, but you might have to wait a day or two to use it."

He waited for an explanation. She was enjoying his confusion.

"Some days we get water, some days electricity, and some days nothing but bombs," she said. "Today's an electricity day. Don't waste your time waiting for something if it's not there."

He leaned against the door frame, watching her. "I've heard a lot about you. I'm looking forward to getting to know you."

"There'll be plenty of time for that later."

He pulled a joint from his headband. "I don't suppose you smoke?"

THREE

IN THE MORNING, ANGELA FOUND André sitting cross-legged in his underwear, chanting on the kitchen floor. She guessed it was some strange religious sect — UFO worshippers, or those people who went off to remote compounds following the former psychiatrist or ex-tax accountant who believed himself to be the living embodiment of some extraterrestrial deity.

"Buddhism," he said when he'd finished. "I was chanting for a protection over the day's activities." He said it in a way that indicated she'd been included.

She averted her eyes from his skinny torso as he stood there in his boxers. Someone needed to feed him, but it wouldn't be her.

"I'll take a helmet over a chant any day," she said.

MORNINGS IN THE COMPOUND BECAME a head-on collision. André was mid-sentence before he got out of bed, pondering the day's activities or commenting on the news spilling from the radio. His endless chatter seemed pointless and annoying. It continued through breakfast as he sat in his checkered boxers, usually shirtless. This seemed to be his regular morning attire, as though wearing clothes were a matter of choice or simply too much effort to bother.

Angela ignored him for the first two days. On the third day she snapped. "Look, I hate to be rude," she snarled. "But could you shut up at least till I've had a chance to drink my coffee?"

His hand absently pawed the sparse hair on his chest. "You don't have to talk," he said.

"Neither do you. And put some clothes on."

Dans la lune. In the moon. That's how she thought of him. He was gone. Absent. Without a camera lens pressed to his eye, he seemed oblivious to everything that passed under his nose.

Over the coming weeks her reports to their supervisor, Martin, were filled with barbs. *Who the hell sent me this drugged-up bimbo?* she wrote. *That drugged-up bimbo is the best videographer we've had in years,* Martin replied. After that the fight was on. *Just what I need — a frigging boy wonder!* she shot back. *He may be a great videographer, but he doesn't know shit about diplomacy, and I can tell you which is more important over here.* Martin's response was immediate. *No doubt he'll learn all about diplomacy from you. In any case, you're stuck with each other for now. Enjoy!*

Despite her misgivings, she guided André through the besieged city, filling him in on its bruised and bloodied history, a story now more than seven hundred years old, buried under the churches and mosques, and echoing over the cobblestones. They passed the site where Gavrilo Princip, an eighteen-year-old Serbian nationalist, sparked the First World War when he assassinated Archduke Franz Ferdinand and his wife Sophie, Duchess of Hohenberg. The same day, Angela pointed out the Holiday Inn housing the Serbian Democratic Party, where the malevolent new Republika Srpska had been birthed.

Patiently, she detailed the precarious balances that allowed both sides of the conflict to exist within the same city, explaining how the UN subsistence flights that kept the citizenry alive also, ironically, prolonged the war. She was a walking encyclopedia, her mind a honeycomb of knowledge. She answered his endless questions, but made no concessions for him. Either he'd make it on his own or he'd break and get sent back to cover local news in Chibougamau or Gananoque. She wasn't going to become anyone's den mother.

Their one-room office housed a small desk and a fax machine, useless without the power that came and went with no warning. Angela constantly had to remind him to keep his papers and gear to one side. Somehow they always migrated to hers, as if he were constantly overflowing his borders. They shared the minuscule kitchen that never stayed uncluttered for long. Both took turns cooking, though neither had any patience for cleaning.

Martin's assessment of her new partner's skills had been accurate. André knew instinctively where to be at the right moment. During an interview with a Serb minister who'd defected from his party in protest against the war, Angela peppered the man with questions. He seemed bewildered. She waited impatiently as he struggled with his English. Getting nowhere, she stopped pressing him. In a far corner of the room, Slobodan Milošević appeared on TV. The minister bolted to his feet. In that moment, an entire history passed over his face as he saw at last how he'd turned his back on his own people and stood looking on from the precarious edge of history. To Angela's relief, as well as her chagrin, André effortlessly captured the moment.

The friction between them mounted. She hated his outspokenness. Oil and water. French and English. One morning in a café, seated with a half-dozen other journalists, André criticized her involvement with Médecins Sans Frontières. She'd paid the humanitarian-aid group a month's salary to bring her to a small town cleansed by the Bosnian Serb Army. MSF had disguised her as a doctor on the way in and as a patient on the way out. The stories of abuse she returned with had been revelatory. Her colleagues had been impressed with her daring as well as her ingenuity.

Despite the chilly morning, André sat dressed in shorts and a sleeveless T-shirt with a frayed collar. He'd been listening to her. He stabbed out a cigarette. She shouldn't have paid them to take her, he announced coolly, smoke rolling from the side of his mouth.

"What the hell was I supposed to do?" she snapped. "Strap myself to the underside of one of their Range Rovers? They have access to places I don't."

"You're a journalist," he said simply. "Offer them coverage for their help. They'll take all the publicity they can get and in return they'll bring you anywhere. You don't need to pay them."

The others erupted in laughter. Angela flushed — he was right. Tactics soon changed: publicity for complicity. It would prove a useful arrangement for both sides in the months to come.

André seemed propelled by a restless energy. His head nodded and his foot tapped continuously. His eyes devoured distance. On his days off, he couldn't sit still. He loved to fix things, talking while he worked. An obstinate door jamb soon operated as smoothly as a well-oiled piston; a repair to the Jeep engine was made in short order even when he had to invent replacement parts from an abandoned tank. In the evenings, he followed Angela from room to room as she turned off the lights, which he seldom remembered to do despite her warnings about sniper fire. His constant talk prevented her from retreating into the sanctity of her own thoughts. She thought she'd go mad. She tried insulting him to get him to stop, but it only egged him on. Once she asked him whether in a Quebec War for Independence he'd work as a journalist or a freedom fighter.

He smirked. "*Merde!* There won't even be a war. When we separate, we're not going to tell you. We'll just disappear one night with the entire province to ourselves. And you English, who are so self-absorbed, will take months to realize that we are gone."

Despite his constant questions, she offered little about herself, as though having a personal life or a past was her least consideration. Occasionally, when pressed, she spoke of an uneventful upbringing in the suburbs of Toronto — what she called her "brown-paper-bag childhood." She mentioned her father's recent death, and spoke warmly of him and the two sisters she tried to stay in touch with, despite the distance. She barely mentioned a mother.

WHEN A MONTH CAME AND went without complaint from the Québécois, Angela grew more tolerant of his babbling and his bohemian attire. For his part, André accepted her jibes just as he marvelled at her meticulous dedication to her work. She rose at 5:30 most mornings to read the reports, if Martin had been able to fax any. Sometimes Martin pencilled comments in the margins: *How are you two doing over there? Getting cosy yet?* Angela remembered him as an embittered ex-pat Brit whose accent got stronger and his snobbery more pronounced the longer he stayed in Canada. She wasn't warming to him now.

If there were no pages on the fax machine when she woke, she listened to the radio broadcasts. Lists of casualties, areas hit by shelling overnight, and weather forecasts came through in English, though she frequently picked up German, French, and Italian, along with the Serb and Croat stations.

She allowed André to read the faxes only after she'd read them thoroughly first. She offered no apology for her possessiveness and he expressed no resentment. He stained the pages with his buttery fingers as coffee brewed and the aroma filled the kitchen. Over breakfast, they discussed their day and tuned in to the UN frequency to learn where the day's trouble spots were. It was illegal, she told him, but most journalists resorted to it. The trick was not to appear too quickly on the scene every time something happened.

In the evenings, André listened to a library of cassette tapes on a portable player he carried with him everywhere. Masses by Josquin des Pres or William Byrd were followed by Aretha Franklin, Kate Bush, Sarah McLachlan. The juxtaposition of styles mystified Angela. His taste seemed to have no connecting threads.

It wasn't the music he listened for, he said. It was the sound of the human voice. One day he made her sit while he played Arvo Pärt's *Magnificat*.

"There are almost no solo voices anywhere in Pärt's music," he pointed out. "That's a political statement in itself. It's a universe where unity and collectivity rule."

She listened to the eerie harmonies, the uncomfortable dissonances that merged and married in their moment of release. She heard in it the shattered life of the city cobbling itself together outside their windows. Like the city, there was an infinite richness hidden beneath the surface austerity.

Angela had her obsessions as well. André often found her poring over her collection of Second World War photographs. They were *noctivagant*, she said. The word made her think of things glimpsed through shade. She handled the images like rare stamps, touching only their backs. The first time André saw her handling photographs he expected to see pictures of her family, but all the faces belonged to pilots and soldiers.

"The second Siege of Malta," she said, in answer to his look.

"When was the first?"

They were sitting in the kitchen, the light so low it barely lit the walls around them. She looked up, adjusted her glasses.

"The first was in 1565," she said, "when the Turks tried to overthrow the island. But Malta's walls were too well guarded. They failed to take it and because of that they lost the Mediterranean. Napoleon held it briefly, two hundred years later. But the second great siege was during World War Two."

She told André how Hitler had underestimated the tenacity of the Maltese, who hung on through two years of unprecedented bombing and near starvation. Taking Malta would have guaranteed passage to the führer's supply ships, allowing unfettered access to the oil-rich Middle East. Failure to take the island cost Germany greatly, and ultimately led to its defeat. She saw

it as history repeating, time curling back on itself. The windows
in photographs. The second Siege of Malta was to have been her
master's thesis, but she'd abandoned it because it seemed removed
from the real world. A month later she'd found herself in the
Mediterranean, visiting places firsthand she'd only read about
and seen in pictures.

She spread the photographs across the table and told him of
the small band of Allied fighters who guarded the island fortress
from 1940 through the end of 1942. Confined there for months
at a time, starving, fighting off the ravages of an illness known
as Malta Dog, and shitting in their own clothes, they waited
without hope for the supplies that only made it in the nick of
time. Most of the pictures showed painfully skinny young men
in their late teens and early twenties.

When prompted, she could recite the names of the men in
the photographs. She knew their histories, their tales of heroism.
She brought the dead to life, one by one, till they became real
to André. It was an English Group Captain, P. B. "Laddie" Lucas,
who championed the flyers, hand-picking rogue fighters and
outcasts from other squadrons. Lucas discovered the maverick
George "Screwball" Beurling, a young blond from Verdun with
a reputation for recklessness and a genius for mathematical
precision in his shooting. Against the warnings of others, Lucas
chose Beurling for his squadron. Under Lucas's command,
Beurling would become the highest scoring ace during the siege,
a virtual one-man air force.

"Verdun is in Montreal," André said. A Canadian war hero
from Montreal — it intrigued him. He leaned in to see the
faces. A sleep-deprived young man in shorts and a cap proudly
displayed a piece of fuselage from a downed German plane.

More shots of Beurling showed him with members of his squadron in various locations around Malta. As she talked, Angela's face was a palimpsest of emotions.

"I think they were trying to make a record of everyone in the event of death," she said. "They wanted to leave a trace of those who'd gone on before as proof that the same things keep happening over and over."

Beurling's skills as a fighter ace helped him learn the secret to making the most of the diminishing fuel and ammunition on Malta. Rather than waste ammunition taking down enemy aircraft, he could mentally calculate his own speed against an approaching plane and take out its pilot with a single bullet. At 350 yards, when most pilots were pulling away, Screwball Beurling was zeroing in for the kill. It earned him his nickname, among other things. His efforts had proved crucial in the fight to keep Malta free.

"He survived nine plane crashes during the war," she said. "After eluding fate so many times, he died a few years after the war in his tenth crash."

"A cat's life," André said.

Angela shook her head. "Murder. The British engineered the crash to prevent his joining the emerging Arab-Israeli conflict. They didn't want him working on the other side." It didn't pay to be too good at something.

A final photo, taken just before his death, showed a man tormented and aged, as though the very nature of his success — killing — had haunted him.

"Any family photos?" André asked.

"Beurling's?"

"No — yours."

She turned the book in her hands. "These men are my family," she said, removing her glasses and closing the pages.

FOUR

ANGELA WAS IN THE MARKET sorting through a bushel of shrivelled tomatoes, dull anaemic stones, when the first shell hit. From blocks away, she knew it had landed near their hotel. The barrage intensified. She walked quickly through the rain-drenched streets as people scattered. The food lineups she'd passed on the way there had evaporated. The aid office was shuttered. Something whizzed overhead and struck right behind her, splintering wood and glass onto the sidewalk. Another shell landed one street over. She broke into a run.

Smoke rose from an apartment complex directly across from the hotel. Most of its windows were boarded up; the vacant holes showed where no one lived. Another shell exploded up the street as Angela hurried inside her own building.

Doors closed briskly along the halls as people made their way to the shelter. Surely André would have taken cover. She walked with the crowd, crossing the courtyard and down the darkened stairs to rooms that had once been wine cellars. They were empty now except for crates of bottled water and emergency tinned food.

Despite the nearness of the shelling, the mood was calm, the faces more annoyed than frightened. Usually people stayed for an hour or so, waiting for signs of let-up, then headed back to their apartments. Angela looked around for André; he wasn't there. She waited fifteen minutes, then picked up her bags and headed up the stairs. Faces watched her go without curiosity.

She found him in his room, calmly taping the building across the street where the residents were hurriedly putting out a fire.

"You should have gone downstairs," she said crossly. "It's not safe."

He stirred, looking up from the lens. "Then why did you come back?"

She set her bags down and watched the scene across the way. Gunfire splattered the walls, sending plaster dust onto the street. Two shells exploded nearby, making the walls rattle. Angela's heart was in her throat.

"It's too late now," she said. "We'd never get across the courtyard."

He shrugged. "It's probably no more dangerous to stay here."

She heard him talking while she changed into dry clothes and put the groceries away. When she returned, he was still rambling. She let him talk as they stared out the window together. Words seemed to calm him, as though turning his thoughts into speech made things more manageable or at least comprehensible. He was talking about his mother.

"I was four when she died," he said. "I'm not sure how much I really remember of her."

Sometimes, he said, he suspected his memories were prompted by a handful of family photos. In his recollections, she might wear her hair first one way and then another. He thought he remembered her teaching him his colours. He was sure he could hear her say *rouge* and remembered asking her to repeat it so he could hear her say it over and over, but other days he wasn't sure it had happened that way at all. In his father's house, a single framed photograph of an exhausted-looking woman sat atop the TV. She held him in her arms, smiling for the camera. He grew up believing he'd caused her death by wearing her out. He'd never been able to age her black-and-white features in his mind. Somewhere she waited for him, eternally thirty.

Angela found herself listening with interest, not condescending or judgmental. "How did she die?"

"Pneumonia. We found that out years later. My father told us she went away, but he never said where," André said. "I thought he meant she'd gone down the road that passed by our house. At night I would stand at the window and stare out at the light on the church steeple, thinking she was out there somewhere just beyond sight."

Of his brothers and sisters, three worked for a fast food franchise in the small town where they were born. A fourth married a rock musician and moved to Quebec City. André was the only one to learn English. It gave him his passport to the world. In his teens he ran away to Montreal where he shared bitter jokes about the English — the "White Rhodesians of Westmount." Later, he moved to Vancouver, got involved with a band of heroin addicts and nearly died of an overdose. A practice that had at first seemed romantic and bohemian became merely stupid in hindsight. He went cold turkey and found the resolve to put himself through school, working part-time at

Burger King. He studied all day and served fast food at night. He fell asleep dreaming of French fries, and foreign countries, and people he'd never met.

Just out of school he made his first documentary, an insider look at motorcycle gangs in Quebec. It won him a National Film Board award. Reports of his bravado spread with the story that the leader of the Hells Angels had spotted him parked across from their headquarters during the taping. When the man walked up to his car and fired a gun in the air, André lifted his head and looked up blankly. The biker was so impressed with his sang-froid that he invited him in to talk with the gang members firsthand. He laughed when he recounted the story. He'd been sitting in the car with his Walkman blaring and hadn't heard a thing.

His second documentary took aim at the unsafe working conditions at the asbestos mines in his hometown. By then his father was manager of operations for the mining company and found himself on the other end of the firing line from his delinquent son, whom he hadn't seen in six years. Their reunion was a disaster. Neither had been in touch since the broadcast.

He stopped suddenly, the words dying on his tongue. "What about you? No memories? You hardly ever talk about yourself."

Angela turned from the window. "I have memories. They're just — not something I choose to dwell on."

She saw herself as a four-year-old twisting and running down a grassy slope, a blur in a white dress, giddy with her escape. *Angela, Angela!* her mother's voice called out behind her. Hands reached out and grabbed her under her arms, lifting her into the air. *Gotcha!* her father cried, as she screamed in delight. Giggles, blond curls, a blue hat flying in another direction. Released, she would immediately run off again as fast as her legs would allow.

Some people understood intuitively when she said her earliest memories were her happiest; others stared as though she'd suddenly begun speaking gibberish. *How could your early life be happiest?* they seemed to ask, without having the courage to say it, as though it suggested the rest of her life was a mistake, a wasteland of despair and grief.

"Was it so bad?"

"No, not really. Just a mother I never got along with."

A few streets away, a stray shell landed without exploding. An eerie silence followed. They waited, but nothing happened. She'd almost forgot where she was, stuck in the middle of a seven-hundred-year-old war in the Balkans. André stood and changed the cartridge in his camera. He stretched and yawned.

"I hope I haven't been boring you," she said. "My family, and all."

"Not at all. I'm fascinated by the peculiarities of the English. All that repression." He winked.

"We come by it honestly. Somewhere in my background I have ancestors who gave each other walnuts for Christmas. An occasional orange was allowed, if you really liked someone. Anything else was considered extravagant."

He laughed. "You don't even have the church to blame. At least I can point to the repressive rules of the Catholic clergy."

"Yes, but we don't have confession. Once I've done something wrong, I'm supposed to feel guilty about it for the rest of my life. We're self-condemning. You, on the other hand, are expected to misbehave to give the priests something to do."

Angela shifted her position on the cushion. Darkness was falling. The fire across the street had been put out.

André watched her. She was enjoying this, he could see, telling a stranger about her family, maybe for the first time since she could remember.

"Go on," he said. "Tell me more. Why was your mother so bad? I'm interested. Really."

"My mother is not so bad. We just never got along." She shrugged. "My mother likes life small and contained. Safety first, last, and always. She was terrified her daughters might do something people would talk about — a disaster for her. She's afraid of everything. I never knew why. It's probably why I'm here right now. I've rebelled against her ever since I was conscious of having a choice. I couldn't take all that suburban hypocrisy, all that fear of whatever constitutes real life. To my mother, social graces are paramount. Surprises are unwanted, almost evil. Boredom is the only virtue worth maintaining."

She began to tell him of her final weekend on the Bruce Peninsula. It was an annual excursion, a get-together she'd loathed for years, and she hadn't been looking forward to it then. She'd arrived on her own, making excuses for Tim without really saying why he was absent. Margaret and her husband, BJ, had been fighting, as usual. Tori's new boyfriend had shown up later, his appearance and his outlook on life designed to zero in on their mother's fears and prejudices. Her father had not been well, but how unwell he'd been only became apparent later. Then Angela had broken the news of her separation. To cap things off, Tim had shown up in the midst of it all. It couldn't have been more disastrous.

Somewhere a bullet pinged off a lamppost. The barrage had shifted away from them. It was getting late. The heavy shelling had ended an hour earlier. Angela stood to go to bed.

André looked up in surprise. "Wait! You can't leave yet. I need to know how it turned out. Tori's boyfriend — what was he like? And how did it go with your husband?"

The darkness outside was complete. She knew he would gladly stay up all night talking and smoking.

"I think we'll leave that for another time," she said. She looked around the room as though remembering where they were, noting that they were survivors, once again, of something as incomprehensible as the war just outside their walls. "Good night."

BOOK II
FAMILY ALBUMS

FIVE

LION'S HEAD, BRUCE PENINSULA, SEPTEMBER 1994.
Hands turned the pages of a photo album where a toddler in blue splashed through piles of fall leaves. Below, a pet collie sported a bow tie, posed as smartly as a small-town politician at a picnic. On facing pages, Angela saw herself as a grinning adolescent in cap and gown accepting a scroll, her passage into adulthood. One page over, Margaret led a Girl Guides parade, while on another, Tori found herself as part of a boating expedition on some long ago holiday. The years between were neatly layered with celebrations — holidays, weddings, picnics — the moments extravagant with emotion.

Prize blooms had also been sought out by the camera and highlighted in their glory: globe thistles, eight-foot-tall hollyhocks, and roses enjoyed their fame equally amid the pages. The trees, too, had been captured. A childish hand had captioned a single snapshot: *Honey locust, an ornamental tree* (Gleditsia triacanthos) *of the senna family. Lion's Head, Bruce Peninsula. Property of the Thomas Family, 1975.*

The sisters sifted their past in a room whose contents — lace curtains, stone fireplace, a wooden rocker — were part of a shared landscape that had been a refuge for more than thirty years. The words that described the scene were not *big, bold, adventurous*, but *small, safe, knowable*. These were their mother's words, her legacy of security in a wilderness of feeling.

The pages unearthed more surprises. Angela scrutinized her teenage likeness warily, noting how her younger self appeared open, approachable. Too knowable. She was no longer so open or approachable.

"Look at my hair!" she cried.

"That was your Jane Fonda period," Margaret said.

"*Gidget Goes To Hell* is more like it. I'm sure glad the '70s are over."

"The '70s are back and they're way cool!" exclaimed Tori, the youngest of the three. The nostalgia radio stations had fuelled her interest.

Margaret laughed. "How would you know, Tori? You were too young to remember."

"I know because I'm the reincarnation of that singer who died of a drug overdose."

Margaret paused to think. Did '70s singers die of drug overdoses? "Karen Carpenter?"

"No." Tori shook her head. "She was just an anorexic who starved herself to escape her shitty life. I mean the blues singer."

Margaret reflected. Billie Holiday came to mind, as did Dinah Wishington. But they'd died earlier. She dug deeper, pulling up a surprising relic. "Janis Joplin?"

"Yeah, her."

Margaret laughed. "She was '60s, darling."

"Oh."

"But just as fucked up as anyone your generation's produced, so don't feel left out."

Pages turned, evoking memories so far off they seemed mythical. A move to the city, the trip to Disney World, Tori's appendectomy. Yet the past remained remote. It could have belonged to anyone — distant relatives, childhood friends — nothing to do with the three women sitting there.

A single black-and-white snapshot revealed a fair young man setting out on a voyage. It was a Tarot card. Upright, it read: *Fair skies and a prosperous passage will accompany the courageous traveller*. Reversed, it presaged darker tidings: *A journey filled with many obstacles to be overcome in time*. Margaret pulled it free of the page.

"Dad was such a babe, wasn't he?"

The sisters murmured their agreement.

Tori looked up. "Why isn't Mom in any of these pictures?"

"That was her Joan Crawford period," Margaret said. "Oops! Did I think that out loud?"

Angela snorted. "*Was?* When did it end?"

A sheaf of news clippings slid free of the cover. Angela snatched at yellowing headlines, cutlines: *Canadian journalist shows courage in African Civil War*. Another, dated a year later: *Toronto correspondent wins press award for war coverage*. Her face appeared again: cropped hair, wary eyes. Definitely not approachable.

"Where'd these come from?"

Margaret shrugged. "Mom must have put them in there. She's been rearranging the albums again."

"Mom? You're kidding! I thought she hated hearing about this stuff."

Angela pictured her mother's disapproving eyes, her hands smoothing the pages into the back of the book where they told of disasters witnessed firsthand. She buried the clippings inside the cover and the journey resumed.

More gardens. An outside shot of the cottage. The locust trees appeared, disappeared, and reappeared as if swaying in the wind. They changed from one page to the next, one season to another. In summer, full; in fall, bursting with flame; in winter, naked; in spring, reborn. Magical. The real trees towered over the stone cottage on the shores of Whippoorwill Bay outside the town of Lion's Head. Three in all, they'd been planted in the weeks following each daughter's birth. They dipped and swayed in the wind that crossed the Bruce Peninsula, eight hundred kilometres of rugged coastline located four hours north of Toronto. The area's history spoke of its own magic. Home to Kitchi Manitou, Great Spirit guardian of the North, the peninsula's giant arm extended upward, dividing the waters of Lake Huron from Georgian Bay. Once the home of the Iroquois and Algonquin tribes, it had become a choice jumping-off spot for vacationing families on their way via ferry from tiny, perfect Tobermory across to Manitoulin, the world's largest freshwater island.

Outside, a lawn flowed from the cottage down to the nearby roadway where a beige Oldsmobile crawled up the drive, as it did every year. And every year Abbie Thomas — she of the "Joan Crawford" fame — immaculately dressed and impeccably thin, stepped from the pages of *Mature Woman's Vogue*.

The car's arrival was a signal. Margaret and Tori made for the door. Angela hung back to study her mother's face through the window, her own reflection superimposed on it. For a moment it startled her as their images joined, a trick in a mirror of the window's glass.

Abbie smiled, her aristocratic head bent toward the scene of greeting. Her hair was knotted in a fashion popular long before. She could have been an opera singer, famous years earlier, coming out of retirement briefly to greet her fans. There was a ghostliness about her — an aura of someone who had survived, of something invisibly held apart.

Angela watched her mother walk to the passenger door and help her father. Conrad planted a cane on solid ground and pulled himself upright. They stood, comrades-at-arms, assessing the cottage and the trees reaching overhead.

"Here we all are for the family weekend!" Abbie exclaimed.

It would be her leitmotif for the next three days. Every year her grown daughters went to great lengths to carry on this tradition, re-enacting their roles as children to please their mother. Her displeasure threatened to devour them all.

Angela emerged from the cottage, her own portrait of reserve.

Conrad looked up. "Here's the world traveller!"

She smiled. "How are you, Dad?"

"Well enough, for an old guy."

He was what she came for. Given time, his warmth could fill the world. The shock of seeing him with a cane settled in a few seconds late. It blurred him a little, like a watercolour left out in the rain.

"It's great to have you back with us this year," he said.

"Wouldn't miss it for the world," she replied. "What's with the cane? Are you looking for sympathy?"

He raised it in the air reassuringly: it hadn't become a part of him. It was merely a prop he used to impersonate someone much older and frailer than himself.

"Just me slowing down a bit. Nothing to worry about." He shook his head, as if even he couldn't quite accept this concession to aging. His arms opened and hugged her, releasing her back into the world.

Angela turned to her mother. "Hello, Mom. How are you?"

They shared a polite shoulder squeeze, cheeks barely grazing.

"Very well, thank you. How was your flight? You look exhausted."

It was instinctive, Angela knew — this criticism disguised as concern. It kept others from getting too near, even a kiss or hug that might affect her mother's composure.

"The flight was fine," she said, making light of it. "The usual bad food, a seedy business type in the seat next to me who wouldn't shut up about the damn Conservatives …"

Abbie cut her off mid-sentence, turning to Margaret and Tori. "Girls, take the groceries in from the car. Don't make your father do it."

Angela felt the rebuke. Thirty seconds in and she'd already broken the golden rule about controversial subjects. No — her mother was not a mirror, unless mirrors lied.

Margaret and Tori took up the cardboard cartons stuffed with meat, eggs, vegetables, juice, cereals, cheese, and milk — an entire grocery store retrieved from the backseat of the car. Angela shrugged and picked up a final carton, feeling redundant even in that.

In the living room, Conrad leaned his cane against the wall and sank into the sofa. Abbie placed her purse on the side table and quickly took in the room.

"It looks better than I expected," she announced, to no one in particular.

"We tidied up a bit," Margaret offered.

"You girls didn't need to do that." Abbie eyed a vase, moved it minutely, and stood back to gain perspective before deciding its ultimate fate.

Margaret and Angela exchanged glances: *The old bird hasn't softened a bit, has she?*

Abbie caught their look. Nervous fingers reached up to pat her hair. She smiled self-consciously, as though she'd been caught doing something in public she normally reserved for private. "Where are the others?" she asked.

"BJ and Markus are out back hunting toads," Margaret said. "We left the girls with BJ's mom."

Disapproval registered in Abbie's face. "I had arranged this as a family get-together. You knew that. Your father and I never left you girls behind when we travelled."

The statement hung there, waiting to be attacked or ignored. Margaret could do neither. After years of appeasement, she remained the middle child who strove for family unity, no matter the cost.

"Sorry, Mom — they're at that age where they want to make their own decisions."

"I see."

Abbie surveyed the room, a teacher taking attendance on the first day of a class that promised to be dismal at best, an unpleasant chore at worst. She noted another absence and looked at Angela.

"Where's Tim?"

"Something came up at the last minute and he couldn't get out of it. He sends his apologies."

Tim would hate the deception, preferring honesty to Angela's negotiated half-truths. He'd tell her to lay things bare from the start, even if it meant leaving herself open to her mother's unsparing criticism. Tim had never understood the slow deliberate moves on the Thomas family chessboard. Angela pictured the last time they spoke, how he'd stood in the driveway outside their home pleading with her to change her mind. Fallen leaves covered the lawn, creating a perfect backdrop for something as momentous as the end of a marriage.

"Will he join us later?" Abbie persisted. "I've been planning for months. Surely my children don't think these weekends just happen?"

"I wouldn't expect him," Angela said, ice in her voice. She would tell them her news when she was prepared to, and not a second before. Her hands shook. She was surprised how little it took to lose her patience after all the years of practice, the years of distance. With an entire world out there — she could just as easily have been in Peru or Afghanistan — somehow she was stuck here trying to appease her mother once again. "Besides, Mom — you changed the dates. We can't all rearrange our lives at a moment's notice."

This was how it always turned out, Angela thought. First one shot, then another, followed by the whole war. If it was going to be a weekend of ambushes and fault-finding, she might as well go home now. Except she no longer had a home to go to.

"Your father wasn't up to coming last month," Abbie reminded them. "He had that terrible flu that was going around. I've already apologized for that."

"Oh, now ..." Margaret made placating sounds to reassure Abbie that their father's illness was not now, and certainly was not ever, her fault. In fact, she seemed to say, their mother was a saint whose earthly rewards could never begin to make up for the hours of tireless devotion to her husband, and to her entire family, who barely acknowledged all she'd done for them.

"Poor Dad," Tori sympathized.

"There's no need to worry about me," Conrad said. "Or use me as an excuse." He looked around at the faces of these women — at times so inscrutable, yet so transparent with their emotional demands. The drive up had been pleasant and the day was still beautiful — the light fell over the bay and lit up the cliffs at Lion's Head. It was far too early to let the mood splinter and the frictions take over.

Conrad transformed, taking on the role of master deflector. He was a trustworthy guide leading them from danger, away from falling rocks and Indian ambushes they might never know had been avoided through his scrupulous care. "How are the gardens?" he asked. "Has anyone been out to see them yet?"

"They look fantastic!" Angela replied. "We took a quick tour when we arrived."

The gardens had been drenched in a thick mist that seemed to have been exuded by the flowers themselves. The day lilies and the phlox, stalwarts they could always count on, stood like sentinels in a grey haze. Beside a stand of black snakeroot that reached above Angela's head the final roses were in bloom, their peach and ochre hues silvered over.

Abbie brightened. "I thought so, too, even from a distance. Mr. McKeough's promised to stop by tomorrow. He's finally going to trim those trees." She looked out the window as if to reassure herself that the locusts hadn't pulled up root and disappeared in her absence. "The storms took a lot out of them last year. I don't want them to go through that again this winter."

She turned to her youngest daughter, who stared off into a distance populated by the faces of dead rock stars. "When is your gentleman friend arriving, Victoria?"

Margaret exchanged a quick smile with Angela: *Gentleman friend?*

"Shep's bus gets in around six," Tori answered, absently twisting a strand of hair between her fingers.

"I hope he'll be on time for supper," Abbie said.

Lines of exasperation formed around her daughter's mouth. "It won't be Shep's fault if the bus is late."

Margaret retrieved the photo album. Other families drew themselves up around the television. The Thomases loved their photographs. Arguments could be displaced with the simple opening of a cover, distracting them with proof of their togetherness. *We're a family like any other*, they seemed to say. The album opened to a snapshot of four-year-old Angela seated on a tricycle. Her dress was smudged with dirt. Her face already suggested independence, even defiance.

"I never could keep you clean," Abbie reflected. "I just stopped trying, eventually. Whenever I tidied you up it seemed to take away all your charm."

Angela reddened, thrown by the inadvertent compliment. Margaret looked pleased. The nostalgia was working.

"Angela was never one to sit quietly," Conrad said. "We knew even back then that she'd be an adventurer."

The shadow of Abbie's displeasure loomed over them again. The habitual wanderings of an errant daughter should not be allowed to darken a bright fall day, it seemed to say. Conrad's usual meticulous care over such things had momentarily failed him. It was as if he'd been out trimming the hedges and come into the kitchen trailing mud, tossing the clippers into the sink.

Margaret did more retrieval work, pushing time back further, past the births of her sisters, before their parents' marriage.

"Dad, when was this taken?"

She held out the album to Conrad, who squinted at a flute-edged photograph of two young men in hunting jackets standing on the shore of a lake so vast its opposite shore was lost.

"That's Lake Superior, so it would probably be the fall of '62, I think. Your uncle Alex and I took a fishing trip right around the time I met your mother."

Tori leaned forward. "I didn't know we had any pictures of Uncle Alex. He was really cute!"

Abbie watched over her daughter's shoulder. "Now how did that get in there?" she said disapprovingly, as though discovering a glove in the refrigerator. She looked at Conrad. "It's hard to believe you two were brothers."

"Yes, we all know Alex wasn't your favourite in-law," Conrad said with a wink to the others.

Angela hid her smile. Her father spoke infrequently about his brother, but the photograph said pretty much everything: the cocky self-confidence bordering on arrogance, the heartbreaking good looks. Her father had inherited the family's more conservative genes, while her uncle, saddled with travel fever and an addiction to excitement, had leapt from one adventure to another, dropping family ties as he went.

That was just his way, Conrad would protest. Alex wasn't heartless, just reckless, but his wildness and his pranks always got the better of him. As a boy, he'd mastered every sport he tackled before moving onto the next. It seemed there was nothing Alex couldn't do. And little he could stick to. At eight, he'd learned to ride his bike hands-free. He showed off for his schoolmates one day, eating lunch from a paper bag as he pedalled around the block. They cheered each time he appeared at the corner, showing them first a sandwich, then a banana, and finally a carton of milk, until he took his luck for granted and collided with a car backing out of a driveway. Conrad was the first to reach him, but his brother sprang up, laughing and unhurt.

A year later, that same bike almost cost Conrad the fingers on his right hand. Trying to imitate Alex, he came down a hill too quickly, hit a pothole and was thrown. Mid-fall he'd grabbed at the wheel, an acrobat reaching for a silvery ring. The spokes sliced three-quarters of the way through his fingers. It was Alex who came to Conrad's rescue that time. At the hospital the doctors insisted they needed to amputate, but Alex protested louder than anyone as Conrad held the hand out to distance himself from the unbearable pain. Conrad would have agreed to anything — even sticking his head in a bucket to drown himself — but Alex argued and, in the end, a graft proved successful. Conrad never forgot he owed his right hand to his brother. He was still paying back the favour more than thirty years later.

Angela watched her mother shut the album on the offending photograph. She had never understood this ongoing dislike, so pronounced it seemed nearly a hatred.

"No," Abbie agreed. "He was not my favourite." Her look softened, as though to say that honour was reserved for Conrad alone.

Conrad raised himself off the couch. "I sure could use a cup of coffee."

Tension deflated; storm clouds vanished over the horizon with barely a sprinkle. Abbie smiled, quietly reassured. She was needed; she must provide, even if it was something as simple as coffee.

"Well," she said, looking around. "Here we all are for the family weekend!"

SIX

LATE AFTERNOON SUNLIGHT SLID OVER the blinds and into the kitchen. A coffee pot, now empty, sat on the counter beside a row of colourful ceramic bears holding signs that read COFFEE, TEA, and SUGAR in elevated letters like a primitive form of Braille. Copper-bottomed pans and gleaming utensils hovered above a central island like surgical instruments, sterile and expectant. The room burned with a quiet fire.

Angela and Margaret stood by the sink. Carrots, onions, and peppers transformed into neatly ordered piles beneath their hands. Abbie dressed a large pork roast in a mantle of cranberries, inserting star-shaped cloves into slits made in the flesh.

"How's work these days?" Margaret asked.

"Busy," Angela replied, barely looking up from her hands. "I was back in Burundi last month."

"Must be fun," Margaret said.

Angela paused. Surely Margaret didn't believe that. The idea of travel may have hinted at excitement, but "fun" was the last word she'd use to describe what she did.

"Did you get my postcard?" she asked. "The one with the dried fish hanging from the trees?"

Margaret reflected. "You'd think I'd remember that. Probably. My short-term memory's shot to hell. I can barely remember what I had for breakfast this morning, or whether I took my Ginkgo biloba to offset the memory loss." She grinned. "What's happening in Burundi?"

"They've had more flare-ups. You don't hear much about it anymore, but the war's quietly going on."

"Are they still shooting people?"

"Only if you're unlucky enough to be a peasant — which most people are." Angela lifted a pile of julienned carrots and plunked them into a bowl. "I half-expected to have my camera confiscated at the border, but either they mistook me for a tourist or I've fallen off the government's least-wanted list."

A bang from Abbie's corner told them she might be displeased by their conversation, though perhaps it had only been a bang after all. It was hard to tell. Angela looked over. Her mother's eyes often seemed populated with unknowable dramas, unnameable fears. The sisters exercised caution, preferring a path of discretion to one of thorns.

"How's the florist business, Mom?" Angela asked.

Angela's childhood was marked by flowers. Blooms transformed in Abbie's hands, enchanted by her touch. Buckets of blossoms filled the house. To Angela, flowers meant wellness. When they were absent, it meant her mother wasn't well. Flowers didn't grow or bloom when she wasn't there to tend them. That was Abbie's law of nature.

"Very well, thank you. Last weekend was the van Beck wedding," Abbie said. "Shirley wanted a plantation styling for the whole house. The in-laws are Americans — from the South. Alabama, I think. We get a lot of Americans. I did everything in crape myrtle, mimosa blossoms, and pink rhododendrons. The mayor performed the service under the arbour in the back garden. Afterwards, they served dinner to two hundred guests on a big covered porch."

Angela envisioned men in tails and ascots, women in flowing dresses and bonnets. "Sounds very *Gone With the Wind*," she said. "Did they hoist the Confederate flag?"

Angela saw her mother's shoulders stiffen at the unintentional affront. Everything was suspect — tenderness, humour, even wisdom. Knives were concealed in words.

Angela retreated. "It must have been beautiful ..."

"It was beautiful," Abbie concurred. "Though I wish young people would make more of an effort to dress." She waved away the thought. "It should be specified on the invitations."

Abbie slid the roasting pan into the oven and closed the door. Angela tried, unsuccessfully, not to imagine the witch in a fairy tale. She watched her mother scoop a platter of hors d'oeuvres from the counter and bear it aloft into the dining room.

Margaret rolled her eyes. "Our very own Scarlet O'Hara."

"It's the torching of Atlanta that worries me," Angela said, turning down a burner.

She picked up a pile of scrapings — red, yellow, and orange vegetable skins — and dropped them into the garbage. The colours spilled from her fingers, the flags of a defeated army.

"How are the twins?"

Margaret beamed. "You wouldn't recognize them. They're almost as tall as me now." She wiped her hands and reached for her pocketbook to retrieve a photograph, but hesitated before handing it over. "It's only a stupid snapshot I took last winter," she said.

Angela held the picture of two grinning ten-year-olds. "Don't be silly. It's a terrific shot."

Margaret warmed to the praise. "That's Cindy on the left. She wants to go into nursing. She's been bandaging the pets for practice. They run whenever she comes into the room, poor things. Karen's doing very well in her skating. She won another divisional. They're talking Olympics in a few years, if she keeps it up."

"The Olympics! That's really something."

Angela stopped to consider these developments. She was always surprised by the progression of family life, as though home should be a static thing without her to record its advances. She handed back the snapshot.

"No up-and-coming comics like their dad?" she asked.

Margaret shook her head. "No, thank goodness. One comic in the family is enough. Markus leaves the room when BJ starts telling jokes. I think he's embarrassed for him. It's sort of funny, but sad too."

"How are you guys these days?" Angela asked. "Happy?"

"Happy?" Margaret shrugged. "I haven't a clue what that might be. The circuit keeps BJ busy. He had a guest spot on the Comedy Network last week. Say you saw it, if he asks." She made a weary face. "We don't fight quite as much as we used to."

Abbie's voice reached them from the other room. "There's no need to fight. You just have to learn to talk things out."

"There's advice for you," Margaret said, lowering her voice. "From the woman who thinks civilization ended with the invention of paper napkins."

Angela grinned. "Too true."

"Have you told them your news yet?" Margaret asked.

Angela was startled. For a moment, she thought Margaret was referring to her separation. Then it dawned on her: her *other* news. "You mean Sarajevo." The word dazzled her, like a light suddenly turned up bright.

Margaret looked at her curiously. "Is there something else? You're not pregnant, are you?"

Angela allowed herself a small laugh.

"Come on — out with it! You are, aren't you?"

"No to both. I'm not pregnant and I haven't told anyone but you that I'm going to Sarajevo."

"Mom's going to be so pissed!" Margaret said.

The clink of silverware reached them from the other room. Margaret lowered her voice further. "Did you wait till now so you could spoil her weekend?"

Angela swatted Margaret with her dishtowel. "I did no such thing! I didn't really plan it, to tell the truth. I just found out last week." She shrugged. "Month."

Suddenly, they were teenagers again, conniving against their mother. But Angela knew better than to annoy their mother. Not here. Not this weekend. She picked up the cutting board and wiped it down with quick, even strokes before snagging it on a hook over the sink.

"How are the phobias?" Angela asked, to change the subject.

"A lot better," Margaret said, averting her eyes. Her voice took on a practised brightness. "The therapy's helping. I don't get nearly as scared as I used to. I may never get on a plane again, but cars are no problem as long as they don't go too fast."

When the fears started, Margaret had tried to explain how everything menaced, how the most innocuous things could fill her with terror. A smudge on the wall or a fallen branch might seem fraught with foreboding. The feel of death was everywhere. *Irrational, but not one bit less frightening for it*, was how she put it. The blank looks she got told her she was wasting her time. Nor could she say why she spent hours rearranging her clothes each morning, her nerves fragile with the effort, till they felt just right. One misstep could send all her artfully contrived assurances crashing to the ground, leaving her in tears and feeling she couldn't go on. Most of all, she was horrified by her children's bewildered faces when she was caught in the riptides of fear and indecision. She loathed BJ's vague disappointment over her paralysis. *But honey — we've planned this for months and the tickets cost* $75. Or how he'd try to reassure her through her tears that it didn't really matter, after all.

Postpartum depression, the doctors said, but Angela suspected it was a genetic legacy from their mother. Her childhood memories of Abbie were of things withered and broken. When Angela was six, Conrad told her that their mother needed to go away for a while. *She was wounded*, he'd said. Angela envisioned a bird trapped beneath a cat's paw, its eyes rolled back. There had been no flowers in the house then. The day her mother left, Angela squeezed her lifeless hand and watched her withdraw, wondering if she'd ever have a mother again. Then one day Abbie returned, her calm restored. They understood she'd come through something none of them could see. Her sister now shared this over-sensitivity to life.

"I kept wanting to scream, 'I can't take it anymore!'" Margaret said. "But I was afraid of sounding like a bad Shelley Winters caricature."

Angela managed a smile.

"My shrink calls it 'Housewife's Disease,'" Margaret continued. "She says a lot of women panic in public because they spend too much time alone. There were days when I couldn't leave the house, that's how frightened I was."

Angela's fears were of a different order — girls and women raped by soldiers, breasts slashed off with machetes, children killed by landmines. That was her reality, though at some point the fear simply became the statistical odds in an equation that said everyone died and sooner wasn't that much worse than later. Knowing this made Angela impatient of all fears — her own or anyone's.

A clatter of dishes in the dining room made them both start.

"Do you need help out there, Mom?" Margaret called.

Abbie's reply took a moment to reach them, as though she were three rooms away rather than right next door. "I'm fine, thank you."

Angela decided to risk the question that had been weighing on her mind the last few hours. "When did Dad start using a cane?"

Margaret's forehead crinkled in concentration. "Sometime in the spring, I think. You haven't seen him since then?"

Angela ignored the question. "Is he all right?"

"As far as anyone knows." Margaret shrugged. "I thought he seemed a little short of breath, but that might just be from the flu. If there is anything wrong, we probably won't know anything until Mom decides it's time for us to hear about it."

As if on cue, Abbie returned to the room.

"I was just saying I hadn't known Dad was using a cane," Angela said. She tried to make the remark sound casual, as though she hadn't been pressing Margaret for information. "Is he okay?"

"Your father's as fine as any sixty-two-year-old workaholic can be," Abbie said. "Retirement hasn't been able to slow him down, and neither have I."

"But is he okay?"

Abbie's eyes narrowed. "Yes, dear. He's fine. I would tell you if he weren't."

Angela looked away. "Good."

AN HOUR LATER, THE TABLE was set. The smell of roasting meat hung tantalizingly in the air. Angela watched her mother check the tight fists of dough rising in the oven. Abbie tore apart a bun and inhaled as the steam rose gratifyingly into the air.

"Did I tell you Elizabeth York's husband left her for the neighbour's daughter?" she asked, closing the oven door.

"I don't think so," Margaret said, catching Angela's eye: *Today's lesson — neighbourhood scandals.*

Abbie removed her oven mitts and laid them on the counter. "The girl is barely half his age. I was surprised to see Elizabeth out pruning the hedges last week. The weekend before that, she turned up at a church social. It just amazes me how she goes on as though nothing has happened."

"Maybe she's happier," Angela said with a shrug. "You can hardly expect the woman to stop living just because her husband left her."

"I suppose you think she should be liberated about it and write an account in the family newsletter?"

"Do people still write family newsletters?" Angela asked, mock-innocent.

"Yes, I forgot. How would you know? Such things don't exist in your world."

The words were a flung glove. Lack of etiquette, even other people's marital troubles were a fault of Angela's lifestyle. People's lives fell apart, but if Angela Thomas had only settled down in one place, they might have been perfectly fine.

Abbie sighed. "It's no wonder my children think I'm old and hopelessly out-of-date."

"No, we don't, Mom," Margaret interjected.

"Yes, we do," Angela murmured.

Abbie's lips pressed into the semblance of a smile. "I know things have changed since I was your age," she said. She reached up to her hair, as though the thought unsettled her. "Even here, in this place, where I thought nothing would ever change. When your father and I first came out here all this land was forest for miles around," she said. "I heard on the news the other day the government just sold that last tract of land down by the bridge."

Margaret reacted predictably. "I can't believe they'd do that! It's one of the oldest stands in the Bruce. They have white cedars there that are incredibly rare!"

Abbie was unsympathetic. "People need jobs," she said. She looked around and clucked in dismay. "I suppose we'll have to use paper napkins tonight. That's all there is." She turned her attention to their handiwork, leaning forward for inspection. "Did you girls put cilantro in the salad?"

Angela and Margaret looked at one another blankly.

"I didn't. Did you?" Margaret said.

"Not me."

Abbie sampled the dish suspiciously. "I can taste it!" she declared. "I won't be able to eat it. You know how it upsets my digestion."

"Mom, there's no cilantro in the salad," Angela insisted.

Abbie pulled out an offending bit of leaf as an intrepid detective might present a single thread left at the scene of the murder. "What do you call this?"

"I think it's Italian parsley."

Margaret grabbed at loose greens around the sink. "It's okay, Mom. I'll make another one for you."

"I'm not trying to cause trouble," Abbie said. "I just asked a simple question. That's all."

She exited, bowl in hand, surrendering her vision of a necessary order into the not-quite-capable hands of her daughters.

Once she'd gone, Margaret breathed out her exasperation. "Can't we do anything right?"

"Of course not. You know the rules."

"Mom lacks nurturing instincts."

"No doubt she used them all up raising us."

Angela watched Margaret negotiating her way through the salad a second time. "Why do you always placate her?"

Margaret stopped and looked up. "Because it's easier. Maybe you don't remember what it's like when she's upset. Tempers running hot and cold, the lectures on good manners and duty and self-sacrifice ..."

"For God's sakes, Margaret — just ignore her. Of course I remember. I remember very well. Or do you think I'm too busy playing war games to care about what goes on here?"

As soon as they were out, Angela wished she could take back

the words, but they'd formed a shape for themselves and gone spinning around the room like a swarm of bees.

Margaret looked away. All day she'd been waiting for a chance to tell Angela how much she'd missed her and worried for her: how she wished they still lived in the same city and shared a bedroom, having long sisterly conversations into the nights. Now, she couldn't say a thing.

Angela saw the effect her words had had. She was appalled by her own tactlessness, regretting her lack of patience for the delicate balances maintained by her family, for the small necessary gestures that held everything in place. She placed a hand on Margaret's shoulder.

"I'm sorry. I didn't mean to snap."

Margaret ignored the hand. "I'm fine," she said, shearing the papery skin off a fat white garlic clove with the tip of a paring knife.

ANGELA DROVE TORI INTO TOWN to meet her boyfriend's bus. They parked the Range Rover and walked down the street to the old train station. Once an optimistic blue evoking vastness and distance, the building had faded into a dull grey along with almost everything else in the town, one more half-forgotten rail link at the base of the peninsula. Inside, there was no longer a station master checking his watch against the arriving trains, just a solitary agent dispensing bus tickets from behind a wicket, her face as tight and faded as the station walls.

There was scarcely even a sense of adventure about the place, merely the fleeting reminder of its possibility in colourful brochures listing the arrival and departure times of the coaches and destinations farther along the shore. Any hint of the past or the once-extraordinary nature of undertaking a journey had all but disappeared, leaving in its place a solitary waiting bench, and a space on the horizon where the tracks ran through as though still awaiting the return of the faithfully approaching trains.

Angela watched Tori bite her nails, resentful and bored with the world. The last time she'd paid attention to her, Tori was still a guileless teenager with crushes on pop stars. That had been a mere two years ago, but light years in a teenager's development. She recalled the disturbing hints from Margaret that the real reason Tori landed in the hospital last spring wasn't from bronchitis, but something more. Angela had been away at the time and only heard the news on her return. "It was nothing," her mother claimed. "She was careless with some sleeping pills — probably too much stress over exams. She'll be more cautious in future." Angela couldn't think what was worse — that a middle-class kid with no real problems would work herself up to a half-hearted suicide attempt, or that they all pretended it never happened.

On the way to town, she made an effort to listen as Tori went on about the state of the world — racism, the environment, political corruption. It was a babble of indignation, as if she alone had discovered these injustices. Her owl-like eyes and heavy makeup only made her seem ludicrous — Rocker Chick Attacks New World Order. Her sentences were full of jargon and buzzwords like *access*, *gender-equity*, *marginalization*. They were the catchphrases of today's university grounds, reflecting the new frontiers of society, the new Bastille they alone must storm. It was a generation that had grown up doubting the effectiveness of everyone who'd gone before them. Angela wondered how they would cope if they had to face any of the world's real problems: starvation, genocide, illiteracy.

By 5:40, a small crowd had gathered. Tori smirked at the expectant faces, their unfashionable dress, and idle chatter. Still, Angela noticed, she managed a smile when the bus shimmered into view and stopped before them. People cheered, finding glamour in the ordinary, as though it brought promise into their lives. For a moment, Tori appeared to feel the same. Shep's head popped through the open doorway. His hair had that just-woke-up messiness, which he cultivated. A goatee defined his mouth and chin. He was lean and sexy, and he knew it. Angela watched him step down slowly, as though his long legs were still asleep in their Gap khakis. One hand clung to a backpack, another to the door handle. A tattooed snake curled down his right forearm, while a doglike animal trotted across the left. He smiled and perfect rows of teeth bloomed.

"Baby, I am so glad to see you! An hour of suburban hell and three hours of cow pastures is enough to make this city boy want to stay in the city forever." He kissed her. "But for you, I have traversed the Circles of Purgatory."

"Then you should be ready to meet my family," Tori told him.

His face approximated horror. "Your family? You mean I'm going to meet your family?"

She slapped at his arm. "You better be ready. I told you, you're walking into the Land of the Amazons."

"Co-o-o-ol!" he intoned, eyes wide. "The tribe awaits!"

Tori turned to Angela. "This is Shep," she said. "My sister, Angela."

"Hey!" He extended his hand. "I've studied your work in my media relations course," he said with enthusiasm. "It's powerful stuff. You're very brave."

Angela always felt surprised when people said they knew her, as if they'd mistaken her for someone else. Still, she wasn't ready to be charmed by him. "It's a living," she said, slinging his pack into the back of the Rover.

SHEP JUMPED FROM THE RANGE Rover. *Wow!* he mouthed. He turned in circles, taking in the stone cottage nestled against the backdrop of trees, and the rugged curtain of rock across the bay, as if the northern lights had touched the earth and petrified. "This is a summer cottage? Amazing!"

Tori smiled. "It's our little family secret. We've been coming here every summer for thirty years. Well, the others have — I've only been coming for nineteen."

He looked up at the trees arching over the roof. They were grand, beautiful, majestic. Yet he knew those clumsy words didn't do them justice. He saw how they swept overhead in the breeze as light filtered through the branches, making them glow from within. He felt diminished by their splendour.

"Are those the trees you told me about? What are they called?"

"Honey locusts. The one on the left is Angela's. That's Margaret's in the middle. The one on the right — the shortest — was planted the week I was born and it'll still be here when I'm an old woman."

"Cool! It's like having a star named after you."

MARGARET STOOD INSIDE THE COTTAGE watching. She noted Shep's clothes — Nirvana T-shirt, the funky cargo pants over slim hips. He made her feel ancient. She wiped her hands idly on the dishcloth, tucked a blond strand behind one ear.

Angela entered. "We're back."

"My, my! Where does she find them?" Margaret murmured.

Angela stood looking out the window over Margaret's shoulder. "Check out the tattoos."

"Mm-hmm! And that ain't all. The girl really has a knack for choosing the ones who'll get under Mom's skin. Do you think she does it on purpose?"

"Of course. Didn't you?"

Shep came in behind Tori and dropped his backpack on the floor inside the front entrance.

Margaret fixed on the goatee, allowing her gaze to trail down his throat and chest. Up close, he seemed much more solidly built. She imagined herself ripping the T-shirt over his head, leaving him bare-chested with just that string of orange beads peeking above his collar. She'd known boys like this in high school. They perspired delicate beads of sweat at the slightest exertion.

"This is my other sister, Margaret."

"Great to meet you, Margaret," he said.

"Likewise." She held his glance, noting his long beautiful lashes, vaguely aware she was flirting with her sister's boyfriend.

Abbie entered behind them. "This is my mother," Tori said, as though introducing a neighbour she couldn't avoid. "Mom, this is Shep Spencer."

Shep put on a winning smile. He hadn't exactly practised this moment except in a dull, dim way, but he'd been conscious of its impending arrival for the entire trip. In fact, he'd been mustering himself — his presence — to be whatever it should be right now, as he stood before the guardian of the gates to a world whose splendour he'd only dimly imagined until this moment.

"It's a real pleasure to meet you, Mrs. Thomas," he said, resisting the urge to bow.

Abbie's face gave no indication whether she would be moved by his attempt to ingratiate himself. Shep's effort seemed to glance off her, falling to the floor by her feet.

"Likewise, Mr. Spencer."

"Call me Shep," he offered.

She noticed the tattoos criss-crossing his forearms. "Are you with the circus, Shep?" Abbie asked, smile perfect and in place.

For a moment he was bewildered, then he caught the reference. Instead of being embarrassed, he extended both arms to display his tattoos fully.

"Oh, right! I got these last year on my birthday."

Good for you, Angela thought. Make no apologies. Don't get caught in her trap.

"What could possibly inspire such an act?" Abbie said sweetly, as though thanking him for a gift.

Shep felt the judgment fall. He lowered his arms and turned to take in the room. "It's a great place you have here, Mrs. Thomas," he said. "It's very …"

He paused to find the right word, which would inevitably be the wrong word, knowing there was nothing acceptable for what he was thinking — that the interior felt remarkably sterile for a stone cottage perched in the middle of some of the most ruggedly beautiful scenery he'd ever seen.

"It's very tidy … and clean. For a cottage, I mean." He stopped, covering his awkwardness with a smile.

Abbie considered Shep's remark in contrast with his appearance, which was neither clean nor tidy in her assessment. "Thank you," she pronounced, with a nod that might signify the queen's acceptance or dismissal.

Before Shep could figure it out, BJ and Markus arrived from the porch. Markus was having a fit of giggles that seemed to have something to do with his father's colourful golf shirt.

"This is my husband, BJ," Margaret said. "And this is Markus, our son-in-training. This is Tori's boyfriend, Shep."

Shep shook BJ's hand enthusiastically. "Hi, how are you? You're the comic, right?"

Angela was impressed — he'd done his homework. She couldn't help admiring that. She'd do the same, though she might not be so quick to reveal it.

BJ caught sight of Shep's tattoos. He pulled his hand back in mock fright. "Yikes! Do those things bite?"

"Cool!" Markus squealed. "Can I see?"

Shep displayed his arms for the boy. Markus examined them in awe and looked at Margaret. "Mom, can I have a tattoo?"

"Hmm. Not today, honey," Margaret answered in her best Carol Brady imitation just as Conrad came down the stairs.

"Who wants a tattoo?" he said, as everyone turned to him.

"Here's my dad," Tori said. "Dad, this is Shep Spencer."

"Pleased to meet you, sir," Shep said, even-keeled, with no attempt to charm.

"Conrad, please." He grasped the extended hand, taking in the tattoos. "Those are real works of art," he said, but without making Shep feel like a failed experiment.

"At least he's on time for supper," Abbie announced. She turned to Tori. "He'll have just enough time to change."

Shep was starting to feel trapped. He realized he should have paid more attention to Tori's warnings about her family. His eyes begged her for his cue.

"Come on," she said. "I'll show you where to put your things."

Grateful for the reprieve, he picked up his pack and followed her upstairs.

"That's certainly an unusual individual," Abbie said when they'd gone.

Her hand reached up to her temple as though to quell a disturbing thought, something unsettling she couldn't place. She made her way back to the kitchen. The weekend must not be ruined by thoughtless behaviour.

BOOK III
IN A PIG'S EYE

SEVEN

Angela sat at the table eating dinner with André when the satellite phone crackled to life. It was Martin. He wanted a story about the black markets. The country's ongoing misfortunes had generated a highly profitable underground economy. A phalanx of warlords and small-time Mafia leaders were benefiting from within, while foreign profiteers circled like hyenas, prolonging the kill in order to soak the profits from without.

Angela knew where to turn. Everyone had tales of bribery and corruption to tell — how the shelling could be stopped for a price, how water had been cut off and restored again once debts were settled. Greed had surpassed ideology as the compelling factor in the war. In one enclave, the Serb Army rented tanks to the Croats to fight against the Muslims for 1200 Deutschmarks a day, while at times the Croats sold their own oil to the Serbs. One night, a paid informer took Angela and André out to hear the gurgling pipelines as fuel was siphoned off in exchange for innocent lives.

Two days after Martin's call, they sat on a café patio. Muffled explosions reached them from a distance. A barrage had started up somewhere. People hurried past in twos and threes. The proprietor served them as if nothing out of the ordinary were happening. Each time he emerged, he looked up as if to gauge his distance from the shelling. Perhaps he had family to worry about, a home to consider. Maybe his wife was there now, gathering the children and bundling belongings they would already have ear-marked: *This clothing and furniture can stay — let them take it if they want — but the family pictures and china must come with us when we leave.*

A young man arrived in ragged jeans and a dirty Metallica sweatshirt. He was one of Angela's informants, sixteen or seventeen. He spoke earnestly, suggesting they go to a public square in a suburb just outside the city that afternoon; they would witness a prisoner drop-off.

"How's this related to the black market?" Angela asked.

"They arrested some men for selling humanitarian aid packages stolen from government buildings, but others have said it wasn't them." He shrugged. "They also arrested four Italian journalists for spying this morning. The Serbs say they're going to start killing foreign journalists."

Angela studied his face. "Why?"

His boot soles, one held on with wire, nervously tapped the tiles beneath the table. "They believe you are turning everyone against them."

"They're doing a fairly good campaign against themselves," Angela said. "Karadžić's daughter is supposed to be the press coordinator and she won't let anyone near her father. It doesn't help them."

Another shrug. "Sonja Karadžić is a pig. Even the Serbs hate her."

André offered him a cigarette and watched as he struggled to light it.

"There is more talk of NATO intervention," the boy said, exhaling. "Though why it would happen now ..."

He shrugged again, his response to everything. Clearly, his belief in outside salvation was minimal. Angela wanted to tell him not to wait for NATO. The world was waiting for NATO to get involved, but no one knew when, or even if, they might enter the war.

André stuffed some money in the pack of cigarettes and threw it on the table. The boy pocketed it, nodded in thanks and left as quickly as he'd come.

They had no reason not to believe the boy's words — he'd passed along valuable tips before. His information had sent Angela to the cleansed village with the Belgian MSF contingent before anyone else got there.

"This could be ugly," she told André on the way back to the compound to pick up their gear. "You don't have to come."

"How ugly can it be?"

"At the camps I visited, some of the prisoners had been burned alive. Others were beaten to death with hammers. The survivors were made to clear out the corpses in the morning."

"Is that it?"

He'd meant to ask if she was holding anything back, but she took it for bravado. "Those were the quick deaths," she said. "Don't forget, it's intellectuals they go for first. That's definitely me and maybe even you."

"Does intellectual mean 'callous'?"

The story of the arrested journalists checked out. Angela and André donned flak jackets, pocketing their press cards and identification badges. Within minutes they passed the first checkpoint in the Jeep. Outside the city, the fields were dotted with ripe pumpkins and neatly ordered bales of hay, as though the war didn't exist. Five minutes later, they passed the UN-controlled area and entered a dead zone of scorched rocket launchers and blackened tanks hunkered alongside the road. Even André was silent as they drove past.

A dried up fountain sat in the middle of a public square. The buildings surrounding it had no windows. Their frames showed only darkened interiors. Bullet holes pocked every wall in sight.

They waited for more than an hour, passing out gum to a few curious children. Suddenly, the square came alive. A crowd rushed in, shouting as an open-backed truck careened to a halt. Three men jumped out, tossing what looked like feed sacks onto the dusty cobblestones. There were four. The children and a few old women watched from a distance.

André grabbed his camera. A soldier standing on the back of the truck jumped down and waved him closer. He kicked one of the sacks and spat on it. "These, my friends," he said, "are the instruments of the enemy. Rapists and petty thieves. Vermin!"

The voices grew as a struggling, blindfolded figure was carried from the truck and up the stairs over the back of the square. A rope was looped around the man's head, the other end tossed over a lamppost.

"Now he will see," predicted the soldier.

Hands yanked off the blindfold. The prisoner blinked in the light and looked wildly around. He shouted as hands grabbed him and shoved him over the edge. His body jerked once then swung slowly back and forth.

André lowered his camera.

THE EVENING, ANGELA AND ANDRÉ stopped at a bar that kept late hours. Over in a corner, an unlit candelabrum rested on top of a piano. Wax drippings hung down like stalactites, time arrested. The place was empty, dozens of photographs of happy partygoers pinned to its walls in mute attestation to its former popularity.

A waiter in a tuxedo appeared from behind a curtain, bowing as he held out menus. His stiff formality was comic relief after the day's morbidity. Angela asked for wine. The man nodded and left.

André looked at a yellowed menu. Most of the items had been blacked out.

"Don't bother," she said. "There's only one thing you can order."

The waiter returned with a bottle, a cloth draped over his arm. He made a show of opening the wine and filling their glasses. Angela was reminded of a dress-up game she'd once played with Margaret, an elaborate ceremony of imaginary dishes and social rituals. Their mother had joined them in the middle of it. It was not long after she'd returned from the hospital, and there had been a sad solemnity to her contributions, like this absurdly over-dressed waiter in the middle of a war.

André had barely spoken since their return from the village. To cheer him up, Angela recounted her tour of Rwanda. One day she'd sat in a hotel lobby for hours waiting to interview a local minister of justice when two men arrived bearing a skinned carcass on a long pole. There'd been no fresh meat for weeks. As the smell of roasting game emerged from the kitchen, everyone — from the most stalwart military personnel and hardened journalists down to the UN workers — had salivated. Later, they'd heard it was a dog killed in the shelling.

The waiter arrived with a meal of overcooked steak, fried potatoes and stewed cabbage. By then, the wine had loosened André's tongue. He began to speak suddenly, almost violently. "Who do you think those men were this afternoon?"

"Hard to say."

They had tried interviewing, even bribing, some of the locals, but they remained mute with fear. No one seemed to know — or want to divulge — who had been killed, and why.

André persisted. "Could they have been the Italian journalists?"

Angela shrugged. "The boy said there were four journalists, but there were five bodies." She shook her head. "There's no way of telling. We'll likely hear about it tomorrow."

He pounded his fists on the table and nearly rose out of his chair. "Why didn't they kill us, too? We're journalists."

She waited till he calmed down. "Maybe they hoped we'd make an example of the others. We may never know. No use worrying about it."

"But why was one alive and the others dead?"

"How am I supposed to know? Stop talking and eat."

She watched him in the dim light — the red headband, the gold earring. A day's growth of beard made him look older, but not much. He picked up his fork then put it back beside the plate. "I never saw anyone killed before," he said. "The awful thing was — it didn't seem real."

He was raw with the knowledge, trying to accommodate the fact that he'd just watched another human being die. Angela saw him struggling, trying to find a place inside him where it didn't cut or jab or demand his attention. This was what made people dark or light, she knew. It was what made them fit to work under adverse conditions, or made them candidates for a breakdown. Those who couldn't accept the facts were overwhelmed by them. She wouldn't sympathize with him. She disliked illusions and preferred them shattered.

She pushed her plate aside and looked around the empty restaurant, then back at him. "Why did you come here? Did you think this was going to be a play war, where no one got hurt?"

He shifted uncomfortably. He removed his headband and tossed it on the table.

"You've seen the food lineups, people starving, the rotting piles of garbage in the streets. You've watched them fight over a ladleful of aid rations. This is reality here. You and I are exempt from the worst of it. We can march in here with our Deutschmarks and order a half-decent meal, all things being relative. I'd say you're damned lucky you haven't watched someone die till today."

He leaned away from the table, balancing on the chair's legs. He put his hands together in a child's version of a church-and-steeple then leaned forward again, the legs landing square.

"So why are we here?" he asked finally. He picked up his glass and swirled it, peering into the redness as though the answer might lie there.

He waited, wanting her to explain things for him, to say more. But she withheld: emotions, facts, sympathy. Normally, he could read people from a touch, decode them with a glance — fears and weaknesses, hopes and despairs. With most people it sat on the surface waiting to be deciphered, though they professed astonishment at his skills to interpret their private natures, describing their innermost selves as though he saw right through them. A personality is a disguise, he'd say. A mask. Follow a twitch to the unvoiced fear, a stolen glance to the hidden desire, the outlines of a sheet to the body lying beneath. With most people it was easy. But with Angela — nothing. Not a clue to give her away.

"You can't question everything that happens," she said. "Just accept that you're here and get on with your job. If you let everything get to you, you'll lose your sanity."

"I feel like a parasite."

Her hand gestured impatiently. He'd offered his uncomfortable — his painful — confession. She'd dismissed him.

"You are. We all are. We're sitting here with full plates while down the street families are making soup out of a handful of beans and calling it supper. Probably after no breakfast or lunch. The blood you've seen on the pavements after a shelling is real. We've watched these people dodging sniper fire as they carry home pints of water. We've seen them taking their shit out to the dump in plastic bags."

He tugged at an ear.

Was she getting through to him? He seemed in shock, his fear sitting on the surface. Understanding would sink in later, if at all. She knew it was a mistake to send these under-experienced and overeager idealists here.

"Look," she said, laying her hands palms-down on the table. "I've been in countries where you can teach people things. How to build better water systems or dispose of waste. Reading, writing — that's of value. Here, there's nothing to teach. They're not repeating history — they're erasing it. The most we can do is bring attention to the plight of the people trapped in this city. Maybe there'll be outside intervention some day because of what we're doing. Until then, don't let your mind run in circles. It won't help."

It won't help either of us was what she'd implied. He lacked her faith in logic. Ideas had no appeal for him. He needed to feel something before he could believe in it. He might recognize the features of a thirty-year-old woman in a photograph, and he could accept that they once belonged to his mother, but he couldn't believe in her love because he couldn't remember what it had felt like.

"Tell me more about your photos," André said. "The ones you study at night."

She repeated the story of the second Siege of Malta, of the small band of pilots and sailors who were its saviours.

"Most of the men were renegades and cast-offs from other squadrons," she said. "They were the war's unwanted heroes. No one ever figured they'd be the key to winning the Mediterranean for the Allies. If it hadn't been for them" — she smiled here — "we might be speaking German today."

What fascinated her, she said, was the symmetry of both sieges. How two invading armies had lost the war almost four centuries apart for exactly the same reason. It was no different from the one the Serbs and Croats were fighting, battling for the same ground their ancestors had fought over seven hundred years earlier. An outline traced beneath history, a fault line running beneath countless lives.

ON THE WAY BACK, THEY missed a turn. Angela reversed and drove faster, the Jeep careening around curves. Curfew was approaching and the streets were a blackened maze. They'd be hard put to find a place to spend the night. So many roads were blocked by debris; others were missing signs to tell them where they were. The darkness up on Mount Trebević might at that moment be concealing a missile launcher holding them in its viewfinder. She fought to keep her panic in check.

They lurched around a corner and found themselves confronted by soldiers standing in front of sandbags and barbed wire. One was short and fat, the other tall and thin. Both had rifles pointed at them. A hand motioned them forward.

"Serbs," she said.

Angela nosed the Jeep up to the barricade. The taller of the guards, dressed in fatigues and with his hair in a ponytail, stepped up to her window. A flashlight played over their faces.

"*Pomoz' bog*," Angela said. A Serbian greeting — God help you. "We're Canadian journalists."

The soldier smirked. "Then God should help you — not me. What are you doing here?"

She pulled out her press card, explaining they were lost. He listened sceptically, retreating with their papers to a small hut while the shorter man kept his rifle trained on them.

Angela eyed the retreating guard. "He's probably checking to see if we're on a list of people he shouldn't fuck with. If we're lucky, they'll give us our documents back and let us turn around."

"And if not?"

"Then either they'll send us away without them or they'll arrest us. God knows what'll happen then."

André was calm. "What about bribery?"

"What have we got?"

"My cigarettes. Your camera. A few American dollars."

"No to the camera."

"Not even to save your life?"

She hesitated. "Maybe mine."

The first soldier emerged from the hut and headed back to the Jeep.

"Know how to make God laugh?" André asked, watching his advance.

"No. How?"

"Tell Him your plans."

The tall soldier conferred with his shorter companion. They both looked over at the Jeep a few times, as though calculating something.

"This doesn't look good for us," Angela said.

"Alternate endings," André said.

"What?"

"We need to imagine an alternate ending — a good ending — to this scenario."

He leaned past Angela to speak through the driver's window as the short guard approached. "Would you like a cigarette?" he asked. He held out an unopened package with some American bills wrapped around it.

The man regarded him suspiciously. He reached for the pack and slipped it inside his jacket. "Your papers do not allow you into this sector," he said.

"I told you — we're lost," Angela repeated. "We're trying to find our hotel. Please — let us turn around and go back."

"How do I know you are not CIA?" the soldier growled.

"If we were CIA we wouldn't be stupid enough to end up on your doorstep," she said.

"Why should I believe you?"

"We're lost," Angela insisted. "We're journalists, not spies. It says so on our papers."

"Papers lie," he said, looking into the back seat. "What is that?"

"It's my camera," Angela said edgily. "I told you, we're journalists."

"What pictures have you taken?"

"None. Here — I'll show you."

She grabbed the Leica, yanking the back open to expose the film. Any shots were better destroyed than to let them fall into the hands of people who might use them against her. She dropped the camera back into its bag.

"See? Nothing."

The soldier scowled and pointed his gun through the window. "Get out," he said.

"We don't want to cross. Just let us turn back."

The tall soldier moved alongside, shining his light in their eyes. Both guns were pointed at them now. "Get out. Put your hands over your head!"

They emerged and stood with their hands behind their heads as the taller man looked through the back of the Jeep and under the seats. He wrapped the straps of the camera bag tightly around his fist. "This I keep," he said.

"*Merde!*"

The guard turned to André. "You are French?"

"Canadian."

"Yet you speak French ..."

"He's French-Canadian …" Angela interrupted. She saw where it was heading. Even if they weren't going to kill them, they could easily justify a severe beating given to two foreigners out past curfew. Rape would not be impossible. "Look, just keep the fucking camera."

"What else do you have?"

"Nothing. Keep the camera and let us go or I'll file a complaint."

"You are spies. I can arrest you."

"Go ahead. Then call the Canadian embassy. You'll just be releasing us in the morning after a shitload of paper work."

Angela suspected they both knew there was only so much huffing and puffing they could do before someone called the other's bluff. The tall soldier hesitated then handed over their documents. "You can go."

They climbed back into the Jeep. The soldier held up the camera and pretended to snap their picture. Angela rolled the window up in his face.

"If we argue he might give back the camera," André suggested.

"We have to get back. We're late."

"It's only a curfew."

"Another few minutes and he would've been asking for the fucking Jeep, if he'd been smart enough to think of it. Anything can happen here after curfew. This isn't Canada. They don't hold referendums over separation issues. They kill people. Try to remember that."

She backed the Jeep around. They arrived at the compound just as the nightly shelling started.

IT RAINED DURING THE NIGHT and the smell of sodden ash filled the morning air. Angela walked the fourteen blocks to the offices of the Belgian Médecins Sans Frontières. From outside, the reddish-pink brick radiated a momentary hope that dissolved the instant she entered its dingy lobby where she had to accept that she was simply in another building in a city comprised of endless cul-de-sacs.

Angela liked the Belgians. They were a cheerful, sober-minded people, though the one time she'd been in their country she found it drab and endlessly depressing. A good place for signing war treaties, she'd thought. She climbed to the third floor, knocked, and entered. The office was in greater disarray than usual due to the previous night's bombing. Some of the staff had slept over on cots.

A voice cried out. "Ah, the Canadian contingent has arrived for breakfast!"

It was Mathilde, a cheerful, dark-haired nurse Angela had met during her first week in the city.

"Coffee?"

Mathilde smiled. "Be right with you."

They dropped into a nearby café where Angela recounted the events at the checkpoint the previous evening. Mathilde clucked sympathetically. A formal complaint would prove useless, they both knew, but she urged Angela to lodge one anyway. With any luck, it might have a cumulative effect with the thousand of other similar complaints. One of the MSF trucks had been overturned in a mortar attack earlier in the week, she said. By the time they got to it, it had been looted and burned, costing them two months' worth of medical supplies. A similar mishap had befallen the World Food Project the previous day when several vehicles loaded with emergency rations for out-lying towns had been hijacked. Her colleagues suspected they were all inside jobs. Like everyone else in Sarajevo, Mathilde was happy to contribute her stories of loss — they were a badge of honour, a membership to an exclusive club.

Mathilde used to tease her for writing everything down; now it had become a game, as she gathered gossip and rumours to pass along over coffee and sweet rolls. Today she had some gems to share. Her team was currently short-staffed because one of their new doctors had been sent home after they discovered he was a morphine addict.

"Can you believe it? No one checked his discharge papers from the hospital he worked in before coming here!"

Even better, Mathilde had met a wealthy Armenian who proposed on their second date. They'd gone to an early afternoon performance of a string quartet, one of many similar concerts given as the city strove to maintain the illusion of normalcy. He'd brought out a ring right after the Dvořák.

"No one's wasting time here," she said with a laugh.

"Did you accept?"

Mathilde smiled. "The ring was nice — but no."

They finished their coffee and Mathilde returned to work. Angela continued on to the *markale* where a direct rocket hit had killed sixty-eight people and injured dozens. It amazed her how it had simply reopened a week later, practicality winning out over sentiment, but what else was there to do? It was full now. She mingled with the women buying dog-eared greens and battered root vegetables. She picked up some onions and potatoes, and left with her purchases.

She returned to the flat. André had gone out, leaving his

unwashed breakfast dishes in the sink. Despite regulations, he'd
left no word where he'd gone or when he expected to be back.
She finished two reports then spent an hour in the developing
lab before going for a walk. By four o'clock, André still hadn't
returned. He'd taken his knapsack, but left his camera and his
bulletproof vest. It annoyed her that he hadn't told her his plans.

At five she started supper, laying onions, garlic, and eggs on
the counter beside a jar of flour. She glanced at the stove: there
was enough wood to get them through the next few days. She
dropped a few potatoes in the sink, scrubbing till they gleamed
yellow-white under her fingers. One by one, she scraped them
against a bottle lid she'd punctured from inside with a nail to
form a rough grating surface. The grated pulp dropped neatly
into the jar. Her mother would be impressed with her domes-
tic inventiveness.

When the jar was full, she emptied the milky contents onto
a towel to wring out the water. The satellite phone crackled to
life. She wiped her hands before grabbing it. It was her contact
at the UN. She sat and took notes on troop movement in
Slovenia for a while. By the time the call ended it was dark outside. Still no word from André. The first batch of latkes was
sizzling when the key turned in the lock.

"When was the last time you had anything from 1893?" she
heard him ask. "And I don't mean sex."

"Are you aware that regulations say you're not to go off alone
for an entire day without telling someone where you are?"

He tugged at the strings of his knapsack, letting it slide from
his shoulders. He reached in and pulled out her camera with a
flourish. "*Voilà!* The magic eye."

"Where the hell have you been?" she demanded, ignoring his stage tricks.

"I thought you'd be able to guess," he said. "I went back to the checkpoint and found out where our friendly border guard lives. Then I went to his home and talked him into giving me back your Leica."

His smile infuriated her. "Don't tell me — it was your natural charm that convinced him."

"Of course!"

Angela turned angrily back to the stovetop where smoke rose from the pan. She flipped the latkes, splattering grease on the stove and floor.

"Of course he didn't just hand it over. I had to negotiate. They like that here, I've learned. I offered to help his sister emigrate to Canada ..."

She turned. "You can't do that!"

He shrugged. "My brother-in-law works for Immigration Canada. I said I'd pass her name along when the time came."

"So you risked your life for a camera?"

"Not just any camera — I know how much this one means to you. After that, I offered him a joint to cement the deal, as you English say."

Angela moved the pan from the burner and turned off the stove.

André sniffed. "Ahh! Potato pancakes. I should have asked if he had any applesauce." He winked. "It turns out our friend Bruno the checkpoint guard is a connoisseur, like me. He went down to his cellar and brought up a small bottle of French brandy from 1893."

He reached into the knapsack again and held up a bottle. It was green, irregular in size and thickness. No labels — just a stamp pressed into the glass.

"Which, no doubt, he looted from some private collection."

André shook the remains, a tempest tossed sea inside the bottle. "No doubt. But it tastes miraculous. Would you like some?" He held it out to her.

She wanted to wipe the grin off his face. "That's a feeble excuse for being out all day without telling anyone where you were going. There's brave and then there's just plain stupid. What you did was stupid. I should report you."

He regarded her coolly and tossed her camera bag onto a chair. He jammed his fists into his pockets and swayed back and forth on his heels.

"Is it that hard for you to say 'thank you'?" he asked. "I don't even care what language you say it in."

ONCE ANDRÉ LEARNED WHAT AGGRAVATED her, her private vocabulary of annoyance, he went out of his way to provoke her. He would leave at any time of day without saying where he was headed. He might be going for groceries; he might be following up on a story.

"Just going down the street," he'd say, if she bothered to ask. When she didn't, he left her to guess. He knew it was childish.

Some nights he stayed out past curfew, purposely delaying his return. Once he stayed out all night. Angela tried to file a missing persons report, but the fax was powerless and the embassy phone rang endlessly. The next day she learned he was picked up by the Serbian secret police, who'd caught him urinating on the wall of a medieval church. He spent the night in a damp, crowded cell until someone from the embassy signed him out in the morning. After that, he stopped being so calculatedly reckless, but still spent most of his evenings in bars and private hotel rooms with other non-nationals. He knew she couldn't discover where he went if he didn't want her to. He also knew he'd fallen in love with her, and feared she might see it in his eyes.

He was twenty-six and had been in love only once, in the days before he'd figured love out. The affair began clumsily, in secret, and ended in tragedy. He'd sworn off love ever since, choosing the solitary life of a wanderer. Despite this, the emotion had followed him through his renunciation of it all the way to the Bosnian city where it threatened to become his own private war. He knew it was as determined to stay the course as he was to shake it.

On the nights he stayed out late, he might return to find her reading by candlelight. She denied waiting up for him. More often she was asleep, no longer willing to second-guess when he might return or worry if he didn't. He envied her her dreams and the people she met there. He wanted badly to tell someone how he felt about her, now that he'd accepted it, but there was no one else to confide in. He didn't dare write in his diary. He didn't trust words. Putting them on a page somehow made them more real than voicing them. The best thing was to leave them unspoken. He knew the Tibetans believed a man could escape a dangerous secret by whispering it into the knot of a tree or a crack in a stone wall, and sealing it up with mud afterwards. His diary had served that purpose before, but now he didn't trust it. Not with this. He wondered if she ever read the pages when he wasn't there. He considered creating a fictitious name for her and writing about his passions for this mystery woman instead, but he rejected the idea.

Instead, he created an inner diary, learning her gestures — the way her fingers moved across the paper when she wrote or how she pressed her palms flat on the desk to stand. He studied the stillness of her face when she looked outside just before shutting herself behind a door or window, as if she wanted to memorize what existed in the space beyond, retaining it in her memory.

At night she slept with her door ajar, leaving herself the smallest avenue of escape. He began to believe, on nights when he came in late, that she wasn't really sleeping. He imagined her eyes opening in the darkness, sensing him without seeing him there, waiting outside her door.

EIGHT

THE BARBARITIES BEGAN TO WEAR on her. Just over the border was Italy and its glories: St. Peter's in Rome, St. Mark's in Venice, the Uffizi, and the Accademia in Florence. There was Botticelli, Uccello, Caravaggio, della Francesca, and the immortal forms of Michelangelo. In Sarajevo, there was only suffering, and death, and more death. One night, the Bosnian National Library burned to the ground, destroying thousands of irreplaceable texts. Beyond the country's borders, the world watched in disbelief the atrocities perpetrated by thugs and criminals.

When the black market documentary aired, Martin called to congratulate Angela and André, sounding upbeat over the satellite phone. The piece had sparked a heated call-in debate on the ethics of wartime profiteering.

"Like the network's?" Angela asked.

"Hey, it's all pay-for-play," he said. "By the way, we've doubled our advertising sponsorship for the next segment."

"I guess I'm supposed to laugh here."

"Only if you really feel like it, darling. Cheer up! Who knows, you may actually be doing some good over there. At least you know the world takes an interest in what's happening."

The follow-up was equally well received, but Angela was wary of success. Television was rapacious, hungry. The images of disaster would flash across the screen, replaced in an instant by hairspray or body wash, a story on migrant farm workers or the lumber industry in Port Alberni. But whether their work had any lasting effect on public consciousness hardly mattered as long as NATO dickered on about whether or not to step in and end the fighting.

What began to matter to Angela more and more were her photographs of people living in the midst of war, a line of half-forgotten lives made visible, glowing bits of history. A French weekly bought her shots of a family huddled under the front of a tank, playing cards during a break in the fighting. Other publications snapped up her photo essay of children playing hide-and-seek behind sheets perforated with bullet holes. She hung the enlarged shots on every available wall in the apartment, slowly populating the rooms with the images.

The next time Martin called, Angela suggested a documentary on the daily struggles in the lives of the ordinary people of Sarajevo — the real face of the war. His response was cool. The network wanted something more upbeat, he said. The war's appeal was wearing thin. It might have been going on too long. The whole NATO thing — will they, won't they — could start losing audiences.

"I think we need something to jazz it up," he said. "Some fun, some verve — something daring. You know how stupid people are — you've got to shock them to keep their attention."

She hated his smugness, as though he had the world sewn up from his third floor office in Calgary. Fifth-rate kippers, she thought, coming over to tell the Canucks how. If Britain's such a great fucking place, then why leave it for a colonial backwater?

"Maybe they're looking for a bit of glamour," she suggested ironically.

"Yes — that's it! Glamour. Let's give them some of that old radical chic."

"I was kidding. Death isn't glamorous right now, Martin. Not over here."

"Then how about a piece on love among the expats? You've really got to sell us this war."

"You want me to sell you the war?"

Static covered the line for a second before his voice burst through again. "Get real, hon — this is TV!"

For a moment she was outraged then suddenly she laughed. "That's the funniest thing I've heard in years," she said.

"Glad you appreciate my humour. You've been getting far too serious on me, darling."

"But please tell me you're not that shallow …"

"Why do you think I'm sitting here in the editing suite and you're in the field?"

"How about a reality-based show then?" she suggested. "I could interview some Serb soldiers as they get dressed for the day's fighting, and then pop over to see what the Croats are having for breakfast, and ask how many Muslims they're hoping to take out that day."

Martin was silent.

"Then in the evening I could do a recap to see who's made it through and who's filled his quota." Still no reply. Maybe she'd finally angered him. She hoped so. "I'll line up potential grieving widows beforehand and have them waiting outside for the news. Would that do it?"

Finally, he spoke. "It needs something, I think. Orphans, maybe. Yes, definitely orphans. Lots of them running around, wailing for daddy."

She laughed in spite of herself. "You're a stupid cunt, Martin."

"God bless you," he said. "I love a woman who can really swear."

"My mother would die if she heard me say that."

"I won't tell her."

WHENEVER SHE COULD, SHE TOOK to the streets with her Leica. Graffiti was rife. Buildings bore the legend *Pazite, Snajper!* Beware, sniper! Elsewhere, *This is Serbia!* had been sprayed across the walls of a hotel. On the building opposite someone had scrawled, *This is Croatia!* A few doors down, someone else had found a moment of trenchant humour amid the destruction: *This is Turkey!*

The war was slipping from tragedy into burlesque. Leaders vied for camera time as they followed their television ratings. Old-school politicians were told to tone down the rhetoric and smile more — optimism before bombast. Meanwhile, gangsters vied for attention like rock stars, carving out celebrity lifestyles for themselves. People followed their antics as if they were soap-opera characters. That month the city's best-known gangster, Arkan, was getting married to Serbia's best-known pop singer. The event was getting scads of publicity.

It was Martin's wet dream come true — his hoped-for glamour amidst all the devastation.

Arkan had recently bought a house near the Marakana Stadium in Belgrade and appeared on television in a First World War uniform, cheering on the Belgrade Red Star football team. Catching onto the fad, restaurants began to serve cheese and wine from the region where Arkan's operations were based. Elsewhere, a rival gangster, a swaggering youth nicknamed Knele, showed up in discotheques wearing open-front shirts and sporting gold chains. Knele had the face of a matinee idol and the sneer of a killer. André interviewed both men and their followers, as he once had the biker gangs in Quebec. Everyone wanted to talk, to be seen on television.

"I don't know about his politics," declared one of Knele's admirers, "but he's a great bank robber. Undoubtedly, one of the best."

Two days before the piece aired, Knele was assassinated by rivals in the lobby of the Belgrade Hyatt. Martin professed his delight on hearing the news.

"Utterly fantastic! The timing couldn't have been better."

Knele had had the instincts of a true pop star.

NINE

"'THE HISTORY OF THIS LAND is long and bloody,'" Angela read out loud over breakfast. She looked over her glasses to where André sat shivering in his T-shirt. His arm snaked across the table for a piece of toast. He'd slept badly through the night's artillery fire. Dark circles outlined his eyes.

"'Accounts of the time spoke of a country flowing in gold and silver until the Turks got hold of it. But by the time of the Enlightenment, when maps were first made in copious numbers, the country of Servia was dismissed as having little left to appeal to reasoning minds.'"

The reading distracted him from his rambling breakfast monologues. He'd quickly become absorbed in her history lessons.

"'The first Serb uprising occurred in 1804,'" she continued, "'but the people of this land were at war long before that. During the uprising, a swine merchant named Djordje Petrović was elected as leader of the Serbs. Petrović soon delivered his countrymen from the Turks. Because of his dark complexion and short temper, he became known as Karadjordje — Black

George. The coat of arms worn by his followers consisted of a pig's head with one eye pierced by an arrow.'"

IN DECEMBER THEY WERE INVITED to a party being given by one of Angela's contacts. The evening air was crisp; sleet bit into their faces as they arrived at the stone mansion, which stood pristine behind iron gates. The neighbourhood seemed almost untouched by the war, its four-block radius largely intact. An armed guard escorted them upstairs along a chandelier-lined hallway where mirrors reached the ceiling. It would have been ostentatious at the best of times, but now it seemed strictly absurd.

The party was underway when Angela and André entered. A jazz orchestra buzzed in one corner. Private parties had become popular because of the large number of people under house arrest. Their host that evening, a UN observer, was an unofficial hostage of the Serb army, who used him as a bargaining tool. Parties were his way of passing the time. He'd recently been granted limited access to the city. In exchange for this bit of freedom, he invited Serb officials and their wives to his socials; they in turn invited him to their weddings and family gatherings.

The homes of political hostages were literally guaranteed safety in the event of attack. The war was engineered to be safe for anyone considered strategic, or a source of revenue. Leaving the city, however, was another matter. A joke went that there were three ways out of Sarajevo. The first was on the UN-requested flights reserved for military officials, public aid workers, and the media. The second, for the daring or the desperate, was an underground tunnel hastily constructed beneath the airport. The third was death.

In truth, the Serb Army ran things. Almost anything could be arranged on their orders. The shelling of certain areas was made to happen or not happen. People disappeared overnight to be escorted safely from the country, or to be killed. Likewise, almost anything was available, but not to everyone. Angela knew this. So did their host, Fred Hatton. His contract had expired three months earlier, but his exit requests had been denied repeatedly. He couldn't leave until someone in the Serb Army gave him permission, so he simply waited.

Fred's home and grounds took up half a city block and included an indoor swimming pool as well as rooftop gardens, though little remained of the gardens. Most of the trees had been cut down for firewood and the larger flower beds dismantled to deter intruders. Angela knew better than to feel sorry for him. She tolerated Fred for the intelligence he passed along all too readily. Once or twice he'd proved useful to her — and she to him, passing messages to his superiors when contact had been curtailed.

He walked toward them, a martini glass in each hand. "Hello, Angela! Good of you to come." He passed her a drink and kissed her cheek. "And who have we here?" he said, sloshing André with the second drink. "Oops!" He gave a peculiar, high-pitched laugh. "Don't worry, there's plenty more."

André brushed off his sleeve and offered a hand. "André Riel."

"Fred Hatton — pleasure to meet you, André. French-Canadian, yes?"

"Yes."

Fred bent to whisper in Angela's ear. "Your date is very attractive. Good for you."

André had combed his hair and retired the headband for the evening. He'd put on a white cotton sweater and black trousers. He looked dashing among the smoked mirrors and potted palms.

Fred gestured with his hand to the room at large. "Welcome to the Sarajevo Country Club. You'll find the most elite in international spies, Mafia chiefs, and military attachés gathered here."

The door opened and a well-dressed couple entered, causing a small stir in the room.

"You'll have to excuse me. That's Milošević's representative," Fred whispered to Angela. "I can arrange for you to speak to him later, if you like."

"Find out if he's got anything to say first," she said as Fred went off to greet his guests.

André surprised her by knowing a number of people in the room. She guessed he'd been making the most of his evenings out to get acquainted with other non-nationals. She watched as he greeted two men she recognized as French photographers. They stood before a life-sized mural of a village wedding, looking like add-ons to a crowd of frolicking peasants. They stepped onto the balcony. Moments later, she caught the acrid sweetness of pot.

André returned almost immediately, looking shaken. "That wasn't pleasant," he said.

"What?"

He nodded toward the large windows. Rows of wooden crosses dotted the field across the street.

"The cemetery?" She shrugged. "It's a war — what did you expect?

He shook his head. "No. Over there."

He pointed off to the left where a makeshift shroud of sheets rose like a small hill. From a distance, Angela could make out an arm here and a head there when the wind lifted the sheets, momentarily revealing the bodies piled beneath.

"They've halted burials," Angela said. "Three gravediggers got shot. They've refused to bury anybody till the shooting stops."

"No, it's not that ..." he interrupted. He turned back to the balcony. "Can't you hear it?"

She tried to distinguish between the noise from outside and the sound of the orchestra. A worried whining carried over the notes.

"Dogs," he said with a grimace.

She looked again. A half-dozen mongrels were fighting over the frozen corpses.

"It seems awfully morbid to be having a party right next door," he said, turning from the window.

Laughter broke out to their left. The band struck up a polka, signalling a change in atmosphere.

"Let's get drunk," she said, retrieving a drink from a passing waiter's tray. She caught her reflection in the smoked glass. Was she always that severe looking? "What did they tell you about me before you left?"

"Who?"

"The day you arrived, you said you'd heard about me. What did they tell you, Martin and the others?" All journalists were gossips. What was the news but gossip on a world scale? But she would never have asked him such things if they were alone. Here it could be disguised as party chatter. Alone, he might see she was fishing.

"They said you were very good at what you do."

"Did they tell you I was impossible to work with?"

He smiled. "Are you?"

"Martin seems to think so. What do you think?"

"I think you're very demanding — of yourself as much as of others. But that's not what they said about you."

"What did they say?"

He hesitated. She half-expected he wouldn't tell her.

"Do you really want to know?" he asked.

"Try me."

"They said you're the best — that I'd never get a chance to work with someone as talented as you — someone with your passion, your dedication, your commitment to the truth. It's all true. But you're also ruthless and unforgiving. I think you see it as strength and independence, but what I see is self-righteousness and a lot of stubborn pride. You won't treat me as an equal because you're afraid I'll think less of you."

"Next time I ask your opinion, remind me I don't want it."

She walked away, flushed by his praise and stunned by his accusations. She'd never known anyone like him before — someone who would say exactly what he thought without first weighing the consequences. In Angela's world, there were always consequences.

When she looked back he'd gone over to a blond who, in her opinion, was neither pretty nor sexually appealing. She watched him walk the woman onto the dance floor and spin her in small, graceful circles. Who would have thought him a ballroom dancer? Angela was jealous to discover he had hidden talents as well as friends she'd never met.

A finger slid down her back. She turned to see Fred, who

had noticed the dancing couple. "Losing the battle?" he asked.

"It's not my fight," she said irritably.

He smiled. He knew better. "What do you think of my little gathering tonight? Impressive, aren't they?"

She glanced around the room. "You certainly make the most of your connections, Fred. Wasn't your father in the Ford administration?"

"You knew my father?"

"Knew of. Of course — he was a brilliant man."

Fred took a sip of his drink. "And you think it's regrettable that I'm not?"

"I think it's too bad you don't use your connections to do something instead of hanging around throwing cocktail parties while civilians are being massacred."

Fred pulled back. "Is that a personal opinion or a professional one?"

"Both."

He sighed. "What would you suggest I do? Overthrow the government?"

"I don't know, Fred. What have you tried? Whatever it is, it's not enough."

"Well, the un's position ..."

"The un just stands around waiting while civilians are shot like fish in a barrel. Why aren't they doing something? Where's nato in all this shit?"

"Whoa! Whoa!" He waved off her questions with an apologetic laugh. "It's easy to ask such things, but not so easy to produce results. You know as well as I do that the un has just so much authority ..."

"The UN has no authority here at all!" she snapped. "That's exactly my point. In the meantime, some of the worst atrocities since the Second World War are happening before our eyes while you entertain thugs and gangsters in your lovely villa."

"Angela —"

She nodded toward a Serb officer chatting and laughing with two alluringly dressed young women. "We all know this isn't a legitimate war. The country's in the hands of criminals. They keep you here in exchange for more time to do what they're really doing, which is staving off NATO intervention while they get rich and attend parties like this one."

Fred's face darkened. "Now you listen! I'd be out of here in a second if I could. I've spent days in the airport waiting to get out, and every time I'm turned back by bureaucratic bullshit. In the meantime, I meet with the people who run this country trying to get them to listen to reason."

Around them, people were watching with curiosity.

"Excuse me," Angela said, waving her glass to the room. "I don't mean to spoil the party, but people are dying out there."

Fred grabbed her by the arm and turned her back to him. "And some of those people are ours," he said tersely. "We are not doing nothing here. It's all a very delicate balancing act that requires time and patience."

Angela glanced toward the dance floor. André and his partner had become the room's centrepiece. Light glittered off the woman's earrings as he swept her around the room, a butterfly discovering its wings. Really, Angela wondered, was a little pleasure in the midst of all this madness criminal?

She turned back to Fred. "Maybe you're right," she said. "I shouldn't be ruining other people's fun."

She put down her glass and headed to the door.

THE HEAT WAS OFF AS she climbed to the third floor. Inside the apartment, the air felt just as cold. The light switches remained dead to her touch. Any reading would have to be done by candlelight, but she had no patience for reading now. She lay in bed shivering for an hour before getting up again. Restlessness propelled her to the roof.

It was past curfew. André hadn't returned. No doubt he was having a good time with his new friends, unless he'd gone home with his blond.

The shelling started up. She couldn't tell where it was falling — a suburb to the west. She watched the diffuse glow lighting the sky. Ammonium perchlorate, polyurethane, and beryllium, if she recalled correctly. Beryllium was a hard grey metal; perchloric acid was a fuming toxin; and polyurethane was some sort of synthetic resin. Together, they spelled bad shit. Especially when they flew through the sky.

The land Karadjordje had stolen back from the Turks was going up in flames. Its cities were rafts on a burning sea. A thousand years of migration and exile, of trade in buttermilk, cheese, and leather had finally delivered the country to this. She remembered from her reading that Karadjordje's tactics had been violent and dramatic, and he occasionally turned them on his own family. He'd had his stepfather executed for refusing to follow orders during a battle. He hanged his brother for rape, and suspended the body outside the dinner hall while he entertained the leaders of his recently restored land. During his short life Karadjordje became an expert in playing world powers off against one another, maintaining a rigid control over the country for eight years.

Under his charge, the majority of Muslims in the pashalik of Belgrade were exterminated, but in 1812 the Turks returned, burning villages and selling thousands of Serbs into slavery. Karadjordje lost his footing. He fled to Russia to plot a new revolution, while his rival, Miloš Obrenović, quietly made inroads with the invading Turks. When Karadjordje returned in 1817, Obrenović's secret agents murdered him with an axe and delivered his head to the Turkish sultan. By then, Servia had become a land where a pig's pierced eye symbolized everything that occurred within its borders.

After Karadjordje's murder, Obrenović ruled the country as cruelly and repressively as the Turks had before him. In Obrenović's lifetime there would be three major rebellions against him, all failures. As the Ottoman Empire declined, his power grew and he lived long enough to found a dynasty.

The last of the Obrenović line died violently with Aleksandar, in 1903. His wife woke one night to shouting from the palace grounds below their bedroom. She rushed to the window in her bare feet, pushing aside the bar in time to see the invaders overtaking the palace guards. Her screams woke her husband just as their door crashed in. She ran onto the balcony where a soldier rushed over and pushed her over the edge.

The king was picked up bodily from his bed and thrown out after her. He clutched at the stone parapet with one hand, until a blade chopped at his stubborn fingers, his fall ending nearly a century of Obrenović reign. Thus Karadjordje, who had delivered the Serbs from their oppressors, who had killed his stepfather and hanged the body of his brother over a gate outside a dining hall, was finally avenged.

All this had happened in the land Angela now watched burn. She'd been standing on the roof a while before realizing she wasn't alone. André stood in the doorway. He walked over and leaned against the wall beside her.

"Enjoy the party?" Angela asked.

He shrugged. "It was okay. And you?"

"Not really. I made a fool of myself, so I left."

"Is that all it takes to make you run?"

"Usually."

They stood watching the glow of bombs pierce the sky. They seemed no more fearsome than fireworks or falling stars.

"It's eerie," she said, "but it's almost beautiful from here."

His fingers slipped into her hand. He kissed her, his body pressing her into the wall to the sound of bursting shells.

"When we get out of here," André said, "I'm going to marry you."

BOOK IV
LILIUM LONGIFLORUM

TEN

Supper was in progress. Seven adults and a child sat around the table in Martha Stewart perfection. Candle flames flickered, caught in the surfaces of the crystal and silverware. Shep was dressed in the same T-shirt and khakis he arrived in, but with a dinner jacket over top. It wasn't clear if this was his idea of a joke, as he pulled it off as though he meant it.

The table was a picture of abundance. Roasted potatoes and yams — skins pinched back and flesh revealed — lay on platters alongside glazed carrots, grilled peppers, and baked onions. Thick slabs of pork, weighed down with a cranberry crust, were artfully draped across a silver serving plate. A welter of greens — Brussels sprouts, broccoli, beans — had been tossed in blue Spode and drizzled with a Béarnaise sauce. Bowls held creamy coleslaw, green salads, and slices of tomatoes and cheese wedged between basil leaves. Knotted buns had been tucked into breadbaskets.

As platters were dutifully passed to the left, Markus directed his attention toward the newcomer with the colourful pictures on his arms.

"I have a dog," Markus said.

"What's his name?" Shep asked.

"Georgie!" the boy crowed. "He's a big son of a bitch!"

A silence followed. It was the moment after a firecracker has been tossed into the neighbour's yard, right before the shattered peace. Conrad was first to the rescue.

"Well, I guess he would be at that."

Abbie drew a breath. "That is no language to be using at your age, young man."

Tori smirked. "No, you'll definitely want to save that kind of talk for when you grow up," she said.

"Sorry, Mom," Margaret told her. "He's been watching too much TV lately." She looked at BJ. "Your influence, no doubt."

Markus continued. "Georgie can sing, you know, Shep."

"Is he good?"

Markus nodded.

"Georgie's a hound," Margaret explained. "When I play the piano he sits beside me and makes these adorable crooning noises like he's singing along. I'm not sure, but it might just be the vibrations tormenting his hearing."

"I wouldn't exactly call it singing," BJ interjected. He was amazed how often the dog got to be a dinner table topic, as though there were a law against intelligent conversation buried in the suburban instinct.

"Well, he may not be Frank Sinatra," Margaret countered, "but Georgie certainly seems to think he's singing."

"What do you call it, Dad?" Markus asked.

"Why, I'd call it how-o-o-ling!"

Markus laughed.

Margaret turned back to Shep. "Actually, he's pretty choosy about his material. He prefers pieces in B-flat minor. Chopin nocturnes are a real specialty."

"I could teach you some Kurt Cobain if you want to widen his repertoire," Shep offered.

Margaret pictured herself sitting beside him on the piano bench, watching his fingers groping for the chords, waiting for the moment he turned to her.

"Hey!" BJ interrupted. "Speaking of moronic, suicidal grunge musicians, how many Gen-Xers does it take to change a light bulb?"

Tori groaned and slumped her head onto her palm. "How ironic to hear you talking about morons, BJ."

BJ ignored her. "Come on! How many?" he urged.

"All right," Angela said. "How many Gen-Xers does it take to change a light bulb?"

BJ's face contorted into an impression of a young hipster in a drug-induced state. "Whoa, dude! Like, who can afford a light bulb? But I can squeegee your windshield for you."

Conrad chuckled; Abbie smiled politely.

"Yuk-yuk. Is that the best you can do, BJ?" Tori sneered.

"I thought you liked being a human experiment, Tori. Just think of my jokes as designer drugs and you'll love them, too."

Margaret nudged BJ and glanced at her mother. That one might have hit too close to the bone. Abbie smiled as though nothing untoward had been said.

"Margaret tells us you've been busy lately, BJ," Conrad said.

BJ brightened. "Did she mention the women's group I addressed last month? I opened a series of lectures by women who'd been abused. You know — wonder-babes like Oprah, from really tough backgrounds. Except these were all Canadian women, so you've never heard of them."

He felt them turning on his words.

"At first I hadn't the foggiest idea what would entertain these people. Here was a roomful of privileged women come to hear tales of poverty and woe that they probably wouldn't relate to in the least. But then it came to me. I did some quick calculations and realized that if each one had her hair done at, say, $125 a crack, and there were 2000 women in the hall, then they'd spent roughly $250,000, plus the tip. I then went on to talk about their dresses, many of them one-of-a-kind. It sort of descended from there." He was smiling, caught up in his tale. "All in all, there had to have been at least a million bucks spent on that one evening alone. Staggering! You could practically prevent child poverty with that kind of money. Needless to say, the organizers made be it clear they were never going to invite me back ..."

"BJ, you're such a jerk!" Tori interrupted.

"Victoria, please," Abbie admonished.

"What? It's true!" BJ insisted. "A million bucks spent on hair and fashion in that room alone. Think of it!"

"It is staggering," Conrad agreed. "We could all think twice about where we spend our money."

Shep had been listening quietly. He had a knack for sitting invisibly in their midst. He lowered his fork and sat back. His voice caught them by surprise.

"Angela? Was that story you won the press award for true? Did you really escape from Liberia on a fishing boat?"

Angela lay down her napkin. A rushing sound filled her ears. She felt trapped, exposed — these things were not discussed openly in her family. Certainly not during dinner. "That's true … I did escape on a fishing boat." Her voice was steady, cool. It's only a story, she told herself. It won't hurt them. She smiled at her mother to reassure her, but Abbie refused to look back.

"What exactly happened?" Shep said. "If you don't mind my asking."

A silence stretched across the table. Abbie looked over at the boy, the stranger among them. How carelessly, how recklessly he opened this box of horrors.

"I was on assignment in the capital when the fighting got fierce. We were ordered to leave, but some of us got caught between the army and the rebel forces. We holed up in an abandoned church for a few days until we could sneak out to the coast."

"It sounds amazing," Shep said.

"Sitting here, it probably does," Angela conceded. "But it was a world of horror every day. It's impossible to convey the extent of it."

"What happened when you got to the coast?"

"I was smuggled onto a boat at night. At dawn we were boarded by government troops twenty miles offshore. The crew hid me in the cargo hold."

From below, she'd heard them swarming over the deck. Even if they didn't find her, she knew they might scuttle the ship. It would be as simple as bashing a hole in its side and leaving them in the middle of the ocean. They would simply have disappeared, a footnote in the war.

At the time, her family knew only that she was missing, along with nine others. For three nerve-racking days they were left to believe whatever they would: abduction, murder, torture. The stories that surfaced from the country were tales of horror and mass murders.

Angela heard someone continue the story. It was her own voice, of course, but it surprised her to hear it spoken with such detachment. It seemed to come from somewhere else, as though she'd lost track of inside and outside, what was real and what not. That was as much as she'd managed to displace herself from the events, as much distance as she'd been able to put between herself and those days.

"I don't know if they were looking for me or just stopping boats from leaving, but they didn't find me. Eventually, I made it out."

She looked at the faces around the table. They knew the story, but she'd never told it to them this directly before, never named things that had been left unnamed till now, in what Margaret had dubbed "The House of Secrets." For every surface, a thousand buried tales. What was of professional interest to her was a nightmare for others, a quagmire of killing, acts of irredeemable horror.

"That's so cool!" Shep's voice bubbled with enthusiasm.

Angela fought her anger. He couldn't begin to imagine the ones who hadn't made it out, she thought. How would anyone ever know they existed? Lily and Montador from a nearby village. And the boy, Toyota, named after the car he was born in on the way to the hospital. He'd been a miracle, surviving diphtheria in a place where there was almost no medicine. No one knew about them. No one except a crazy journalist who chanced her own life to reach them.

On her return there were public talks, auditoriums crowded with people sitting on the floor or leaning up against the walls. They plied her with questions: *Were you brave?* No, just incredibly lucky. *Did you ever think you would die?* Yes, every day. *How does your family feel now about what happened?* For that, she had no answer.

She suspected what they really wanted to know was how such things could happen to someone like her. Was she daring or crazy to have put herself in such a position? She resented this curiosity. It was as if they sensed that nothing exciting would ever happen to them, so they were free to wonder about her life, her adventures.

I can't say for sure why it happened to me, Angela told them. *I love what I do and Africa is just one of many places I might have ended up. There's no lack of violence around the globe. It could happen anywhere. To anyone.* It became her standard response.

"Weren't you afraid?" Shep asked.

He was a child asking about the dangers in the woods after dark. A cheap scare was all he wanted. None of her family had any idea, Angela thought.

"I don't think fear covers it," she said. "Fear is being followed down an empty street at three o'clock in the morning. This was different. It moved too fast. I was mostly numb at the time."

"What would have happened if you'd been caught?"

"I would've been killed. The army had a habit of shooting people rather than arresting them."

Her mother looked away, refusing to witness this public obscenity. A fathomless moment passed.

"Anyway, I wasn't," Angela concluded. "Killed, I mean."

The table relaxed, as though she'd been telling them a horror story and at the last moment chosen a happy ending for her tale. In that instant, she hated them for wanting to be let off so easily, without earning it. No, it wasn't hate, she told herself. It was anger. Resentment. She needed to round it down into something manageable. There was enough hate in the world.

"I suppose this is as good a time as any to tell you I'm going to Sarajevo next," she said.

She handed it to them like an unexploded bomb. The candle flames recoiled.

Abbie's intake of breath was audible. "You're going there? Why?"

"I've been asked to cover the siege. I know the background, so it makes sense for me to go."

Abbie shook her head. Sarajevo, Liberia, Burundi — none of these names meant anything to her. Nor could she think why they should. They might as well be the ends of the earth. In fact, they were. Why would anyone risk her life for such things?

"I'll be safe this time," Angela said.

"You were supposed to be safe last time," Abbie snapped. "That's what you said then."

There was a pause. Hands reached out for second helpings as eyes reverted to plates. Angela suddenly resented her father's reticence, her mother's disapproval, everyone's discomfort.

Conrad cleared his throat. "Of course we trust Angela to look after herself."

Abbie stood and began to gather the plates, as though taking back the meal. She retreated to the kitchen. Angela looked around the table. Maybe she'd gone too far. What could she say to her family, who'd never seen the things she had? Your fears are big only until you've stepped over them, she knew. But for them it was like bridging the Niagara Gorge.

"I'm sorry. I shouldn't have brought this up now. I forget how upsetting it can be for all of you."

Conrad reached over and squeezed her hand. "You had to tell us sometime. We know what your work entails. Your mother can't help worrying for you."

Markus, unsure of the emotional current at the table, timidly ventured a question. "Aunt Angela? Are you Superman?"

There was mild laughter from the others.

"No," she told him. "But sometimes I wish I were."

"Hey, Shep," BJ called out. He was tired of all the serious talk. "What super power would you choose if you could have just one?"

"I don't know, BJ. Is Russia still a superpower?"

"Ha-ha." There was always a smart-ass in the crowd. BJ persisted. "No, really — what power would you choose? Strength?" He flexed his biceps. "Flight?" Birdlike movements with his hands. "Invisibility?"

Markus piped up. "I want to be invisible!"

"Hey, buddy boy," Shep responded. "Most people spend their entire lives being invisible. You don't need to ask for that one."

"What about you, Angela?" BJ asked.

"I'd ask for the power to be in two places at once." She looked around her. "That way part of me could be here with all of you even when I'm away."

"That's not a super power, that's schizophrenia," BJ said as Abbie emerged from the kitchen. Her return threw him. His ears turned bright red.

"Where's your family, Shep?" Conrad asked.

"I don't really know," Shep said. "We haven't been in touch since I was sixteen. My dad was in the army when I was a kid, and we moved around a lot. He and my mom split up. I left home as soon as I could." He shrugged. "It wasn't a healthy scene."

"Don't you keep in touch?" Margaret asked with concern, sensing the boy in the man. Her amorous feelings for him suddenly transformed to something maternal.

"No." Shep lowered his eyes. "I don't really want to."

There was a moment of assessment by the others, as though suddenly made aware of gaps in their own lives in light of what he'd just told them about families who weren't together by choice.

Conrad weighed in. "It's not where we come from, but where we end up that counts."

"Absolutely," Shep responded. "That's what I told myself when I was a kid. What I do with my life is totally up to me."

"And what is it you plan to do?" Abbie asked.

"Right now I'm still studying," he said, animated by his telling. "I'm not sure what I'll do when I graduate. Maybe something in politics or the media. They both affect our lives more than we realize."

Conrad took the volley. "You and Angela share something in common then. She can talk a blue streak about politics and the media when she gets going."

Shep nodded excitedly. "Think about the way words get used," he said. "'War,' for instance. There are many kinds of wars: political, economic, social. Or 'family.' What's 'family'? And what happens when you don't fit into the traditional meaning of the word?"

"The family is sacrosanct," Abbie snapped, the lid closing down on her decree. "It doesn't matter whether you fit in or not."

A spoon clattered against a dish. Shep slumped in his chair. He knew better than to take her on in her territory. He searched for another posture, something between charm and appeasement. He was a chameleon; he would be anything she wanted. The only problem, he knew, was that she didn't want him to be anything at all. Not here in her cottage amidst her family. Not in her future, either, he feared. He sat up straight and smiled. "Anyway," he said, "that's all in the future. Right now I work at a coffee bar."

"In management?" Conrad asked hopefully.

"Nope. Just a *barrista* at Starbucks."

At least, Conrad's face said, Starbucks was an established institution. Everyone had to start somewhere.

Shep wouldn't leave well enough alone. "Or rather," he corrected, "I did work there. I had to quit to get time off to come out here."

"You quit your job to come here for a weekend?" Abbie's face registered rock bottom for any sense of responsibility or reliability he might have had. Her look was of someone who might spare change for a street person, but never strike up a conversation.

"It's not a big deal," Tori said. "They'll take him back."

"Just like that?" Conrad asked.

"Sure. I've done it before," Shep replied.

Abbie rose abruptly. "I'll see if dessert is ready."

"I'll give you a hand, Mom," Margaret said, following.

Shep looked around the table. "Did I say something wrong?"

"Congratulations," Angela said. "You've just joined the long list of people who've disappointed our mother."

IN THE KITCHEN, ABBIE LEANED against the counter. Margaret watched her anxiously.

"Tattoos and coffee bars," Abbie said of the black clouds on her horizon. "I wonder what else this boy has in store for us."

Margaret touched her shoulder. "He's young, Mom."

"That's no excuse." Abbie turned to her. "And I suppose you knew of Angela's plans to go to that place?"

Margaret hesitated. "I …"

"I suspected as much. Why would she be going there? Did you encourage her? You've always had an irrational hero-worship of your sister."

Margaret was caught by surprise, as much by her mother's accusation as by her own reaction. "Mom, it's her news. Her life. Why don't you ask Angela about it?"

For a moment, Abbie looked as though she'd say more, then turned her shoulder to her daughter, sheltering herself from a cold wind.

AT THE TABLE, CONRAD PUSHED aside his plate. He felt the brusque edges of fatigue pulsing inside him. He heard the muted conversation in the kitchen. They all heard it. There was only so much eating they could do to pretend they weren't listening. He exhaled loudly. It was as much exasperation as he allowed himself in front of the others. He knew his wife's worries and the walls that contained her fears, just as he understood his daughter's need to rebel. They were so similar, he thought. A mirror, a pond. Though neither could see it.

"I hate to turn in early," Conrad said. "But, if you'll excuse me, I'd like to rest for a while." He looked for his cane, lying like a thin shadow against the wall behind him. Angela and Shep both reached out for him, but he stopped them. "No, I'll get it. Just tell your mother I've gone to lie down."

"I'll help you, Grandpa," Markus said.

Conrad smiled. "Why, that would be nice of you."

Abbie and Margaret returned to the table bearing bowls and spoons and a steaming dish of pudding. "Coffee's coming," Abbie said, mustering a voice of cheer. She set the dish on the table and looked around, suddenly flustered. She reached up to her hair. "Where's your father?"

"He went upstairs with Markus," Angela said. "He said he needed to lie down. Is he all right?"

It was more than a question, but less than an accusation.

"Of course your father is fine," Abbie said quickly, and turned to the steaming pudding. "Who would like hot blueberry buckle fresh from the oven?"

ON THE WAY UPSTAIRS, CONRAD stopped to catch his breath. He flexed the fingers of his right hand, looking down to where they gripped the railing. His brother's shadow again. It followed him wherever he went. Alex had been an escape artist. There was nothing he couldn't slip out of. Right out of college, he'd gone south and joined the United States Army, distinguishing himself in Vietnam. After his discharge, he married and divorced, then married again. Half a dozen jobs passed in quick succession, none of them keeping his attention long. His approach to both marriage and work was that if he wasn't having fun, then it was time to move on. And he had moved, leaving his new wife behind. Malaysia, the Philippines, Mexico, Cuba, and even Tanzania held his interest for a while, but it seemed he had a permanent itinerary, moving constantly till mortality caught him up. He'd survived Vietnam and the carnage of two marriages, only to be cut short by a Malaysian peasant on a tractor, hauling a load of hay and death on a lonely highway.

Conrad looked down at Markus, who waited patiently for him to continue his climb. A door on the left opened into a bedroom appointed in staid oak furniture. Bright floral wallpaper tried to make up for the room's gravity, with blossoms and bows caught mid-air, forever falling. A window opened onto the bay, luminous in the fading light. Markus helped his grandfather lift his legs onto the bed before climbing up beside him.

"So," Conrad said, breathing slowly and carefully. "Are you having fun yet?"

The boy's hands fidgeted between his knees. He was torn between saying something nice — "If you can't say something nice," his mother had told him repeatedly, "then don't say anything at all" — and letting his grandfather know how he really felt, which was that he was bored among all these adults who argued endlessly and looked so unhappy.

"It's all right," he said finally, choosing the middle ground and looking out the window toward the lake. He squinted, closing his eyes just enough to keep the water in sight while removing all the trees from the periphery of his vision. He felt safest when he shut everything out like this.

"You know," his grandfather said, "I've been thinking. Why don't we do something fun together tomorrow?"

Markus opened his eyes, restoring the trees.

"Can we go fishing?"

"You betcha."

"Just us?"

"Sure."

Markus thought it over for a second. "And Shep, too."

"What about your dad? Should we bring him?"

The boy looked down at his knees where his hands moved in a private sign language, his true thoughts hidden in those small gestures.

"Only if he doesn't tell jokes."

Conrad smiled. "We'll probably have to remind him. And what about your grandmother? Should we invite her, too?"

Markus reflected on this, too, wanting not to offend. "I think Grandma has to dust the furniture," he said at last.

Conrad nodded solemnly. They lay there, the youngest and oldest among them, bookends to a life. "She's not much fun, is she?"

"Don't worry, Grandpa," Markus said. "It's not her fault."

ELEVEN

LAUGHTER HUNG IN THE AIR as Markus appeared in the doorway of the family room. He stood there, a solemn dwarf innkeeper come to see about his disorderly guests. His father and mother sat together on the sofa. His aunt Angela was in the armchair. Aunt Tori lay on the floor by the fire with Shep. Markus crawled up on the couch and put his head on his father's lap. BJ ran his fingers through his son's hair, cradling a highball in his other hand.

The room was soporific with heat from the fire. Extraneous gestures or unnecessary words seemed at odds here. BJ raised his glass. Shep had just asked him how he became a comic.

"It all started with a sincere talent to annoy people. When you can get under people's skin, the word spreads fast. I started doing stand-up at open mike nights. There were a few spectacular failures and some rousing successes. That's how I got onto the circuit. Once you're plugged in you can go anyplace."

"Do you enjoy it?"

"I live for it."

It was electric, dazzling. When he was on a roll, the words

shot out like fire. He felt whole for those few moments onstage. He could have told them he'd been on TV twenty-six times. By this measurement alone he could probably call himself famous. He calculated that each appearance generated between 200,000 and 300,000 viewers, give or take, which added up to roughly six and a half million people who'd seen him. And that wasn't counting the club audiences. He was getting recognized in the street lately. Still, he was careful not to say too much for fear of setting Margaret off. She hated being left alone at night while he entertained people with too much time on their hands. Careless, casual people whom she would dislike if she met them.

"Hey, BJ," Tori interjected. "What do your initials stand for? Big Jerk or Blow Job?"

BJ smirked. "You know, Tori, I like you. I truly do. But I sure hope I never see you working with subatomic particles."

"Will you two stop?" Margaret said wearily. "You're worse than the kids."

"I am a kid," BJ retorted. "And proud of it." He sat upright, trying not to jostle Markus. He squared his face with his hands as though framing himself in a television screen, and thrummed a fanfare. "It's BJ Robinson on Comedy Central's *Adolescent Hour!*"

"BJ thinks TV is reality," Margaret interjected.

BJ gave her a hurt look. "My biggest fan," he said. "But she secretly revels in my fame and glory." He rested his hand on the back of her neck and tugged gently at her hair. She winced. He'd said too much, obviously. Lately, she could become distant and brittle without warning. "What I do is nothing. Angela knows more about TV than I ever will," he said, hoping it would take the heat off him. "I may appear on it now and then, but she and her gang make it happen. They're on the right end of the camera."

"I don't know if that's true," Angela said quietly. The rushing sound that overtook her at dinner was racing in her head again. She saw herself on the streets of a small village. A crowd of refugees moved in a long slow line in the distance. She knew exactly where the first rocket shell would fall, how everyone would scatter when it burst.

"It must have been so cool to win that award!" Shep said.

It wasn't cool, she thought angrily. It was indecent. It was obscene and heartbreaking to stand up there a year later and talk about absent friends.

"That award was a bribe for people like me who risk our lives so the rest of you can sit around watching it on television. That's how they get rid of radicals these days, by giving us jobs that'll get us killed off. They probably don't teach you that in media relations."

Shep was silenced.

Feeling betrayed by her anger, Angela turned to Margaret. "Maybe we should do those dishes."

ANGELA STOOD AT THE SINK watching Margaret run the water. The detergent bottle wheezed in her sister's hands and spewed out the few last drops. Angela passed plates from the sideboard to the counter where Margaret slipped them gently underwater. Red rims circled white centres before disappearing beneath the suds.

"I think my social skills could use some refining," Angela said at last.

"I guess the war'll do that to you, huh?" Margaret said. "Don't worry about it."

Angela picked up a tea towel as Margaret handed her the first clean plate. They grinned as the dish changed hands.

"I thought plates came after cutlery," Angela said.

Margaret laughed. "You know, I was eighteen before I realized not everyone's mother arranged the dirty dishes in order before washing them. The girls in my dorm used to make fun of me for doing it."

"'First comes glassware, then comes silverware,'" Angela began, and Margaret joined in. "'... followed by the dinnerware, and last come pots and pans!'"

They laughed at the hold memory had over them. Utensils clinked against the bottom of the sink. Angela held out the dry cloth like a net waiting to catch something. "Any good family gossip?" she asked, accepting another plate.

Margaret plunged her hands under the water, her eyes darting around the room as though afraid of being overheard.

"I'm not supposed to say anything ... but Aunt Jane's dating again."

"Good for Jane! It's been years."

"She's seeing a golf instructor. He's got all his hair and teeth, and he's not bad looking, either. What's more, he's fifteen years her junior. Mom's scandalized!"

Angela whooped and nearly dropped a plate. They made horrified faces at one another, and laughed even more. It felt like they were kids again.

"How's Tim?" Margaret asked. "You haven't said a word about him all night."

"He's fine." The answer was quick, nonchalant, a drawer sliding back in place.

"You're so lucky, you know. You go running off all over the world and he's right there waiting for you when …"

"You've got BJ. He's …"

"BJ's an adolescent jerk." Margaret raised a hand to her mouth. "Oh, God — I can't believe I just said that."

Remorse crossed her face. She panicked whenever she spoke too quickly and truthfully, as if waiting for the punishment that must follow. It might be the hand of God or it might be her genetics, striking her down with depression or the edge of madness. It could simply be her husband coming home at 4 A.M., not saying where he'd been. The private earthquakes that destroyed in silence.

"Some days I just feel like giving up," she said. "Every month's a stretch to pay the mortgage. We've had to borrow from Mom and Dad more than once …" She wiped at a tear. "Our life is a mess, if you want to know the truth. BJ frustrates me so much I can't bear to have him touch me anymore. I won't let him." She spoke as though it were a shameful secret. "I wish he'd grow up. Some days he seems more like a child than a husband. I think, 'Is this the man I married? Did I grow up while he stayed a kid, chasing his juvenile fantasies of fame and glory?' Whenever I try to discuss it, he gets angry. I tell him to be satisfied with less, but he always says he's on the verge of a breakthrough. It could happen any time." She shrugged. "Or not."

"What else could he do?" Angela said in a way she hoped wouldn't sound condescending. "You wouldn't be happy being married to a chartered accountant."

Margaret sighed heavily. "Do you always have to be so damned practical? Can't I just rant a little?"

"Of course you can. You can say whatever you want."

Margaret felt filled, suddenly, with desolation. There was an awful sense that everything important lay behind her and she could never retrieve it. It was as if the bottom had dropped out of her world and she'd vanished from it altogether.

"I used to enjoy my life. It wasn't perfect, but at least back then there was a promise of more. Now I just feel trapped. I don't recognize myself anymore. I'm the wife of some guy who tells jokes for a living. But who is that? I used to think I enjoyed going to BJ's shows and being this really popular couple, but now I just go to discover who I am. And I have no idea who that is. It scares me."

Angela wanted to comfort her, to say the world was a fine place and that good things happened to people who deserved them, but she no longer believed that. She, too, often felt in search of herself. With each assignment she moved farther from home, slipping away. Sometimes she thought she found herself out there — wherever *there* was — but she always left herself behind again and returned feeling divided, as though both selves couldn't exist in the same place.

"Don't underestimate yourself," she said. "There's so much you can do." Platitudes, nothing more.

Margaret turned her head as the tears welled up. Angela was extraordinary at everything she did, whereas she, Margaret, was barely competent. Not even competent. She'd merely painted a patina of competence over her life, a life that was badly flawed. She wasn't really the person standing here now, nor had she ever fully inhabited the woman she was supposed to be — mother, wife, sister, or daughter. She was a fraud who had never belonged anywhere and habitually floated through the lives of everyone around her like a rootless ghost. She reached out to touch the countertop, gripping the hard surface as though to assure herself she was real.

"The truth is I don't have your strength, Ange. Or your ambition. You forget how lucky you are."

Angela hoped she wasn't about to hear of some long-buried sibling rivalry between them. She'd rather it remain buried with all the other emotional failures in her family. "What is this — 'your-brilliant-career-versus-my-dismal-marriage'?" She sensed Margaret bristling, and wondered if the anger lay deep or on the surface, like scum covering healthy pond water.

"What it is," Margaret said, "is me stuck home all day with three kids while my moron of a husband goes out to play. That's my life. I'm always wishing I'd done something — I mean really done something. I'm the one who can't follow her dreams because I'm always helping BJ or the kids follow theirs. And what's worse is, I resent myself for saying these things, because I really love my family!"

The tears were flowing freely now. Margaret hid her face in the dishtowel.

"I know you do," Angela said, putting an arm over her shoulder. "But it's okay for you to say you feel angry, or ripped-off, or unfulfilled, or whatever else you feel. It's okay."

Here, Angela thought, is my sister at twenty-eight, gorgeous and warmly giving. Margaret had never accepted that she should just sit back and enjoy her undisciplined mind and her decline into what would otherwise be an easy and uneventful life — a life that half the planet would envy. Yet she found it pointless, and pushed herself into neurosis because of it. It was the story of half the Western world. Where else would people purposely and systematically turn good fortune into bad because it wasn't exactly what they wanted?

UPSTAIRS IN THE BEDROOM, CONRAD was awake. Abbie checked his forehead. It felt feverish. She walked to the window and opened it, looking out into the blackness as the cool air rushed in. The waves on Whippoorwill Bay sighed like a distant warning. Even in shadows, she couldn't hide her worry.

"What's the matter?" Conrad asked.

"Does it show?"

His eyes were tranquil. They radiated calm. "You're not worried about me, I hope?"

"You?" she snorted. "There's nothing wrong with you that a good rest won't fix. You're just trying to scare me."

He raised his hand — the old achy, wounded hand — and touched her cheek. She gripped his fingers and pressed them to her face. There was nothing she worried about more than his health. When the weather changed she waited to see if he'd develop a chill, watching for the signs, clamping down on them with all the energy she could summon. He wondered if she fooled herself when she said she didn't worry for him.

"What is it then?" he asked.

Her mind caught on a tag of annoyance lying behind her unrest. "Why don't my children respect me?"

"They do respect you," he answered. "And they love you, too. But you can't expect them to see eye-to-eye with us about everything."

She looked up. "Eye-to-eye with me. The girls get along fine with you. I'm convinced they look for ways to get under my skin."

"They see the world differently than we did, that's all. Where we saw opportunity and enterprise, they see unfairness and exploitation. They care about things we never thought about at their age."

"Why don't they care a little more about me?" she said. "Or am I just being selfish?"

Her eyes drifted over the dresser top, to the pill bottles and the opened thermometer case. Inside the drawer lay a catheter tucked away beside more pills, a heating pad, and lotions.

He followed her gaze, guessing at her real unrest. "I'm all right. Everything's fine."

"Yes," she said, with a soft intake of breath.

The Thomas family, she knew, boasted a half-dozen octogenarians and one nonagenarian who still lived on her own, sharp as a tack. But one brother drank himself into the side of a hay wagon, while she married the one with a faulty heart caused by rheumatic fever in childhood. At first, the loss of energy and a slowing pace had merely seemed Conrad's response to retirement, but they'd consulted one doctor and then another: he suffered from congestive heart failure. His heart, always steadfast and true to others, was unable to supply his organs with the necessary blood. His fate lay in the hands of God, if not his genetics. Nothing could stop it when the time came, but then, too, no one could name the time. With proper care, Conrad could just keep going. She couldn't see it otherwise.

He brought his hands to either side of her face and drew her down to him. When they met, he would never have held her like this. How fearful she'd been the first time he offered her his arm to help her from his car. She'd seemed a hollow reed that might snap at any moment. Slowly, he'd given her his strength and his patience. There'd been a restlessness churning inside her, a constant wind. Whatever it took, and for however long, he would find it in himself to be there for her, he had told himself. He'd felt that way the very first time he saw her, sitting with Alex in the Red Grill in downtown Sudbury. His brother had been in the middle of explaining something about canoes when he just stopped talking. Conrad turned to see the big brass doors at the front of the store whoosh to a close as a young woman in a lime green dress stepped inside.

Alex stood and invited her over to their booth, introducing himself and Conrad, and asking her name. Though she looked fragile, she hadn't been standoffish at all. In fact, she was rather playful. Conrad was tongue-tied watching his brother, envious that he could speak so freely to such a pretty girl. He suspected they already knew each other, but he never let on.

It was ten minutes to nine when she'd arrived. The waitress had been snarky about serving them. The store was closing in ten minutes, she reminded them, and the shake machine had already been wiped down. She'd have to do it all over again. No, they insisted with a laugh, they must have another shake. A strawberry shake for her. He couldn't recall how the evening ended or where they'd gone afterward, but he never forgot his first sight of her.

A year later, they arrived at the cottage one morning not long after her release from the hospital. At first he'd taken her only on short trips, not wanting to tire her out. That was where it began. They were forbidden to go beyond the town limits, as if her world stopped at its borders, but they quickly began trespassing those bounds. Soon they went farther and farther, eventually all the way to the Bruce Peninsula.

The gardener, an eccentric Englishman named McKeough, greeted them as they wandered around the medieval-looking grounds. He informed them that the owner, Mr. Grey, was anxious to sell the property as his wife had recently died.

McKeough was very good with visitors. He sensed the trauma in Abbie. He saw it in plants and he could see it in people. He stayed with her words when she spoke. He noted her cropped hair, the circles under her eyes. Perhaps it was just the summer heat and her swelling pregnancy. He could detect no trouble between the young woman and her husband, who was so careful and gentle in his manner.

He walked them through the grounds, pointing out the various beds. He listed the types of flowers and the care each required, a neighbourly introduction, revealing which among their number could be difficult to deal with and which might make congenial friends. The lilies won Abbie's heart that day.

McKeough pointed to a bed of maroon flowers almost hidden from view. "These shy things," he said, "are called down-facing lilies, preferring to share their beauty with the soil. While these ones," he continued, turning to a patch of orange fingers splayed upward, "love the sun and are called up-facing."

Abbie brushed the petals with her fingers, bending to smell the blooms. McKeough waited before moving along to the next bed. "The ones that look you right in the eye," he said, "are the outward-facing lilies. The truly beautiful ones — though I try not to show favouritism in front of them — are known as trumpet lilies. To these belong the black trumpet and the Easter lily — *Lilium longiflorum* — such a familiar emblem of resurrection."

Conrad watched his wife's face come to life. That was when he knew he would give her all of this. She was enchanted with the grounds and the gardener, whom they kept on when they bought the place. It was he who taught her the Latin names for the plants.

At times during their walk that morning, and occasionally in the years to come, Abbie sensed a woman in a wool cloak bending carefully over the beds. Had McKeough described Mrs. Grey, the owner's late wife, or had she merely imagined her? She couldn't remember. She'd been hugely pregnant then, watching her shadow with fascination as it moved along the ground. Afterwards, Abbie felt it was this woman who'd given her the chance to put her life back together, to retrieve it from the overgrowth and weeds. *Lilium longiflorum.*

On her next visit she planted a small locust tree, with McKeough's approval. There would be two more before McKeough died at the very good age of eighty-five. Now his son tended the gardens, pushing back the weeds that ravaged the beds and the roots that threatened the rock walls. It was this man who would trim the hedges and prune the locusts before winter set in.

"Prune vigorously in the early spring," the elder McKeough had said, "but thin lightly in the latter part. With flowers you can deadhead all summer long if you like. It encourages the blossoms and promotes stronger growth. Fall is the time for cutting back."

It was sound advice. Fall was the time for culling the weak and infirm for the good of the plant. It was what young McKeough — though she felt ridiculous calling a fifty-year-old man *young* — was coming for tomorrow, to see them through the long arduous winters of the Bruce Peninsula.

"A garden must be maintained. If you don't prune for two or three years, it shows," old McKeough had said. "Plants grow straggly and produce stems that can't support the weight of their blossoms. When that happens, it's work to coax them back into shape."

She'd been standing at the window looking out. The memory of McKeough dissolved. She turned to Conrad. Thirty years, she thought. We've been coming here all this time. How could it possibly stop? Conrad had taken the news much more calmly than she had: the heart muscles had simply worn themselves out. Left to himself, he would just sit there and wait to die. He had accepted the inevitable, but she would not.

"Please don't worry about me," he assured her. "I'm all right."

She nodded. "All right," she said. "I'll try."

He kissed her forehead.

"Tell me something," she said. "Have you been happy all these years we've been together?"

"Of course I have. Don't you know that?"

"I don't mean just 'happy.' I've always wondered if it's been enough. For you, I mean."

"More than enough," he said. "I've never thought otherwise. Don't you know it's what's kept me holding on this long?"

She looked like she would cry. "I just want what's best for my family," she said. "It's what I've always wanted."

"I know."

TWELVE

SHEP TRACED HIS THUMB ACROSS Tori's brow. The glow from the fire lit up their silhouettes like the horizon at daybreak. The flat of his palm moved down her cheek, along her neck and past her shoulder, sketching her into existence. He'd never felt so content, lying beside Tori in her family cottage with the trees, the bay, and the mountains right outside the window. There was so much life around him. It gave him a sense of belonging. It suggested permanence, a solidity he could touch.

With both eyes closed, Tori imagined the friends she might be meeting at the Red Lion Pub or other boys she could be talking to on campus. No matter where she was, she felt she was missing out on something. Regrets carved away at her, water on limestone. She'd half-convinced herself when she swallowed those few pills that she really was trying to do more than grab attention. Was there anything more final than dying? It was an act of empowerment, taking her life into her own hands. Still, she knew it would also be a punishment — for her family, friends, and the teachers who'd neglected to see in her a singular vision of life.

She'd convinced herself the world was dishonest. She hated the vague dissatisfactions people lived with, the hypocrisy of not speaking up in order to spare the feelings of others. She despised the emptiness of modern life, its blatant consumerism: childproof caps, prefab houses, lifestyle television, takeout food, the destruction of the rainforests — the whole damned, dissatisfied, empty lot of it. That's what her death would have meant. But when she thought about it, she couldn't decide — was it power she wanted or was it punishment?

She couldn't help feeling like an exceptional being trapped in a world of mundane events and ordinary people. It seemed as if all the really cool people were dead: Janis Joplin, Jim Morrison, John Lennon and Dean ... No — it was *James* Dean, of course. The rest of them were frauds. Even Elvis. Well, he was more of a joke, really. What had he ever sung that was meaningful? Not that she could name a single song.

But it would be an unforgivable waste to die before she'd accomplished something. There'd be nothing gained by dying before she'd left her mark on the world. Still, they'd all be scandalized to learn she'd walked among them contemplating her own death. More — she seized on it — they'd be terrified by it.

She opened her eyes. Shep smiled.

"Would you stay with me if I got pregnant?"

Shep's smile vanished, but his answer came quickly enough. "Yes. Are you?"

She watched him closely, amused by how she could stop time with a word: *pregnant*. The very power it held, like *love*, or *death*, or *mother*, or *father*. It was almost tangible. She waited, holding

off. He couldn't make her answer if she didn't want to. Earlier
that day, Angela had told her she had no real understanding of
power, how quickly it changed hands. By force, ownership,
subterfuge. She didn't care.

Tori smiled and patted Shep's head as though rewarding a
dog. "Nope — just checking," she said, and turned back to the
fire.

ANGELA LEANED AGAINST THE KITCHEN sink, watching Margaret fold the tea towels. The dishes were all put away. Her
sister's tears had subsided for now.

"I still do it," Margaret said. "I still placate Mom when she
gets angry. My shrink says it's because I feel guilty. She says …"

Angela interrupted. "Never mind what your shrink says.
What do you say it's because?"

Margaret shrugged, as if she'd put her own thoughts aside
and must now locate them again. "Sometimes I think I'm trying
to hold the pieces of the past together. The place where I was
happy." She corrected herself: "Relatively happy. It's not as
though our childhood was all that great."

Margaret dropped a folded towel over the oven door handle
and sighed. Her lip quivered. She felt ungrateful again.

She took a breath and gripped her sides. "How do you do it,
Ange? How can you just close yourself off to everything?" She
was afraid of angering her sister, but secretly hoped her words
would cause pain, and that she could get away with it. "How
can you just walk away and leave everything behind each time
there's another story for you to chase?"

Angela had an unsettling moment of recognition. What she knew was that she no longer wanted to be with her family. She'd closed off the space between herself and them. Whatever she had become, whatever she was searching for, she no longer felt at home with them. She knew them too well — their fears, their weaknesses. She had to go away, to leave them behind, because they couldn't help her.

"Maybe I've lost my capacity to be surprised," she said. "Maybe that's what you call my 'closing off' to everything."

As a teenager, she'd felt imprisoned by family life and sought escape in the names of places. She saw how she could change the world with the spin of a globe. Restless with insomnia, she stayed up late devouring maps, geography textbooks. She would drive to the airport and watch the planes taking off in the early morning light. She grew up dreaming of distances, places whose names were magic when spoken aloud. Later, she discovered them. Only no one told her that once she found them she could never return.

"What are you looking for?" Margaret asked.

Angela saw herself as that four-year-old in a white dress with her tricycle. It was the photograph her mother had commented on earlier. Suddenly she was running from something. Some*one*. She heard herself shriek and laugh as she turned to avoid whoever was chasing her in that pristine world she was born into by what seemed no more than an accident of good fortune. The response came so quickly she knew it was true.

"I'm looking for answers," she said. "Things that don't fit the narrative I was brought up to believe in." She was peering at the world through her internal lens again.

"And you think you'll find those answers in Sarajevo, or wherever you go next?"

"I don't know."

"Aren't you afraid of anything?" Margaret asked.

"Only Mom's coldness when she shuts me out. Nothing terrifies me more than that."

Margaret closed drawers and cupboard doors, shutting down the world around them into a more manageable shape.

"I worry for you," she said. "I truly do. What will Tim do while you're gone?"

"I've left Tim."

Margaret waited, as though there must be more: *I've left Tim for the weekend*, or *I've left Tim at the bus stop and told him I'd be back for him shortly*. Something shifted as the words took on new meaning.

"When did …?" Margaret fumbled for words. "Couldn't you tell me …?"

Angela shrugged and shook her head, as if her life surprised her. "I really didn't mean to keep it a secret."

Margaret suddenly glimpsed the distance between them, frightened to see it there. "Oh, no. Please don't let this happen to us." She pulled Angela close, holding the world together for herself and her sister, who wandered about in it without fear. "Please don't keep secrets from me. We promised one another that."

Angela squeezed back. "Okay," she said. A feather on the breeze.

BJ, HAPPILY DRUNK, WAS HOLDING court in the family room and rolling a joint. Tori and Shep lay on the floor, legs intertwined, just out of reach of the fire.

"Do you kids know why it's called premenstrual syndrome?" BJ asked.

"Why?" Shep said absently, taking the joint and lighting it.

"Because mad cow disease was already taken."

Tori groaned. "That's the worst joke I've ever heard, BJ."

"It's really sexist," Shep said, trying to hold the smoke in as he spoke.

BJ ignored the remarks. "What's the definition of a long-term relationship these days?" he said.

"What?" Tori said, her eyes on the joint.

"Six consecutive one-night stands."

Tori and Shep made eyes at one another, even while laughing. "You don't have to entertain us, BJ," Shep said, passing the joint to Tori.

"You kids should lighten up. Just accept that the world's going to hell, then sit back and enjoy the show." BJ's eyes swam in the firelight. "What do you believe in, anyway?"

"Nothing," Tori answered.

"We believe in everything, only Tori doesn't know it yet," Shep countered, watching her toke.

BJ snorted. "What the hell does that mean, 'We believe in nothing and everything'?"

"It means," Shep continued, "that we're a part of everything in the physical universe and that everything, ultimately, is nothing in the grand scheme of things." He rolled up his sleeves to reveal his tattoos. "You see these? These aren't just any tattoos." He pointed to his right arm. "This snake is Typhon in Egyptian mythology. Typhon portrays the descent of spirit into matter. And this," he said, pointing to the other, "is Anubis, the jackal-headed god who represents its reawakening."

"Oh, right! Aren't they friends of Rocky and Bullwinkle?" BJ said.

"Not quite."

"And who are you in this ultimate revolution of being and nothingness?" BJ asked, taking the joint back from Tori.

Shep smiled. "We're just particles of change that make the universe a beautiful place to be."

BJ shook his head. "That's so far fucking out I can't even begin to ridicule it."

"It's all about enlightenment, man. Get with the program."

"Who needs enlightenment when there are good drugs?" BJ said. "Enlightenment is boring. It's too autocratic, too demanding. Insanity, now … that has possibilities. It holds the promise of entertainment. Better yet, there are no rules. You can be insane any way you want to. It's totally democratic."

BJ took a final toke and threw the roach into the fire.

Markus stirred and looked up. "Dad, are you finished telling jokes? I want to go to bed."

"My other biggest fan," BJ said, looking down at Markus. He stood and stretched. "Okay, cowboy, let's you and me go round up some mad cows." He picked Markus up and swung him around in his arms. "See you in the morning," he said to Tori and Shep. "Whoever the hell you are."

ANGELA STOOD IN THE HALLWAY outside her bedroom listening to the soft slap of linen coming from inside. Her mother was punishing the pillows and enforcing rigidity on the sheets, making up for the order lacking in the world. The room was a simple one. Abbie had named it Tiger Lily. It had been Angela's for as long as the family had owned the cottage. Her sisters' rooms were Ladyslipper and Foxglove, magical names for rooms set outside of time. As a child, Angela had loved the nightly rhythm of crickets beneath her window. *Let's hurry up and eat supper*, she would announce to the dinner table. *I want to go to bed so I can hear the bugs sing.*

Angela wasn't interested in crickets now. Nor was Abbie. She straightened, taut with efficiency, turning to regard her daughter.

"I've left extra blankets, in case you get cold." She might have been a maid going off-duty.

"It's a nice night. I'll be fine."

"You can open the window if it gets too warm. The insects have all gone."

That was her mother, Angela thought. All eventualities had been prepared for, be they famine, flood, or flying pests. She'd made prevention into a religion.

"I'm sorry if I upset you with my news at supper," Angela said.

"Mothers know better than to expect anything from their children." This was spoken as a truism, something beyond question.

Abbie went back to her straightening, as if the whole world could be fixed with good hospital corners. This was where it always broke down, Angela thought. Coldness, followed by anger. What if she just slipped past it and pretended it didn't happen?

"If mothers don't expect things, does that mean their children aren't obligated to give them anything?"

Abbie sighed in a way that suggested Angela didn't understand how hard she made it for everyone else. "You don't owe me anything," she said. Her eyes flashed with concern, her hands approximated a gesture of care, but there was no comfort or familiarity in her voice. She'd practised the externals of her role while neglecting to carve out its essence. "How does Tim feel about your going away?"

"I've left Tim."

There was a barely perceptible rise in Abbie's features, as though they'd been talking about a change in the weather.

"When did this happen?"

"Last month. Right after I got back from Calgary."

There it was, Angela thought. It was finally out in the open and it wasn't nearly as big as she'd expected. It hardly took up any space at all.

"When were you planning on telling your family?"

Angela heard the unspoken accusation, the long-standing disappointment her actions entailed. But the truth must be embraced, she reminded herself, whether it was a bullet, a mortar shell, or a sinking boat crammed with refugees who'd been looking forward to their new lives in a better place.

"I thought I'd just let it pile up with all the other family secrets," Angela said.

Abbie held, the briefest of hesitations. "I have to say I'm not surprised. I always thought you married him to spite me."

Angela felt stung. "You know, Mom, it's amazing how you can make everything turn out to be about you."

"It's not about me at all. It was obvious you never really loved him. I hoped I could make you see that at the time."

Angela saw herself as a criminal who believed her crime would never be discovered, only to learn it had been apparent to everyone all along. She turned to the dresser mirror and caught her mother's reflection over her shoulder. The lower half of the room lay in darkness; their upper bodies floated like islands in pools of gloom.

"How can you ever know when it's love?" she asked quietly.

Abbie's face softened. "After more than thirty years, I still don't know. But I do know that you endure, despite the problems."

This was the mortal world after all, Abbie thought. You lived in it when you could, you endured it when you couldn't, and always you forgave it and accepted what it offered. Love was never where you looked for it. It could disguise itself as a million things and hide in the strangest places. In a star, a tree, a fallen leaf. Or in the smile of an infant as you pointed out stars, and trees, and fallen leaves. The most beautiful, tender things could be the most troubling. Sometimes you simply learned to live with the unanswerable.

"You should have had a child. To help cement the marriage," she said.

Angela shrugged off the suggestion. "That virus in Africa," she said. "I have only one tube and half a uterus left. It wasn't exactly an option."

"You could have adopted. You still can."

"I'm not so sure I could love someone else's child."

"You learn to love." Her mother said this as if it were an infallible recipe that produced the expected results every time.

"What if the child turns out to be an ungrateful wretch? Like me, for instance."

"I suppose you could call it just deserts. If you weren't such an insatiable ambitionist, that wouldn't be the case. You're lucky all it cost was your fertility. Why do you run all over the world risking your life? What's out there?"

"A kind of peace."

Angela offered this, hoping it would make up for the anxiety she'd caused, for her inability to explain what drew her away. She'd seldom met anyone who knew what it meant to talk to a nineteen-year-old soldier who said he was doing what he did because it beat brick-laying, lying to his parents about where he was posted so they wouldn't worry for him while the fighting was on. Or when a young man told her he'd joined the army because his parents had been threatened with death if he didn't. Or how she believed she was doing something worthwhile when she visited the family of a thirteen-year-old who'd left the house wearing her favourite blue dress and red fingernail polish to attend a friend's birthday party, never to be seen again. How could she tell her mother she did it for them, to make their stories mean something?

If she'd chosen to do anything else, it would still have taken her to the edges of the earth. She might have become an Arctic explorer or an archaeologist sifting sand in the desert, but she could never have stayed home, like her mother and sister, fighting off imaginary demons.

Once, in Rwanda, a mine disposal technician let her detonate a landmine, placing a long thin prod in her hand to set it off. She poked at the ground till it flashed and roared, blasting soil and bits of metal into the air. She was secretly thrilled by it. She saw her life in that moment, pieces flying off out of control, danger everywhere. That was the meaning her work gave her.

"I don't understand why you're so intent on throwing your life away," her mother said.

Angela felt the anger flash. "The truth is, Mom, I'm glad I didn't have kids, because I might have turned out like you."

Abbie had been waiting for this, harbouring grudges she bore against the unknown and unknowable world of her eldest daughter.

"I won't tolerate your rudeness. If you can't be civil while you're here, then you can go back to wandering the world."

Angela watched her mother's outline disappear in the mirror as the door closed backwards on itself.

BOOK V
THE CENTRE OF THE UNIVERSE

THIRTEEN

"'Just outside the town of Niš lies the famous Ćele Kula, or Skull Tower,'" Angela read. "'The Serbian leader Karadjordje had pointed out to Napoleon, as well as representatives of the Turks and Russians, that Niš belonged to Serbia. In 1809, an army of 16,000 Serb soldiers was dispatched to reclaim it, digging five trenches to fortify their position and filling a cave with ammunition. In May, the Turks attacked the most prominent trench on Čegar Hill under the command of Stevan Sindjelić. The Serbs fought them off five times, but they succumbed during the sixth attack when the Turks filled the trench with their own fallen soldiers, crossing over on the bodies of the dead.'"

André reached across the covers and pulled her close. He loved the careful rhythms of her voice bringing history to life. Mornings were an entirely different affair now that Angela woke to his peaceful breathing instead of his fitful babble before she'd had her first cup of coffee.

"'When Sindjelić saw that the Turks had broken through, he ran to the powder cave and fired his gun into the gunpowder magazine, killing three thousand of his own men and twice as many Turks. If nothing else, he had spared his men the gruesome fate that awaited Turkish prisoners — impalement or beheading. After the battle, the Turkish pasha Hurshid ordered a tower to be built of quicklime and embedded with 952 skulls of the Serbian men who died in the explosion as a warning to the Serbian people.'"

André sat up quickly. "Is that true? It's incredibly gruesome!"

"Yes, it's true."

She waited till he settled back down before continuing. "'In 1833, French poet Alphonse de Lamartine wrote of his travels in the Ottoman lands. He described coming upon the tower, seeing its whiteness gleaming in the distance like fine marble. Sitting in its shade, he glanced up to see row upon row of skulls, bleached by the sun and cemented into sand and lime. *In places*, he wrote, *tufts of hair still clung to the skulls like lichen, disturbed now and then by the wind that blew through them, making a mournful noise. May the Serbs keep this monument!* he wrote. *It will always teach their children the value of the independence of a people, showing them the price their fathers had to pay for it.*'"

THE FIGHTING HAD SLOWED WITH the onset of winter. For a while, it seemed as though an unofficial truce had been declared. One night the power came on suddenly at 3 A.M. They spent two hours doing housework — ironing clothes, washing dishes as the water heated up, showering for the first time in weeks. All their faxes were sent, all their stories accounted for. In the daytime, they spent more time with their colleagues. They tried to disguise their burgeoning romance from the others, but a native sensitivity to the undercurrents of human behaviour made it impossible to hide anything from journalists for long. Even the lack of grumbling had the others on the alert.

"You butter your toast without bitterness now," remarked an acerbic comrade one morning in the small café around the corner from the compound.

IN FEBRUARY, AN UNEXPECTED OFFER came from Martin — a month's vacation in Mexico.

"What's this?" Angela asked. "Generosity from the mother ship?"

Martin's voice crackled over the phone. "There is a bit of an opportunity for you, while you're there," he said.

"I knew there was a catch!"

"You'll love this. It's your kind of thing — social rebellion and all that," he'd said over the phone. "I need an update on the Zapatista Rebellion in Chiapas. The Mexican army just broke the ceasefire brokered by a Catholic priest who's said to be pro-Zapatista."

Angela had followed the story with interest, as indigenous tribes in the southeastern province declared war on the Mexican government. Led by a guerrilla in a balaclava, three thousand peasants took over several small towns the day NAFTA was ratified. Fashioning themselves after Emiliano Zapata, a hero of the Mexican Revolution, the new Zapatista Army of National Liberation cited centuries of unfair treatment and neglect. Several hundred died in skirmishes with the army, but within days nearly half of Mexico rallied in support of their cause, as did much of the world.

"Subcomandante Marcos and the other leaders have managed to elude the government till now, but it looks like their time may have come," Martin continued. "The government wants them rooted out permanently. Those poor Che Guevaras. The peso is down and investment has fallen drastically. They've been waging a pretty successful media campaign on the Internet. But get this: did you know the natives believe this war was prophesied in a sacred text called the *Chilam Balam*, written hundreds of years ago?"

"What exactly will we be after down there?" Angela asked.

"It's hard to say — everyone is leaving, disappearing into the jungles. I doubt you'd be able to find Marcos, but there must be someone who'll be willing to talk, provided it doesn't cost them their lives. Maybe they'll show you the magic book. I'd love to get a copy."

Whatever else, it promised to be a respite from the larger theatre of war.

Angela and André packed their bags and waited for a flight out. When the directive for evacuation came, they were ready. A sudden call sent them to the airport where they waited another twenty-four hours, sleeping on the floor, before boarding the UN flight. Despite the unfinished business, they felt relieved to give up the unrelenting grey and overriding gloom of the place they'd called home for the last few months.

FOURTEEN

Mexico unfurled in a blazing tapestry of mountains, deserts, and searing heat. Light assailed their vision, cutting everything down to shape and shadow. Water was driven underground in an extensive system of limestone caverns, where it flowed beneath the land, invisibly nourishing. It was a perfect *trompe l'oeil*. The earth burned above while the water ran in secret tables below.

For the first few days, Angela and André endured the hotel life in Cancún, but found themselves unable to relate to the giddy tourists lounging by pools and bars. They wandered pointlessly across empty beaches and sprawled on rocks at sunset, while their minds stayed alert for the sound of tanks and falling shells. Nothing came at them out of the sky but the unsettling light.

A market in the old town yielded stalls of fruit, vegetables, carob beans, chilies, handmade clothing, and jewellery. They bought flowery shirts and shorts, laughingly posed as honeymooners. Their skin darkened. The heat made them feel drunk in the daytime, but left them restless at night. On the third day,

they packed their belongings in a Jeep and headed south, at last
back in their routine.

Jungle shadows offered coolness in the narrow margins where
the Jeep hugged the edge of the dirt roads. After hours of seeing
nothing but trees, the ruins of Chichén-Itzá reared above the tree-
line. They climbed its massive pyramid, an elaborate calendar.
Each year on the vernal equinox, the sun hit the steps at a
particular angle making the feathered snake, Kukulkhan, descend
in a ripple of sunlight to the applause of tourists. The edifice had
long outlasted its creators, who had disappeared into the jungle
as though they'd slid off the map, escaping time entirely.

Angela and André stood silently together on bleached cliff
edges above the well of sacrifice, while parents shouted warnings to children to stand clear. Below, the fetid water glinted
in the midday sun. A tourist pamphlet told how the Maya
weighted messengers with stones and cast them in to send
appeals for rain or bountiful crops to the lords of the underworld. Those who stayed afloat till the glaring light of noon were
freed. They read how the Maya had worshipped rain, blood,
milk, semen — the sacred *itz* that gave life. Chichén-Itzá: *At the
mouth of the well of Itzá*. To be sacrificed was an honour.

Angela snapped a half dozen shots of André balancing on one
leg at the edge of the well. His face mocked her. His rain dance,
he called it.

They left the ruins and headed back to the sparse coast, past
Cobá and Tulúm, following the pathway of the Maya. With one
hand on the steering wheel, André fished around in his headband
for a joint.

"I think I should try this stuff," Angela said.

André lit up and passed the joint along. Angela took in the harsh smoke, sandpaper tearing her throat.

"I don't feel a thing," she said.

He laughed. "It's not instantaneous."

She tried again and waited another five minutes. "I still don't feel anything."

He watched as she removed her shoes and propped her feet on the dash. "Maybe not," he said, "but this is the most relaxed you've ever been."

She snorted. "Is that all there is to it?"

"What were you expecting — the Second Coming?"

The Jeep snaked along the ghostly ribbon of black outlining the shore. By the time they reached the campground, the sun had disappeared, its afterglow spreading over the water. They paid for a cabana and deposited their belongings inside the thatched-roof hut. It was already dark as they plunged into the waves. The surf pulled at their legs, washing away the strain of the long day's drive.

Starlight bounced along the crests. Angela stood, amazed as stars spilled from the water, running off her skin, quicksilver explosions catching on her arms and legs. She pointed them out — the ocean was burning. André laughed and shook his head. Water didn't burn. She was stoned. Then he saw it, too: sparks catching on the waves. Watery stars. Nitrogen in the algae igniting on contact with oxygen, she explained. *Dinoflagellates*. André laughed even harder. Were all those big words just sitting somewhere in her brain, waiting to be used? She was laughing, too.

AT NIGHT THEIR BODIES CELEBRATED, easing over and under one another. André was the most talented lover she'd had, an explorer with a gift for discovery. His hand on her drew a map of possibility, etching meaning on skin as it rode over hills or lingered in sweaty plains. His palms plied the inside of her thighs. His tongue rolled across her abdomen, moving down to tangle in her forest. All of her silhouetted by candlelight, moonlight, light of setting sun, starlight. Reflecting off the dark surface of the water.

At night she slept curled around him, his penis wrapped in her fist. When they woke they lay without moving, feeling what it was to lie like that, a mountain and its shadow. In the daytime they kept to themselves, a tribe apart. They wanted no company other than their own, no sound but the murmuring of sun and surf, stopping only briefly to chat with strangers who chanced by their small point of land. They absorbed the solitude, the rhythm of waves meeting sand, and entered into it.

On the third night they came across a secluded cove. The air was cool. They built a campfire from driftwood and wrapped themselves in rough blankets. André had taken a peyote button he'd bought from some teenagers on the beach. It made him restless and dreamy. He explored the dark around them, the air full of tangled lights and intricate paisley patterns. He swam out till he knew she could no longer see him. He stayed there treading water, watching her by the firelight and assessing his need for her. He was gauging his ability to withstand the distance between them, like an endurance test of extreme cold or heat, before venturing a little farther. This far. Now this far. No — that was enough. Finally, he capitulated to his need and returned.

When he reached her she was going through her collection of photographs, the firelight flickering on her face. Even here she'd brought those talismans, her phantoms from that other world that mesmerized her and took her away from him.

"This is an English boy named Norman McQueen," she said without looking up. "He was just twenty-one when he died. He was liked by everyone in the squadron. It was a complete shock when his plane went down."

André saw a lean young man with curly blond hair, his face turned partly from the camera as he negotiated the tricky steps of a ruin near a beach.

"Before his crash, Norman willed his camera to his commander, Laddie Lucas, whose own camera had just been broken. I think Norman knew he was going to die. All of Lucas's most famous photos were taken on that camera."

"How would you know if you were going to die?"

She looked up, the flames retreating from her face. "I think it would feel like you were getting ready to go off somewhere for a long time and you'd want to say goodbye to everything."

He was quiet for a moment then he said, "I think it would feel like you needed to experience everything all at once, to cram all of life in while you had the chance."

He watched Angela turn the pages, willing herself into the lives of the men in the photographs. She called up what she knew about each picture: where they were taken, why, by whom. History without beginning or ending. Windows in time.

She pointed out the squadron's Flight Lieutenant, an attractive boy with the strange name of Raoul Daddo-Langlois, and described the intense friendship he'd shared with Lucas. They'd been a formidable duo in Malta, famous for their exploits during their brief time together. Daddo-Langlois had died in Malta. It was Lucas who, later in life, had borne his friend's name into history with his photographs and his recounting of their exploits.

Angela turned more pages. Daddo-Langlois' face appeared from time to time: shy, happy, diffident. She mentioned his Arab-French background.

"All these men," she said, "grouped together like that. Do you think many were gay?"

She looked up to see him watching her in the firelight. Without the headband, his hair fell forward over his features, framing his cheekbones. He pulled the blanket close around his shoulders.

"I'm sure some of them were gay, only they didn't call it that. And sometimes it's just sex, but they didn't call it that, either."

For the first time since it happened, he began to speak about Jacques. How it had begun when he and Jacques were in high school. Not a seduction, but a mutual curiosity. Smoking up, touching experimentally under the covers during sleepovers. A stray hand, a not-quite careless caress. At first it was something allowed, then encouraged, consented to. It had gone on from there, becoming more daring, more explorative. Through sixteen, seventeen, and going on eighteen. It lasted nearly three years.

"We did everything with each other," André said. "And there was nothing we wouldn't do for each other. We both felt it, even if we never said it out loud. But when I called it 'love' he became afraid. Then someone found out — or guessed — one of the boys at school. It turned ugly."

Listening, Angela sensed things about him she hadn't noticed before. The labyrinths of his mind had neatly concealed the paths lying in front of her. Here were secrets, abilities, unexpected people in his past. The shadowed outlines of his life. A mosque, dismantled brick by brick, that remained in memory.

"Sex is easy for men," he said with a shrug. "Does it make me less attractive to you now?"

She touched his face, as if memorizing him should he shape-shift and disappear. "I like knowing there are things about you I can never claim."

Everything outside their circle of light had disappeared. He watched her eyes to see if they would retreat to that place inside her only she could see, arranging the world to please herself. But she stayed with him.

"I tried to tell him it was okay, it didn't matter what the others called it. It was our name for it that mattered."

"What did the others call it?"

"Dirt. Disgrace. *Sacrilège.*" The last word made French to invoke its fullest meaning.

"What happened? Where is he now?" Discovering a door into the past, a hidden cave before her eyes.

"He killed himself." He raised his eyes to the dark. "I admired him. And I loved him more than anything, but he couldn't face himself."

She didn't ask more, fearing to be an infidel trespassing. The wind blew into the fire. The flames reared up and retreated, a cavalry ambushed.

"Tell me about your mother," he said after awhile.

To his surprise, she did, though when she spoke it was with effort.

"I was afraid of my mother the whole time I was growing up. One word from her could devastate me for weeks. I tried to be close to her, but it never worked, somehow. She wouldn't let me. I think I closed myself off to her eventually. Sometimes I think I travel just to avoid being around her."

She picked up a stick and stirred the flames. A flurry of sparks, fiery insects flying into the night.

"She spent time in a psychiatric hospital, but I don't really know why. My sister Margaret thinks she tried to kill herself before we were born, but I can hardly believe it. She's too tenacious for that."

Nothing more came, as if speaking those few words completed something. Chipping away at an old stone. David laying Goliath to rest.

An arm slid from under the blanket, a coppery snake emerging from its basket of reeds. André pulled the tape deck from his knapsack and pushed a button. A tinselly melody burst forth, nearly drowned by the surf.

He pulled her up by her hands and they began to dance, twisting and turning in the dark for the length of a fiery samba, followed by a raunchy blues song, and finally a slow foxtrot. A classic — "These Foolish Things (Remind Me of You)."

Singing along with Billie's heartache — of cigarettes and lipstick traces, of hearts with wings and other foolish things — they twisted the ends of the blanket, stretching it above the fire, spinning in the dirt like planets around a sun. André jumped across the flames and grabbed her, still dancing but joined at the pelvis now, till they fell laughing onto the sand.

The smoke leaked away as they kicked wet sand over the embers. Their talk and their dancing had exhausted them. They trekked silently back. André sat cross-legged in the cabana rolling a joint. Angela watched him crawl into the hammock, where it was strung like a giant smile in the air. A match flared. The red point arced away and back with its vapour trail. She left him and returned to the beach.

The waves whited over with a sigh as she dropped her clothes on the sand. The moon glared down like the noonday sun. The water moved restlessly, as though eating something. Once, in the Caribbean, she'd sailed at night without any lights, the boat, the sky, and the water at one. Disappearing in time.

She leaned back and floated. Overhead, the stars were perfectly still and whirling around her at the same time. It made her think of that moment when you were dancing and suddenly the music stopped yet you moved with your own momentum as the beat continued in your brain, your pulse winging you along with it.

A surge broke over her head and she came up sputtering. Her feet reached down, but the bottom had vanished. She looked back to the beach and was startled to see the far-off shore. A second surge crashed over her head. The water held her in its grip and pulled her farther out. There was nothing to hold onto — just the darkness above and below — no telling how deep the water was. Her instinct fought the riptide, though she knew she should go with it till it released her. Another wave, bigger than the others, took her and held her down. She choked and swallowed with each successive crash, unable to surface long enough to clear her lungs before the next one roared overhead.

She glimpsed a honeycomb of light, a cruise ship inching across the horizon. She pulled air into her lungs, choking, but unable to cry out. She thought of her family: if she drowned, they might think she'd walked away from them. But she could never walk away from her family. They were like the dead. She had carried them with her for years, looking for a place to lay them aside. Another wave pushed her under till she felt herself tumbling against the sandy bottom. It seemed forever before she surfaced again, panicking for air, spluttering as she broke through.

Off to the right, a seaweed sketch danced on the dark water. She barely glimpsed him through a chance surfacing. *André!* Black arms slapped a black branch toward her. It landed right in her hands, slipped free again. The water pulled, taking her down to the lords of the underworld. André flailed at her, keeping his grip on the stick. For a moment he lost his footing and seemed to rise up out of the waves in sheer panic. He whacked the stick down with both hands, just missing her. This time she seized it and he pulled her toward him, both of them floating, holding onto each end as though they were still dancing.

He choked out a command: *Swim!* They moved slowly, the suck of the sea pulling and releasing them briefly before starting in again. Suddenly, he found the bottom and stood, an astonished fisherman reeling in a mermaid.

They collapsed on the beach together and lay there panting.

André gripped her arm so hard it began to hurt. "What were you doing?" he choked out, his words barely coherent.

"I just went swimming," she panted.

"Don't ever — do that — to me — again."

"Oh, yes — everything happens to you!"

For a second she thought he might cry. He choked back a sob and buried his face in her shoulder. He'd saved her, the horror of it only now apparent to them both.

Afterwards they though of it as a marker, a rite of passage: *Those who stayed afloat till the glaring light of noon were freed.*

Later, she tried to explain what had happened. "It sounds weird, but even while it was happening, I knew I would live. I never saw myself not getting back to shore, even when it seemed hopeless."

He nodded. "You imagined an alternate ending," he said knowingly. "Like that night at the barricades."

That was all. They didn't speak of it beyond that night, didn't name what had transpired, as though the speaking might unleash some further danger. From that moment on, she would owe him her life.

FIFTEEN

THE DEMANDS OF WORK DREW them on. They left the coast and drove into hills. The heat slipped away as the hills became mountains, but the light changed little. They stopped just outside San Cristóbal de las Casas, where the uprising had begun. A clock in the town square, over the city hall, bore a bullet hole in its face between the numeral three and the centre where the hands met. Not from this revolution, but from the last one, in 1911. A daily reminder of the constant struggle the people faced.

For a moment, it seemed as if they'd returned to Bosnia. Trucks lumbered past with soldiers in army fatigues and carrying rifles. Two white travellers inspired fear and suspicion in the natives, a small, sparse people who called themselves Chamula, Zinacanteco, Tenahapa, Tzotzil. These were the people fighting a surprise rebellion against centuries of poverty and neglect by the country's leaders.

Angela's instinct was to grab her camera, but she'd been warned against it. The natives believed photographs could steal their souls. It could be dangerous even to be seen with a camera. Children threw stones at insensitive tourists who disregarded the region's laws, which forbid the use of recording devices. There was the added risk of arrest. It was a punishable crime.

"Even something as simple as a cactus will be keenly guarded," Martin warned her. "They believe even the damned plants have souls."

"Then what am I supposed to shoot?" she'd asked.

"Get anything you can, hon," he'd said. "You're the best. Just don't get caught."

The city lay nestled in the hills, colourful and tidy, Florence displaced by an ocean. In the narrow streets everything moved single file: people first, followed by bicycles, cars, pack animals, and carts. Everywhere they went they were surrounded by young girls in colourful dresses selling candy and Chiclets for a few pesos. When André held out a tube of Pringles, they converged on him as though he'd conjured a feast.

With the heavy military presence, there were no obvious signs of insurrection. Still, they moved cautiously. They'd been warned their chances of being kidnapped were high, though by which side was unclear. They met a few other journalists, but the tourists had disappeared like rabbits running down holes.

Everyone but the children ignored them. No one approached or seemed curious about their presence. On the third day, they asked a maid at the hotel and two waiters in a café how they could meet anyone who spoke for the rebels. The maid, all in white, looked terrified, as if they'd asked her to spit on the floor of the church or slap a priest. The waiters seemed to have no opinion on the subject, but agreed to pass the word around for a handful of American dollars.

The next afternoon they ambled through the *zócalo*, looking over the wares on display. A few of the locals were dressed in the loose-fitting trousers and serapes of the Chamula tribe. The man who approached wore a pale pink shirt and shorts, designating him as Zinacanteco. Two ribbons dangled freely from his hat to indicate that he was a bachelor. A married man would have worn his ribbons neatly tied.

He walked up to them and smiled nervously. "Signor," he said to André. "You want to meet the people. *¿Si?*"

"*¡Si!*"

"Go to San Juan Chamula in the market. Someone will come for you."

The man slipped away as though pulling free of their grasp. *Where in the market? What time?* But he was already gone.

They made the trek to San Juan Chamula in the early morning and found themselves in a small dusty town that seemed to have blown in from the nearby hills. Costumed men carrying marimbas and drums wandered in search of somewhere to set up, while women lit fires to bake tamales and teenagers were left in charge of soda-pop stands.

Angela fingered the woven tapestries and leather crafts displayed on whitewashed walls and makeshift racks. The presence of two gringos evoked stares, but no fear. A roaming band struck up a song, and several young women began to twirl through the market in brilliantly coloured dresses adorned with suns and moons. As the dance ended, a boy came around with a hat for donations, but he shyly avoided André when he held out a coin.

Tall green crosses marked the square. Each one had pine boughs strapped to it, the needles dried to a rusty orange. The church was empty of pews. Instead, the floors were covered by more pine boughs. The air hung heavy with incense smoke. The interior glowed with the light from hundreds of candles, some placed on the floor among the branches, others set on stands along the walls.

Small knots of people crouched on the floors around the candles, chanting or praying silently. Hands rotated plastic bottles of water or Pepsi over the flames, hinting at their belief system with its mix of Catholicism and Native ritual. Angela fretted that she hadn't been allowed to bring her camera inside the church. It was eating away at her.

They still had no idea who or what they were waiting for.

Outside, a crowd had gathered in a far field where half a dozen men with burning brushes set fire to the ground. Smoke rose in grey-green tufts as three near-naked figures began to run barefoot along the fiery path.

"What are they doing?" André asked.

"Purifying themselves," Angela said. "They're cleansing flesh and spirit."

When the run finished, the men were cheered. Youngsters in sandals stomped out the remnants of the flames as everyone turned back to the market. A round-faced boy leading an old man edged toward them through the crowd. The man's face was wrinkled beyond description. His eyes were jet, his hair white. He might have been more than a century old.

The boy brought him forward. His grandfather wished to speak with them, he said.

"I am Don Alejandro," the boy translated for the old man. "A Tzotzil Indian."

He was the guide they were seeking. He was offering to take them to meet his people.

IN THE MORNING DON ALEJANDRO waited outside their hotel. He'd brought three horses — two mares and a stallion. Each carried a sleeping bag rolled behind the saddle. The maid said he'd been standing there since five, but she'd refused to wake them till six-thirty.

The boy Pablo hadn't come with him, so they had no way to communicate. They tried to determine how long they'd be gone, pointing to their watches, then up to the sun. The old man raised an arm and seemed to beckon them on. He might have been indicating the direction they would travel or warning them of an approaching storm. He motioned to the ground, as though describing a small animal, then pointed ahead and nodded. They surmised that the boy was to meet up with them later.

They packed travelling kits and cameras, and made arrangements for the Jeep. Don Alejandro helped them mount the mares before he straddled the stallion. The horses bumped down the road, a mini-caravan leaving the waking town. They soon got used to the slow gait and occasional stumble as a hoof slipped on rock. Half an hour outside of town, Pablo appeared on a horse of his own. He waved at them from a distance and when they got up close thanked them for coming. He seemed unable — or unwilling — to divulge their destination. There was little to do but follow.

For another hour they went down, and then the ride climbed again sharply. There was nothing but dust and rock, and a surprising coniferous forest. If there were people, Angela and André never saw them, though they knew the land around them had been populated for millenia. The air was thin, and the sun more searing because of it. To get lost here would have been death.

At midday, a sound rose to meet them, rhythmic, like hundreds of seeds shifting in a hollow gourd. It increased in pitch and volume, filling the air with a pulse that rose and fell. At first it sounded like a distant plane, but the noise persisted with no sign of anything above. It seemed to come from a cluster of rocks just off the path. Angela expected to see a swarm of winged insects take to the air at their approach, but eventually the sound died away without revealing anything.

André rode as if he'd been born to it. The bright plumage of his headband looked like it belonged at last. By early afternoon they entered a grove of trees stripped of all but their uppermost leaves. The trunks were covered in fierce-looking thorns. The path wound skilfully around the trees, channel markers charting a course through treacherous shoals. The horses seemed to take greater care not to stumble, as if aware they were on dangerous ground.

The sound of falling water reached the travellers' ears, the dry air turning moist and limpid. In a place like Eden, a long thin cascade spilled from a plateau high above. Water slipped over stone, splattered and rose briefly again in a fine spray. The pool was clear and cold, its bottom unseen. The horses bent to drink. Pablo turned in his saddle and said they would rest here.

They wiped their faces on their sleeves and sat in the shade eating fajitas and beans. With hands cupped, they drank from the trickling rocks. André stripped to his boxers and jumped into the pool. He swam across until the downpour forced him back. Finally, on the third try, he gained a hold on the rocks and scrambled up out of sight behind the falls. Angela heard him calling her from behind the water, bodiless.

Soon, they refilled their water flasks and rode north for several hours before making camp. Pablo helped the old man unroll two small tents. Their hands travelled in well-timed movements, unfurling the canvas. Later that night, the wind tore through the site, turning the tents into ships about to set sail.

Angela walked a few paces from the campsite and stopped to look back. Camera raised, she aimed at the boy and pressed the shutter before her conscience got the better of her. Pablo looked up just as she lowered her arms. She was struck by his look of trust. It was the only picture she took without permission. Later, when the roll was developed, she would discover a dark blur with oblong slashes like eyes. If she hadn't known better, she would have thought she'd captured a wolf, something feral. She seldom missed her mark and for a while she obsessed over the faceless shadow, recalling how Don Alejandro had seemed to describe an animal when indicating the boy.

They sat on rocks next to the fire while the old man carefully turned strips of meat wrapped around sticks. The fat hissed and threw smells in the air as it dripped onto the stone. When they were done, he laid the branches across a tin plate. Pablo unwrapped a bundle of tamales. They ate with their hands and drank goat milk from animal-skin flasks to wash it down.

Don Alejandro began to speak. He spoke at length before Pablo interrupted to translate whatever he had words for. The boy's descriptions were brief, his English limited. It was hard to tell what was left out. Before the Spanish came, he said, the Indians worshipped a tree called the ceiba. The ceiba was the source of all creation and it stood at the centre of the universe. The Maya called it the World Tree and dressed it in human clothing. A holy scarecrow. When the Spanish arrived the World Tree was transformed into the cross of Christianity, its original meaning buried. It was the cross with the pine boughs they'd witnessed in San Juan Chamula.

Eventually, the Maya staged an uprising against the Spanish in the Caste War of Yukatán. They established a town, Chan Santa Cruz, as their capital and remained there independently for half a century until the Mexican government reconquered the area in 1901. The last of the Maya tribes were then scattered across the peninsula. Don Alejandro, the boy insisted, had taken part in the original revolution, and had returned to his people to lead them again.

"There is a book," the boy told them. "It says the punishment comes again and war returns to the land."

It was the *Chilam Balam*, Angela realized. The book foretold of the return of power to the Maya at the end of time. The natives had a magic tree and a book of prophecy firing them up. It was no wonder they believed they could take on the entire government. After Pablo and the old man went to bed, Angela and André sat by the fire.

Angela looked up from the flames. "So Don Alejandro think he's returned from the last century. He looks old enough, that's for sure."

The night cold was coming on. The wind shifted and the flames cowered to the rock. They leaned in for warmth.

"What do you think of this book of prophecy?" André asked.

She shrugged. "War's a constant. Do we need prophets to tell us that?"

He smiled. "You're such a pragmatist."

"I'm an empiricist. I believe in reason."

"I thought you were a journalist. But I don't mind as long as you believe in emotion, too. I'm French, after all."

She looked off in silence. Mountain peaks sketched out the horizon where it unravelled in darkness.

"What are you thinking of?" he said after a while.

"About the ceiba. The World Tree."

"I want to see this tree," he said.

"If you were a tree, what kind would you be?"

"An oak," he said. "Something that lives for a hundred years. And you?"

"A locust tree. A honey locust sitting on the edge of the Bruce Peninsula."

"You're nothing, if not precise."

IN THE MORNING THEY ROLLED their tents and climbed stiffly back onto the horses. Angela hoped it wouldn't be another long day of riding. The boy assured them it would not. Sometime before noon they came across a hand-lettered board tacked to a tree. It was the first sign of anything human they'd seen since the previous afternoon. She knew they were in the Chiapas Highlands close to the Lacandón rainforest. Oaxaca lay to the west and Guatemala to the east, but where they were on any map was impossible to say. They had come to a land where places existed only on certain days of the month: a farmer's market might be hurriedly raised and disbanded again every fourth Saturday after the exchange of crops, the performing of music and dance, the drinking of sugar-cane liquor. Who could say the where of their location? Just "here."

A little past one o'clock, they passed two men in dust-covered overalls carrying hoes. The brown faces studied them with careful gravity. After another twenty minutes they arrived at a gathering of thatched huts with roofs supported by poles, the walls covered in mud and plaster. It looked temporary, yet at the same time as if it had been there forever.

Children gathered to watch their arrival, but didn't approach as they had in San Cristóbal. The riders dismounted. Their horses were taken from them to be looked after. Don Alejandro seemed to be describing their journey to several solemn young men. The new arrivals were led along a path to a long low hut where wooden crates circled the expanse of an axe-hewn stump that served as a table.

Two ancient men and one woman, all nearly as old as Don Alejandro, greeted them. A young woman entered — their translator. The old ones were the village elders, she explained. She welcomed them and thanked them for coming, her English only slightly better than Pablo's. They all sat and listened as the elders spoke at length. The progress of the talks was slow and painstaking.

They'd been invited because they were gringo journalists who could send their tribe's message abroad, that much was clear. But apparently there was something more. One of the old men, called Father-Mother, spoke at length. Through the translator, he indicated they were to write down his words and bring them into the world. While they expressed solidarity with the Zapatista rebels, he said, his people did not admit to being part of any group other than a generalized movement known as the People's Coordinating Committee. They feared retribution from government troops, who had already assassinated group leaders and routed their families.

At the conclusion of the talk, the elders thanked the journalists again for coming. Outside the hut, they were joined by a shaman in a plum-coloured waistcoat decorated with lightning bolts. A leather pouch hung from his neck; similar bags were tied at his wrists and waist. He withdrew a handful of crystals, scattering them on the ground. He repeated the procedure, mulling over the stones each time. Satisfied, he returned them to the pouch. He nodded to the translator.

The shaman had something special to show them, she said. The crystals had approved their intentions. She bowed and left. Angela and André quickly gathered their belongings and followed the shaman, with Don Alejandro and Pablo trailing behind. Would they be shown mass graves or evidence of torture of the people at the hands of the army? Did the elders hope the evidence of genocide would be presented to the world? They did not go far. The shaman stopped at a grove of canopied trees spreading overhead.

"Ceiba," Pablo said happily. The World Tree.

To the left, a series of mounds covered in grass and moss caught Angela's eye. Her instinct said there were bodies buried there, but as they drew closer she saw the ground hadn't been disturbed for a long time. If this was evidence of mass murder, it was not recent. The shaman scrambled into a small opening in the earth.

"*Cenote*," Pablo said to their inquiring looks. An underground cave spring.

They eased down after him. Inside, a natural shelf in the rock held a series of irregular clay vessels. Don Alejandro retrieved several, holding them up one at a time to catch the light. The sides were engraved with images of stingrays, turtles, feathered snakes, and jaguars. "Very old," was all they understood of Pablo's explanation.

The shaman opened one of his leather bags and removed a handful of gold-coloured pellets.

"*Copál*," Pablo informed them. Tree gum resin.

The shaman gathered brush and made a neat pile, then pulled out a matchbox with a trucking company logo on it. He lit the fire, throwing the pellets into the flames as smoke rose in sweet wisps. The ground around them was strewn with burnt *copál* and corn kernels. He lit a candle and guided them through a low, narrow passage. The space opened into a chamber that echoed with breathing and shuffled footsteps. A hundred feet above, needles of sunlight reached down and stitched together the outlines of a pool. The shaman lit more candles, affixing them to the rocks until the cavern was illuminated. He nodded to André, pointing to his camera case.

"He wants you to tape this!" Angela whispered excitedly.

The shaman shook the crystals from his neck pouch again, placing them around the cave. From another bag he retrieved a small clay burner. More *copál*. Smoke streamed up to the roof and gathered there. He drank from a bottle of clear liquid and spat on the ground before passing the bottle to André.

"Make one spit for the gods," Pablo told him.

André followed suit, passing the heady grain alcohol to Angela. He kept his camera focus tight as the shaman untied the largest sack and removed a brown and white chicken. On being freed, the bird squawked and squirmed until the shaman placed a hand over its eyes. He stretched it over a rock, quickly severing the head and feet with a knife. Blood seeped down the side of the stone. The shaman placed the dismembered parts on the ground and began to chant. The cavern resonated with his voice. Then suddenly the sound stopped.

"Ask him what it's about," André said to Pablo when the ceremony was over.

The shaman spoke briefly. Pablo turned to André. "He say it is for good eat and strong fight," the boy told them.

"Why did he want me to use my camera?"

Pablo again conferred with the shaman. "So it not be lost when ..." He struggled with the words. "When we finish," he said at last.

"Finish what?"

The boy thought carefully.

"By soldier."

André exchanged a glance with Angela. "When they kill them," he said. He nodded to Pablo. "Tell him it won't be lost."

André pulled the tape recorder from his bag and slipped in a cassette. Music filled the cavern, an opening phrase, richly resplendent, growing with confidence as a choir entered. It was a baroque anthem. Angela thought she knew it, but couldn't bring to mind what it was. She looked up to see André gesticulating wildly in the air — a swarm of bees, perhaps — but, no, he was conducting, his arms moving in a frenzy. He was offering the anthem with its ecstatic notes, its sacred moment of belonging, to this miniscule, ancient heart of the universe, as the *forever and evers* of Handel's "Hallelujah Chorus" bounced from stone to stone.

Pablo smiled. Don Alejandro, who had remained silent through the ceremony, suddenly laughed an ancient croak of a laugh. The shaman joined in, laughing as the chorus shouted from rock to rock, rebounding on its own echo, a massive fugue emerging from the depths of the earth as it reached its fervent climax.

Crawling back through the passageway, they stopped while Don Alejandro pointed out the figures on the earthenware pots lining the walls.

"World begin here," Pablo translated. "Maize god plant seeds for stars. Here is home of ceiba — the World Tree."

Don Alejandro passed one of the jars to Angela. A human figure emerged from the mouth of a feathered serpent, a meta-physical birth. Next to it stood the World Tree. She nodded in understanding. The jars told how the Maya's ancestors had come to this place with the World Tree at its centre. *Be fruitful and multiply*. They were guardians of the culture flowing from the roots, up the trunk, and out the leaves of a tree they believed had given birth to the world. It was their history they were protecting, as important to them as the war they were fighting, this lifeline into the darkness stretching back thousands of years.

BOOK VI
GREY LIONS

SIXTEEN

Angela rose before the rest of the house and walked down to the beach. The cliffs of Lion's Head had just begun to emerge in the dawn light. She watched the ghostly outlines take form. In summers past, she would wake every morning before sunrise and come down to crouch at the shoreline, waiting for the darkness to withdraw. Slowly the massive sculpture would appear, a curtain of rock dividing water and sky. It was her private Genesis, as though the forces of creation were still at play. For Angela, lions had symbolized beginnings. She waited for it to appear now — a grey lion, ancient and prophetic.

BY THE TIME SHE RETURNED to the cottage, the world had started again in earnest. Flowers had bloomed in her absence: an inverted pyramid containing bright *heliopsis* rested on a base so small it defied gravity. The kitchen table yielded platters of steaming eggs, crisp bacon, piles of hot buttered toast. Plates, napkins, utensils, and pitchers of juice sat off to the side. It was a gleaming self-serve morning in a daffodil-yellow and robin's egg blue world.

Angela sat by the window, fingers knotted around a mug. Margaret hovered in shorts and a Barney T-shirt, keeping out of the path of their mother who frequented the byways of food delivery. Abbie was immaculate, looking as though she were hosting a formal city dinner rather than a country breakfast.

BJ came down the stairs in a ratty dressing gown — feet bare, hair damp and limp behind his ears. He groped for coffee, discovered the pot empty.

"Caw-feeee!" he groaned, casting around for an audience. "It's bad enough to realize I can't drink the way I did when I was eighteen, but surely you don't expect me to get through the day without caffeine?"

"I'm making a fresh pot, BJ. It should be ready in a few minutes," Abbie announced.

He shook his head from side to side. "Clearing ... clearing ..." He stopped and looked around as though he'd just been transported from another planet. "Was it just my nausea or was the house shuddering this morning?"

"That was Shep chopping wood," Angela said. "For all his city-boy talk it turns out he's quite an able-bodied woodsman."

"So the kid has some use other than to annoy his elders." Not content with insulting the absent, he turned on Margaret. "Do you know you pawed me in the middle of the night? Was that self-defence or a pathetic attempt to revive our sex life?"

"Sounds more like a nightmare to me."

Angela rose with her mug. "I'll let you two have your private time."

Abbie raised a pair of tongs, waving them about. "I want everyone to get along today. Just enjoy yourselves and have fun."

"Jahwolt!" BJ replied. "Efferyvun vill now haff fun!"

Abbie's stern look couldn't veil her amusement. For some reason, BJ got away with these comments when no one else did. "Help yourself to breakfast, BJ. Coffee will be ready shortly."

Abbie stepped out to the porch where her youngest daughter lay stretched on the deck chair. She glanced with distaste at a navel piercing glinting in the sun.

"Good morning, Victoria."

Tori's eyes blinked open. "Morning, Mom. Did you see all the wood Shep chopped?"

"Yes, I believe I did."

"It would be nice if you showed him a little appreciation today. It might help him feel more accepted."

"If Shep wants to feel more accepted, he might try looking more acceptable," she said, and continued across the deck.

Tori scowled and wrapped herself in her arms. BJ emerged and stood beside her, warding off the sunlight with his hands.

"Hello, little sister."

He fumbled for his sunglasses in the pocket of his robe. Mr.-Hip-and-Cool-I've-Been-on-TV, Tori called him. Her friends had laughed at him when they caught his stand-up routine at Yuk Yuk's. He made such an effort to be with it. Old hipsters never knew when to fade away. How old was he really? Thirty-two? Thirty-four? Who cared anyway? He was ancient.

Conrad appeared with Markus from the far side of the cottage. "Good morning, all!"

"Morning," Tori called out.

"What's everyone doing on this beautiful day?"

"Recovering," BJ mumbled, slinking off to a deck chair.

"I'm going to do some gardening," Abbie called from the lawn. "Mr. McKeough is coming by to see about pruning those trees."

"Wonderful!" Conrad replied.

Abbie looked around to survey the group. "And I believe the girls are going into town," she said, pleased to tuck everyone into tidy itineraries.

"I want to go to town!" Markus interjected.

"No men allowed," Tori told him.

"I'm not a man — I'm a boy!"

"Sorry, kiddo. This afternoon is for the three Thomas sisters."

"The sisters are doin' it for themselves," BJ chanted from his chair.

"You got that right, bub," Tori shot back.

"Hey, you!" Conrad said to Markus. "I thought we were going fishing today."

"Fish!" Markus chimed, momentarily distracted from his disappointment. He looked up with suspicion. "Is Grandma coming with us?"

"No, I don't believe so. Grandma doesn't like worms."

Conrad looked around to where his wife had wandered along the walk. Late-season pansies fidgeted in bursts of purple at her feet. The ground was dotted with leaves from the locusts and the rusty needles of a hemlock spruce. The garden backed onto mossy hills that levelled off at the far edge before giving way to the forest. A rock wall wended through. Stone owls and squirrels dotted its length, crumbling under lichen. A pond bridged the ground between nature and nurture where the haunted asymmetrical branches of a jack pine clawed the air. Further back, a bur oak unfolded, and the graceful canopies of sugar maples rose in bright yellow balloons. All this had been here before Abbie arrived.

She looked up at him and waved. The garden was her thank-you to Conrad as much as it had been his gift to her. He'd been with her on that first day. He with his graciousness, his grasp of each moment's needs. She'd known he would always be there for her, ever since the moment he stood beside her in this garden. She'd thought she was waiting for the future to arrive. It already had, but she'd failed to recognize it. And so she married him. Because he rescued her and put her back on the road of possibilities, saving her from her fears and her loss. For every rose, a thousand thorns. He'd freed her from all that.

She cupped a bloom and inhaled — not just the flower, but the leaf too. Not just the flower and the leaf, but the stem as well; right down to the roots earthing themselves in the dung-nourished loam. She snipped one rose, then another, their brilliance falling beneath her hands. They are the best of me, she thought.

She turned to see Angela watching, the first child she'd brought to this sanctuary all those years ago. How long ago that was. And how quickly it all changed: life, love, this moment we call "now" even as it tripped hopelessly over into the future. Her daughter stood before her, waiting. What had she got to give?

"I thought it would be nice to have roses on the table tonight," Abbie said.

"Can I help?"

Angela had mustered the energy to play Good Daughter. It was a role she always assumed in her father's eyes, but hardly ever in her mother's. If she concentrated, she might sustain it long enough to get through the weekend. With practice, it might even start to come naturally, though that was probably asking too much.

Abbie held out the shears. "I'll hold the branches back while you cut."

Angela accepted the unwieldy instrument. The blades grasped a stem and bit down. A single blossom fell at their feet. It seemed a triumph of sorts, one more step to get them through the day as mother and daughter. What could be so difficult in that?

But, no: "Snip a bit lower, on an angle," Abbie instructed.

A second flower clung briefly then fell beside its sister. Angela felt the sudden pricking of a thorn.

"Ouch! Damn it!"

Abbie reached for the hand. Angela withdrew it, biting her finger to relieve the pain. Hadn't some fairy-tale heroine been poisoned by a rose from her mother? No — it was an apple. And it was her stepmother.

Abbie clucked. "You can't have roses without thorns."

"A metaphor for life?"

"No, dear. It's just common sense. I'm not as clever about such things as you."

Angela wondered if her mother realized how hurtful she was. Her instinct was to strike back, but she willed herself not to, drawing on her instinctive respect for silent dangers: unexploded landmines, candles left burning behind boarded-up windows. Things that threatened only if you failed to understand them.

Abbie frowned at a blemished leaf. "Black spot," she intoned darkly, as one might say *rheumatic fever*. "It's the damp. It can be devastating once it starts. I hadn't noticed it before, but then we've hardly been out all summer. It's getting to be too late now."

"Is this enough?" Angela held out half a dozen roses to go with the ones her mother had already cut.

"That's fine, yes. That's perfect!"

She'd done it then. What more to say? Leave while it was perfect. "I should go. The girls are probably waiting for me."

"When you're in town," Abbie said, "would you pick up some bread?"

"Sure. Anything else?"

They were like neighbours who'd lived beside each other for years, still discussing the weather and casting around for anything that might put them on common ground besides this ordinary patch of earth they shared and the fence they watched each other across.

"Some dinner rolls would be nice."

Shep called out from the far side of the porch, where he'd set up his Polaroid for a family portrait.

"It's got a timer," he explained, "so I can be in it, too!"

He was pleased with himself, as he lined them up with his hands. The men stood in back, Conrad next to BJ, who refused to remove his sunglasses. Tori and Margaret were on the right, with Markus at their feet. In the centre, Abbie cradled her flowers. Angela stood on her left, awkwardly wondering whether to rest an arm casually over her mother's shoulder. It seemed silly to be standing together but not touching. The arm reached out, but the moment felt forced. Angela tried to look relaxed as Shep raced toward them and the shutter snapped.

"Oh, look — here's Mr. McKeough!" Abbie freed herself from her daughter's arm as a man with greying hair strode toward them, a ladder and a canvas bag slung over his shoulder.

He planted the ends of the ladder on the ground and nodded. "Good morning, Abigail."

"Good morning, Scottie," she called out brightly. The keeper of the trees, she thought. He had none of his father's generosity of spirit or his boundless humour. He seemed rigid and upright, like his ladder.

"Morning, Scottie," Conrad called out.

"Morning, Connie. I've come to save those trees for another year."

"Well, do your best."

Abbie followed McKeough with her armful of roses.

Angela turned to her father. It was the first she'd seen him since last night. He'd left his cane somewhere. He looked good, she thought. There were no signs of illness in his face, no trace of weakness. But it wasn't much of a diagnosis.

"Good morning, eldest daughter," he said.

"Good morning, honourable father. Did you sleep well?"

"Beautifully, as always."

A sudden clanking made them turn. McKeough had dropped the ladder. He picked it up and settled it against a tree trunk. Abbie stood beneath the locusts, directing him. The leaves swayed overhead in a sudden rush of wind.

"It's amazing how they've grown, isn't it? I'm always reminded of my childhood when I come to this place," Angela said.

"And I'm reminded what an old man I've become."

Conrad slipped his arm around her, this daughter who contained so much energy, rushing from calamity to crisis. They wandered toward the pond, stopping where the water seeped through as their weight pressed down. The pond had no formal boundary, no precise point where there was no water. Fallen leaves had gathered and turned brown, lining the bottom with a decomposing blanket. Angela studied her reflection on the surface.

"You know, when I was a kid I imagined a whole world hidden beneath the surface of the water looking back at me. Another Thomas family with a life completely opposite from ours."

"You mean with three boys instead of three girls?"

She smiled at his gentle humour. He caught her staring at him as if she were looking for signs of something beneath his skin.

"How are you, Dad — really?"

"Well enough, for an old guy."

If she'd hoped to take the conversation further, she saw now she would be trespassing. He was far less guarded than her mother, but just as adept at keeping the shroud drawn over family secrets. He squeezed her shoulder as if to say he felt her thinking too hard.

He glanced up. "Look at the light. Isn't it beautiful?"

She followed his gaze. The clouds had turned luminous above the cliffs across the bay. It was him, she realized. He was her grey lion, embodying the grandeur of this land.

"I think I hear the fish calling," he said. "I'd better go get ready before I find myself in trouble with the younger generation."

He ambled back toward the porch. Angela watched him for a moment, thinking he seemed slower than she remembered.

"Catch something for supper!" she called out.

He stopped and turned. "You betcha!" Always a smile.

MARGARET STOOD TO ONE SIDE of the Range Rover, taking in the huge tires and the high step up. She looked back to a small blue Tercel as her sisters watched from the front porch. She shook her head and pointed sheepishly to the blue car. Angela and Tori resigned themselves to the smaller vehicle. They piled into the front while Margaret lowered herself cautiously in the back, handing the keys over Angela's shoulder.

"It was just too big," she said, apologetically.

Angela looked in the mirror. "That's why it's safe. Just tell me if you start to get scared, all right?"

"I'll be fine as long as you don't go over twenty."

The car slipped into gear. Angela glanced in the mirror again. "You're kidding, right?"

Margaret shook her head. "Sorry."

Tori rolled her eyes and turned to the CD player. The ragged voices of the Indigo Girls filled the car as the sisters added their own harmonies on top.

"They sound like ugly Stevie Nicks twins," Margaret announced.

"You say that every year," Tori replied.

"Do I?"

"Where to, ladies?" Angela asked.

Arms dangled out windows as they passed deep forests, the shade of solitary hours mingling with rotting needles and fallen leaves. The dust rose in plumes behind the car.

"Uh-oh! We forgot to help clean up after breakfast," Tori said. "Mom'll be having a fit."

"Maybe she'll recruit Shep for kitchen duty," Margaret called over the music.

"He'd do a better job than we would. He's the only boyfriend I've ever had who likes to do housework."

"That's what they all say before the wedding."

"What wedding?"

Angela smirked.

"Do you know the two things every woman needs to learn about men?" Margaret asked.

"No."

"One, never take them seriously. Two, never trust them. For instance, you need to learn how to decipher their speech. To a man, six equals eight."

Tori turned to look back at Margaret. "I don't get it."

"When a man says his penis is eight inches long, you can be sure it's really six."

"That's because women measure with rulers, not their imaginations," Angela added.

Laughter filled the car. They were remembering past trips, all the previous summers that included this same journey down the highway.

"And never forget — the fastest way to get what you want with a man is by crying," Margaret told them.

Tori made a face. "That's so pathetic."

"I know, but it's true. Men are like that," Margaret said.

IN THE KITCHEN, CONRAD HOVERED over his tackle box, sorting through lures, flies, and sinkers. He picked up a hand-painted wooden chub, marvelling at the faded grey-green on its sides, the yellow eyes and white underbelly. His father had given it to him more than half a century ago. One day he'd pass the entire collection over to his grandson, who shared his passion for quiet hours spent casting out and slowly reeling back again in tranquil coves.

Abbie came in from the porch. "Scott's going to trim all those branches on the west side," she told him.

"That's good. I'm sure he can use the extra money."

"They've been scratching against the windows. If we have

visitors next year, it will keep them awake when the wind is up."

Conrad said nothing. They'd already discussed the improbability of a return. Had she forgotten? No, she was just reassuring herself again.

Abbie looked at the breakfast table and shook her head. "I guess I'll have to clean up by myself."

"I'll help you if I can use some of those leftovers for bait."

"You certainly will not," she scolded.

He stood behind her as she surveyed the ruins of the morning meal. Hands pressed gently onto her shoulders. He felt an unexpected moment of joy unfold inside him.

"Abbie Thomas, have I told you that you are, without doubt, the most beautiful grandmother I've ever seen?"

She smiled and let him charm her, feeling his tongue graze her neck — moist, warm. Something surfaced deep inside her, cracking open like a sigh.

OUT ON THE PORCH, BJ corralled Shep to try out his routine about the collected wisdom of men in love and marriage.

"When we fight," he said, "they cry. That way we can give in to them without losing face."

Shep grimaced.

"I know — it's complicated," BJ agreed, mistaking disapproval for confusion. "For instance, when a woman says 'yes,' she really means 'no.' And when she says 'maybe,' she still means 'no.' But if she says 'I'm sorry,' she means 'You're going to be sorry.'"

Mr. McKeough passed them, shouldering his ladder. "Aye, laddie. And when she says 'You need to learn to communicate,' she means 'Better just agree with me or you'll be even sorrier.' That's the time to worry."

Shep grinned.

"One more thing," BJ continued. "Never measure yourself, if you know what I mean. You'll only be disappointed. You're never as big as you think you are."

Markus sat holding a can of worms bedded in peat moss. He looked up as his grandmother joined them.

"Hi, Abbie," he said.

"Don't call me that. I'm your grandmother." She turned to her son-in-law. "BJ, I'd like you to take Markus to the store with you to buy some milk. Take the Oldsmobile, if you like."

"But we're going fishing with Granddad!" Markus protested.

BJ and Shep exchanged glances.

"It will only take a few minutes, and Granddad can wait."

"Okay, cowboy, you heard the lady. Let's go," BJ said. "Milk, it is. Regular? Menthol? Unleaded?"

She watched them walk away then turned to Shep. "I want to thank you for chopping all that firewood this morning."

"Don't mention it. If you ever need a log cabin built, I'm your boy."

He flashed his most winning smile. Abbie ignored it.

"Why don't I be blunt?" she said. "If you don't mind my asking, what plans do you have for Victoria's future?"

It took his breath away, how she placed the responsibility for Tori's future on his shoulders. But if she'd hoped he would defer to her or try to reassure her in any way, she was disappointed.

"The future's a pretty big subject, Mrs. Thomas. Right now we just want to see how we get along together before we make any long-term commitments."

Abbie looked at him skeptically.

"I know you think we're young," he said, "but Tori and I share a very solid affection."

"Oh, affection!" she snorted. "I know all about affection."

Her gaze was powerful, animated by something he couldn't discern. It felt like an attack on everything he represented, everything he professed to believe in and was deluded enough, it seemed to say, to think he could offer her daughter.

"Do you honestly think affection is enough to build a lasting relationship on?"

He thought of telling her they didn't use words like "relationship," or even that it was none of her business, but clearly she thought it was.

"We need to make sure we can be friends," he said, looking her in the eye. "As well as lovers."

Abbie wanted to say more, but stopped herself. He might have tattoos and no visible future, but she sensed something about him she was unable to sidestep.

"Just don't break my daughter's heart, Mr. Shep Spencer," she warned. "Or I'll break your head."

She retreated into the cottage like Floria Tosca after murdering Scarpia.

THEY WERE WELL PAST LION'S HEAD. Its peak diminished behind each curve as the car moved on to new territory. The Indigo Girls had given way to the scarecrow voice of Willie Nelson. The breeze nearly blew the lyrics right out the windows.

"When I met BJ, I thought he was the sweetest, funniest person I'd ever known," Margaret said. "He was so charming. He actually paid attention to me back then." She still recalled a wisp of a boy with a flashy red car and a mouth that never seemed to stop talking. When had it turned on her? "I hoped he'd bring me some relief after our repressive upbringing. I didn't understand then that humour comes from repressed anger."

"Repressed anger?" Angela said. "You'd think Mom would be a lot funnier."

"He knew I loved gardening," Margaret continued. "One day he showed up at my gate with a bunch of blueberry plants and handed them to me over the fence. He said, 'They told me they wanted to live here.' So I planted them next to the raspberry canes. The next time he came over I told him I'd introduced the blueberries to the raspberries. He looked at me kind of funny for a moment. Finally, he said, 'And what did the raspberries say?'" Margaret slapped her thigh. "Isn't that great?"

The water appeared suddenly, a long corrugated mirror reflecting the tree-dotted hills. Angela pointed off from the road. The boathouse was overgrown and derelict, its windows broken or missing like rows of uneven teeth.

"That," she announced, "is where I lost my virginity to a 'townie' boy named Tommy Higgins who always smelled of fish."

Margaret and Tori looked over at the boathouse.

"Couldn't he afford anything better?" Margaret asked.

"Believe me, he didn't need to."

"What did he look like?" Tori said.

"Long and willowy, with shiny black hair down to his shoulders. He had high cheekbones and heavy-lidded eyes that made you want to fall right into them."

"Dreamy," Tori said.

"That was one boy who didn't need to measure with a ruler."

"What happened to him?" Margaret asked.

"He proposed to me, but I'd been accepted into university. Last I heard, he got married."

Margaret shook her head, laughing. "Somehow I can't see you as a small-town wife with curlers in your hair, pushing a stroller through the grocery store."

"Except maybe I'd be happy now," Angela said, with a glance in the rear-view mirror.

Margaret sighed.

THE WHINE OF A SAW reached through the cottage like a long dull ache. It seemed as though the trees were grieving. Abbie had spent the last half-hour arranging *objets d'art* on a Mexican slate-top table, slowly whittling the pieces down to three: a green enamel bowl, a framed photograph of the girls sitting on the grass behind the cottage, and a jade bust of a Japanese princess with an ornate headpiece. She stepped back. The simplicity pleased her. It was perfection of a kind, a small triumph of the day.

She picked up the photograph album to tuck it inside the sideboard, but stopped and carried it upstairs to the bedroom instead. She sat with it unopened on her lap, staring out the window.

Outside, BJ and Markus had returned with the milk. Shep hailed them as they came around the corner. "Hey, BJ! Hey there, buddy boy!"

Markus looked intently at Shep. "I'm not buddy boy. I'm Markus."

"Then who's buddy boy?" Shep exclaimed in mock surprise.

"You are buddy boy," Markus declared.

Abbie watched BJ disappear inside the cottage with the milk. She opened the album and removed the snapshot of Conrad and his brother, holding it at a distance. Looking at them now, it was easy to see Alex wasn't the handsomer of the two. Conrad was much more ... beautiful. Yes, that was the word. He was beautiful. Alex looked — what? Smarmy, she thought, with his hair slicked down and his playboy's grin, as if he'd just conquered the world. What had he thought as he lay dying on some Malaysian highway? Had he struggled against his death, or climbed into it like a child climbing into its mother's arms? Had he finally understood the consequences of his actions, the effect they'd had on others — Conrad trying to fill his older brother's shoes, the grief he'd caused her? "You're my girl," he'd said, whenever a serious look came over her. But he never said "only."

It was a different garden that day so long ago. Petals had littered the grass beneath the oak tree. Willows might bend, she thought, but an oak could only break. *And so did my false love to me* ... And that, surely, was a very silly thought for a woman of her age, she told herself. A mistake, that's all it was. Not intentional cruelty. A mistake compounded by the unreality of a sudden summer storm and his seemingly chivalrous offer to keep her safe and warm. Had she thought he meant for her whole life? How ridiculous! How silly and stupid. Just a mistake, really. Love was a mirror in which you either liked or disliked what you saw. He'd run as fast and as far as he could.

A dreadful mistake.

Below, she watched Conrad emerge onto the porch with a battered fisherman's cap on his head. He was still beautiful, she thought. And regal. That evening in the department store over milkshakes, Alex had flirted and talked so much she'd barely noticed his younger brother. It had been one of those rare moments when everything in life changed, though she hadn't recognized it at the time. A door opened to another world. You either entered or walked away. Conrad had been the right choice, all along.

"Is everyone ready to go?" she heard him ask.

Of course they're ready to go, she thought. Who wouldn't be ready to rise and follow when the captain calls?

"Are you coming with us, Shep?" Markus asked.

Shep messed the boy's hair. "Who's Shep? I'm buddy boy!"

Abbie smiled absently at how easily the men got along. Her gaze turned back to the figures in the photograph. "You damned fool," she said, unsure whether she was talking to herself or the figure on the page. She replaced it in the back of the book, carefully closing the cover on it.

"I'll just go up and say goodbye to your grandmother," she heard Conrad say.

THE SISTERS SWEPT DOWN THE streets of a small town, looking upbeat and very out of place. Little had changed in the decades they'd been visiting there. They passed curtained houses, a dress shop, and the family bakery where strawberry, lemon, and pecan tarts always crowded the front window. In a used-clothing store, they tried out odd bits of clothing. Angela pulled on a pair of gloves, the lace faded to a yellowed ivory. Tori held up a vinyl handbag with a plastic rose for a clasp. The other customers stared at the out-of-towners making a spectacle of themselves.

Knowing they were being watched made the sisters laugh and clown even more.

A by-the-pound table held an assortment of oddities for their makeshift parade, as they dredged the remnants of lives from the bottom of a fabric bin. Margaret dug out matching his-and-her cowboy outfits, holding them up for show. The "his" legs were unnaturally long, as though they'd been tailored for a stilt walker.

"These would be perfect for you and Shep," she said to Tori.

"Oh, right! Like we'd go anywhere looking like that."

Margaret winked at Angela. "You kids are too fashion conscious these days. Why, in my day we wore any old rag so long as it was made of denim."

Tori spied a shelf of disembodied Styrofoam heads, their eyes painted wide in expressions of joy or astonishment. "Church lady hats!"

She pounced on a form festooned with strawberry blossoms and a veil. Margaret chose a sleek black number.

"Very Jackie O.," Angela intoned, watching Margaret adjust it in the mirror.

Margaret pointed to a pillbox hat with a long plume. "Look — a dead bird. It must be a Martha Stewart creation!" She placed it on Angela's head. "Definitely you!"

The clerk stood proprietary over the cash register, watching the sisters as though she'd just tuned into an unexpected news broadcast.

They left wearing their new hats, a mini-parade of Easter bonnets, and stopped in at the bakery with the tarts in the window. Back then, it always seemed they were entering a child's world of icing sugar confections. Frosted cakes, sweet buns, and every type of cookie lined the shelves. Smiles greeted them now. Clerks in immaculate uniforms and hairnets stood behind the counter, maternity nurses slipping swollen loaves of bread into bags like newborn babies.

Out on the street again, Angela removed her hat. The town's novelty had worn off, its other-worldliness fading from view as if she'd stepped from a cinema back into the light of day. It wasn't smart or pretty, just small and faded. In reality, it was an unpleasant place she would never have wanted to live in.

They drove back in silence, watching the landscape passing in reverse. Angela's shrine to lost virginity approached and receded again, assuming its proper place in time past. It was like reviewing life backwards, seeing all the wrong choices in close-up.

CONRAD FOUND HIS WIFE STARING out the window, a photo album open on her lap like a prayer book. As he entered, he saw their life together, a richly intricate carpet rolled out farther than the eye could glimpse. He'd never stopped being amazed that the woman who walked into Kresge's wearing a green dress that evening had been married to him all these years.

Without looking up, Abbie said, "I don't think Shep is the proper sort of boy for Tori. He thinks affection is what it takes to hold a marriage together. Can you imagine?"

He wanted to say something — that affection wasn't so bad. That it led to stronger bonds over time. Hadn't it? Of course it had. But no words came. That was when he felt it — the mortal ache, the cold that was always with him. His features distorted, possessed by pain. His hands reached for a bottle. The contents rolled across the dresser and onto the floor. Little yellow and pink capsules tumbled everywhere.

Abbie turned at the sound. Her husband's face suggested regret over the spilled medicine more than pain. He staggered and slumped to the floor.

"Grandpa, we're waiting," Markus called from outside.

BOOK VII

WAR WITHOUT END

SEVENTEEN

Spring found Angela and André back in the heart of the conflict, documenting the growing flood of people streaming away from the fighting by tractor, truck, cart, or on foot. Taking with them what little of their lives they could carry, the lines of human misery crept forward, a giant centipede wriggling in the dirt, the road behind them strewn with abandoned belongings.

The Bosnian Serb Army shot down a United States Air Force F-16, bringing further condemnation from NATO. The army began an all-out offensive, attacking and killing UN troops. Two days later, NATO planes struck. Fear of retaliation against non-nationals grew. Martin put Angela and André on evacuation alert.

Foreign aid workers were arrested. A man went berserk, killing three Red Cross nurses. Soldiers looted supply stores and hijacked vehicles, shooting anyone who tried to stop them. In Pale, UN staff members were chained to bridges and ammunition dumps. The scenes were broadcast live on television as a warning to NATO to suspend the bombing.

When Angela and André returned, colleagues and relief

workers stared in disbelief. The Belgian MSF office was in a frenzy as the entire staff prepared to leave.

"Has no one told you there's a war on?" Mathilde scolded. "Everyone's waiting for word to transfer out and you come rushing back like you missed the place!"

The UN suspended humanitarian airlifts. Aid was reduced to a trickle as the Serb Army refused to grant the convoys safe passage across their territory. The toll in human lives mounted sharply. Directly contradicting its mandate, the UN began helping people flee the fighting rather than return to their lives. Villagers stood helplessly by as their homes burned. There was nothing to return to.

The entire country seemed to be in flight. Everywhere, people walked or sat on the sides of roads with their bags packed, waiting to be evacuated, while armed vehicles lumbered past. Rumours leaked out on the wind. In one town, it was said, more than 6000 Muslim men and boys had been killed to prevent them from joining the fighting.

Angela and André moved against the tide, piling camping gear into the Jeep alongside cameras, helmets, bulletproof vests, and first aid kits. They slid along like a finger on a map: Teslić, Banja Luka, Doboj. Every day their work took them into sectors and towns formerly inaccessible to them. In the country, miles of devastation surrounded them. Checkpoint guards expressed disbelief that they were headed into the fighting instead of away from it. The soldiers they met were mostly old men. The young men and boys had all gone to the front. A few civilians wandered among the ghosts of former neighbours, the thousands who'd been killed or exiled in the last three years.

The two journalists passed the blackened remains of a town where a single windowless wall stood against a grey sky, a doorway leading to nothing. Smoke rose from the earth in columns. Here and there orange flames licked at the greyness, a tiger slowly devouring its prey.

At the edge of the town, a boy emerged from the smoke and asked them for ten dinar, shyly accepting their handful of coins. Did he know where the detention centre was? *The place where they kept the men? Yes, of course. Everyone knows.* Would he take them there? More coins held out. He nodded.

They followed him down the road. On the town's outskirts they came upon the solitary building off to the side of the road. The boy left them as they entered the open doorway and crept through a long narrow passage. The ground was strewn with the charred remains of what might have been cooking fires.

It was a deserted gymnasium. Someone had been there recently — a checkered jacket hung off a door handle; a wooden box contained hoes that were probably prisoners' work tools. Smaller rooms held mattresses tossed haphazardly on the floor. There was little else. Whoever had been there had been made to vanish with little trace.

THEY HAPPENED ON THE BURIAL by accident. The misreading of a map and a slight detour to get back on track brought them to a rise above a farm where a dozen men were digging a pit. Bodies lay heaped beside it. Angela raised her camera.

At a word, the men dropped their shovels and began to push the corpses into the trench. This wasn't the sacred interment of loved ones. These were people in a hurry. Some of the corpses slipped in easily; others had to be dragged in by arms and legs. It appeared all the dead were men. It soon became clear the trench wasn't deep enough. Bodies began to pile over the edge, creating a small rise. A soldier climbed on top, dragging the remaining bodies up by hand.

André crouched beside Angela as she took the shots. A voice in her head intoned the Gloria Patri: *As it was in the beginning, is now, and ever shall be, world without end* ... The words stuck in her brain like a tape loop while her fingers pressed the shutter. She felt the lightness overtaking her, felt herself floating directly above the scene. She was on a clifftop on the Bruce Peninsula, watching eagles drift effortlessly below her. People who returned from the dead described scenes like this. They left their bodies to float over operating tables and car wrecks, deciding whether to stay or return to their lives. The lightness disappeared and she found herself beside André again, an entire roll of film finished. For those few moments she'd felt linked with the dead. Below them the dirt flew through the air, covering the tower of death that pointed not to the sky but to the future, to unfinished history.

Angela slipped the film into her pocket and popped in a new roll. This is a good day, she told herself. How odd, to be thinking that. She looked at André. He caught her eye and nodded at the cabal in the distance.

"Better hurry. We don't have much time left."

THEY HEADED WEST, STOPPING ON the banks of a shallow river, the remains of a bridge jutting up from the water. Two medical supply trucks had tried to cross and got stuck in mud up to their axles. A blue-and-white armoured personnel carrier passed without slowing, followed by a second and a third. André tuned into the UN channel. The call for help came from a nearby town. Angela looked over at him.

André shrugged. "Let's go," he said, as the Jeep edged into the water.

The road was empty. They reached the village in ten minutes. Green smoke roiled like curdled milk and hung overhead as families emptied from their homes. The atmosphere felt pent up, ready to explode. All afternoon, the sky had been cheerless, the light threadbare. Now, toward the end of day, it had opened into a boundless blue.

"There doesn't seem to be much happening," André said, scanning the town through his binoculars.

"Look for the APCs."

They drove to the town square and saw the armoured personnel carriers in the distance. A helicopter hovered overhead. A rope dropped and someone on the ground grabbed hold of it, pulling himself up as the chopper moved off.

Angela stepped out of the Jeep. André grabbed his camera and followed. A cracking sound split the air. *That was too close!* Angela was about to say, when a hand of flame threw her against the vehicle. In a second that splintered into a thousand fragments, she saw the sun shining, people running silently, a car tearing away. Time slowed. Then just as suddenly, it sped up again. She sat up and looked around in a daze. André lay beside the Jeep, the camera rolling away from his arm as if it were trying to escape.

There was a second blast. Bodies fell from the sky, thudding to the ground. Some lay still; others struggled. Those who could began to run. Angela stood shakily. She pulled André toward her, sickened by the ragged pulp on the side of his face. Blood leached into the ground. Sounds came to her in an incomprehensible buzz. There was a *whuff!* and her hearing returned.

The air flashed again. The helicopter shuddered, and fell, sucked right out of the sky. A black cloud bent away from it. Men with guns streamed into the village, firing as they ran. An old man dropped. A woman slumped against the wall of a house. A soldier pirouetted on one leg, kicking out at her.

Angela pulled André toward the Jeep, his feet dragging behind him. "Are you all right?" she yelled.

She yanked open the door and pushed him in. "Can you hear me? Do you know where you are?" She thought she got a nod. She pulled off her jacket, pressing it against his face to staunch the blood. He cried out.

She jumped into the driver's side, put the vehicle in gear, and raced onto the road. Three minutes outside the village, a personnel carrier passed them heading the opposite direction. Angela reversed and gave chase. She overtook them and swerved in front, planting her foot on the brakes. The vehicle came to a halt inches from the Jeep. The top lifted. A surprised head popped out.

"I need a doctor!" she screamed.

The man appeared confused. A second head emerged and spoke in halting English. They were a German team. There was an MSF camp on the far side of the mountain, the man said, but snipers had the road covered. She demanded they take them there. He refused. They were headed for the village to help with the evacuation. The lid slammed shut and the vehicle lurched off the road, skirting her Jeep and heading for the shelling.

She turned the Jeep around and sat in the middle of the road, with the faint gleam of headlights thrown onto the pavement ahead. It would be dark soon. Nothing came toward them.

Blood seeped through the jacket where André held it to his face. He kept adjusting it against his forehead. His face was white, his breathing thick and wheezy.

"I've got to get you to the MSF camp," she said.

He gazed at her absently, as though he had no opinion on the matter.

"It'll be dangerous," she warned.

He tried to speak, but coughed instead. He persisted till he could make himself heard. "Know how to make God laugh?"

"Tell Him your plans."

His fingers squeezed hers. She squeezed back and switched off the Jeep's lights.

EIGHTEEN

LIGHTS OFF, THEY HEADED EAST up the mountain. Fog slipped
between the trees and across the road like ghost fingers, making
the driving hazardous even as it camouflaged their progress.
Somewhere to the right, the mountainside dropped hundreds
of feet unseen in the darkness. Above, she imagined snipers
lying concealed, guns at the ready. Useless even to think about
the mines they might run over.

Behind them, in the rear-view mirror, the sky was purple,
outraged. The sound of shelling covered the noise of the engine
as they crept forward. They were halfway up the mountain
when something occurred to her. She reached her hand behind
and felt around on the floor. Her camera was there, but the pack
with their food supplies and identification papers was missing. The satellite phone was gone, too. She glanced nervously at
the fuel gauge. Without lights, she could see only black. She
couldn't remember the last time they'd fuelled up. She felt in
her vest pocket for a lighter and flicked it. The indicator had
crept past empty. Her fingers clenched the wheel; fear balled
in her chest.

She strained to see through the darkness. If there were snipers hidden in the rocks, they could be no more than a few feet away. She held her breath, as if that might help conserve fuel and carry them safely over the top. She had no way of knowing how far they'd come or how far they had to go. She looked over at André. He was watching her.

"Tell me about your childhood," she said, trying to sound cheerful.

"Didn't have one," he managed, his voice dry, raspy. "Want yours."

"No, you don't."

But the words spilled from her anyway. She told him about the honey locusts behind the family cottage on the Bruce Peninsula, about climbing Lion's Head Point to stand a thousand feet up in the clear blue air over Georgian Bay while sails glided far below. She described mornings in the yellow kitchen where her father made soft-boiled eggs and cut the toast into finger-length pieces for dipping. "Soldiers," he'd called them. It was lost to her now.

"Was it good? A good childhood?"

"Yes," she said, finally. "Despite everything."

Despite the mother who seemed to resent her no matter how hard she tried. The mother who devoted herself to order and beauty that somehow became lifeless where the two joined. Angela couldn't help wondering what her mother would think of this suicidal Jeep ride through the middle of hell.

She held André's hand between gear changes. It was the only palpable sign in the darkness that she wasn't alone. It had been more than fifteen minutes since she'd checked the fuel gauge.

She was convinced they were riding on fumes when the road took a sharp turn and dropped quickly. She geared down to neutral and breathed deeply for what seemed like the first time since they'd started. Ten minutes later, at the foot of the mountain, she put the Jeep in gear and risked the headlights. Ghostly shapes loomed on either side of the road. Miraculously, she found the medical post. It was the only place with a light. She tore into the building where an astounded staff of three sat around a radio listening to news reports. They all jumped up at once.

"I've got a wounded journalist in my car."

"How did you get here?" A British accent.

"We drove across the mountain."

Astonished faces stared at her. "No one can cross that road without the UN."

"We just did."

As they carried André in from the Jeep, a fresh-faced doctor named Steve told Angela what he knew. They were trapped inside Bihać, a small pocket in the mountains. There was no way of telling how long the fighting would last. They'd had no supplies in more than a week and ran out of antibiotics two days ago. The UN operated a helicopter air bridge to bring in food and supplies. It was due within the hour.

She accepted a cup of coffee as he left to examine André. Twenty minutes passed. She heard the droning of a helicopter and went outside where the *whuff-whuff* of blades swayed everything down to earth. Steve returned. He'd ordered André to be medevacked.

They'd bandaged his head from ear to ear. His eyes were closed. She wasn't sure if he could hear her, but his eyelids struggled open. His fingers sought her out. She bent toward him, folding his hand in hers.

"Alternate endings," she said. "I'll make you one."

She kissed his lips and whispered to him, as though sealing an unbearable secret in the crack of a wall.

The helicopter crew ran in with supplies. The stretcher was loaded and the chopper lifted off into darkness, the shadow of a bird flying into the shadow of a mountain.

Afterwards, Angela shared supper with Steve and two nurses. They gave her five litres of gas once she promised not to attempt the mountain pass again. In town, she might find one or two working hotels. If not, she was welcome to come back.

THE VILLAGE APPEARED OUT OF the fog like a shipwreck looming up from the ocean floor. Angela drove along its silent streets. Nothing moved. A sign glowed in the headlights: Hotel Drina. The windows were boarded shut, but a light pierced its door-frame. The old man who answered her knock listened patiently as she explained that she was a Canadian journalist and her papers had been lost in the shelling. She was desperate and had nowhere else to stay. He shrugged and opened his hands in a gesture of acceptance.

"Many people no longer have papers. I can give you a room."

She signed her name in the registry book. Hers was the only signature on the page. She flipped back through several months of blank pages, then the entire year, and the year before that. Nothing. He led her upstairs by candlelight. He apologized for the state of affairs, but assured her the room came with a heater and as many blankets as she wished. He lit the heater for her and set the candle on the bedside table. For the first time, she realized she was shivering.

"Please," he said, with a sweep of his hands, as though encouraging her to enjoy all the comforts of the room.

The door closed behind him and Angela collapsed on the bed. Time became an elastic thing that stretched or shrank to cover the world. She couldn't tell whether it was still early, or late, or how long she'd been lying there. From behind the boarded window came the distant boom of shelling. Her watch dial flared. A quarter to eleven.

She came back downstairs. She saw herself, gaunt and pale in the mirror over the stairs. The old man sat at his desk. He nodded when she asked if he had anything to drink. He wandered off and returned in a few minutes with a bottle of vodka and two glasses.

He chain-smoked as they sat and drank together, leaving one cigarette burning in the ashtray to light another. Life was good in the pocket, he said, as though the war raging outside were a minor disturbance, temporary in nature. When it was over business would resume, life would go on.

That was when she saw the telephone. It still worked, he said proudly. A miracle of telecommunications amidst all the fighting. A wave of homesickness overtook Angela. She dialled her mother's number. As she waited, it occurred to her there would be questions. What would she say — that she was the lone guest in a hotel at the foot of a mountain covered by sniper fire? That she'd spent the evening listening to rocket shelling after seeing her lover shipped off to hospital by helicopter? What could that inspire but fear and worry?

The rings echoed in her ear. Suddenly her mother's voice sounded from halfway around the world. Angela felt a surge of panic. She hung up and came back to the desk. There'd been no answer, she said. The man nodded. She was welcome to use it any time, he told her.

Fatigue overtook her. She climbed back upstairs and quickly undressed, sliding under the covers. The orange glow of the burner gave a faint contour to the room, though it failed to bring much heat. She felt ringed by loss and emptiness. More than anything, she longed to hear André's voice.

She woke to violent shivers, her body drenched in sweat. She'd been dreaming of him. He hovered over her like a bird, arms planted on the mattress at her sides, blowing gently on her breasts to cool her as he lowered himself into her. She arched her body to meet his, but he slipped away again.

She listened to the sound of falling shells, sometimes close, sometimes farther off. She slept again and woke just before dawn from a dream in which her head was a balloon filling with hot sand. She opened her eyes to see the curtains billow in and out of the room. Sunlight streamed in so thickly she could have gathered it in buckets. She heard waves and saw children playing on a beach. It pleased her, though she knew the windows were boarded shut and there was no beach for miles.

Frank Sinatra was singing right outside her room, some nonsensical song about ladies and tramps, ermine and pearls. It was a song her father used to sing. He'd wandered around the garden at the cottage humming it underneath the honey locusts. Frank was winding up for the finish. He peered in the window and tipped his hat: And that was why the lady was a *SMASH!*

The words weren't quite right, but it didn't matter. Sinatra drifted away; the curtains continued to billow. The shell had struck very close. Even half-conscious, she'd felt its reverberations through the floor.

BOOK VIII
TANKS

NINETEEN

The white rental car turned up a pebbled drive. Its driver had come a long way, but his journey wasn't over. He stepped out of the car and looked around. There was no sound save the weeping of branches high above. At the back of the cottage, a small boy sat with a young man he didn't recognize. The boy looked up.

"Uncle Timmy!"

"Markie Mark."

"This is Shep," the boy said, pulling his new friend by the arm.

"Hi there," the other said, offering a hand. "Shep Spencer — this week's social experiment for the Thomas family."

"Tim Weaver — Angela's husband." The words felt wrong, as though he were usurping someone else's identity. "I think."

He looked around the empty grounds. "Where is everyone?"

"Granddad went to the hospital," Markus said solemnly.

Shep and Tim exchanged glances. "They've been gone a couple of hours," Shep said, in lieu of any real facts.

They had just gone inside when the Range Rover pulled up the drive. BJ stepped quickly out of the driver's side and over to help Abbie. She looked up to see her other son-in-law emerging from the front door.

"Tim ..."

"I just heard. How's Conrad?"

"They're keeping him overnight at the hospital, but everything's going to be all right," Abbie said. Her voice was strong, sure of what she was telling him.

"I'm sorry for showing up unannounced on your doorstep at a time like this," Tim said. "I know you weren't expecting me."

She waved away his concern. "You couldn't have known."

"I'm sure I can find a motel somewhere. I passed a couple on the ..."

"You're still a part of this family, as far as I'm concerned," Abbie interrupted. "Stay here tonight, in any case. It's likely we'll all be leaving tomorrow when Conrad returns."

"Of course," Tim said, regretting the timing of his appearance more than anything. "What did the doctors say?"

"He needs rest." Her self-control vanished for an instant. "Conrad hasn't been well lately. I foolishly insisted we come out here this weekend, despite his health."

"Don't blame yourself. It won't help."

Her hand reached up nervously to her hair. The voices of the dead railed at her. The past was always present. "No, we can't change the past."

HALF AN HOUR LATER, ANGELA pulled into the drive and parked beside the rental car beneath the pine trees. She looked over at the new vehicle and frowned.

"Visitors from town?" Margaret conjectured.

"I wonder."

She entered the cottage carrying the loaves of bread and ran right into Tim. Here was her husband, who had travelled thousands of kilometres to be there, appearing suddenly as if resurrected from the dead. Caught in a burst of sunlight from the open door, his face almost blinded her.

"Your dad's in the hospital," he said.

His words flashed like something out of control. Margaret and Tori stopped behind her.

"What happened?"

Angela felt ambushed. She thought of her father's cane, his shortness of breath; she'd sensed all along that her mother's quiet reassurances were false. It was a shock to think something so huge might be taken away without warning.

Abbie appeared behind Tim. "It's all right. Your father's going to be fine. We'll know more tomorrow."

"I should go," Tim told Angela.

"There's no sense rushing off after coming all this way," Abbie said.

She relieved Angela of her packages. Tori and Margaret followed her wordlessly to the kitchen as Tim stood waiting for a cue from his wife.

"Mom's right," Angela said. "Stay."

She stood before him offering hospitality, but nothing more.

SUPPER WAS ODDLY FORMAL UNDER the circumstances. Abbie seemed to have gone all out, as though making reparations for the disturbance in their plans. The family weekend would not be thwarted, her efforts declared. The roses cut earlier in the day sat astride the table — tender, remorseful. Conversation was laboured, as though they were a people piecing together fragments of a past they'd forgotten or misplaced.

Abbie occupied the head of the table, opposite the empty place at the far end. "Did Markus have enough to eat, Margaret?"

"He didn't want anything. He was very upset when Dad didn't come back from the hospital."

"Bring him some leftovers when you go up. He might wake up hungry later on."

Tori brooded. BJ watched as she emptied her wine glass, then poured another, leaving her food untouched.

"Whoa, cowgirl! You'd better eat something if you're going to drink like that." He pushed a bowl of potato salad toward her. "Take it from someone who knows."

"I'm fine," she snapped.

"You won't be tomorrow if you keep that up."

"Thanks for the advice, shithead."

Abbie's head jerked up. "Victoria — manners!"

Tori's mouth quivered. "Oh, yes — good manners are so important at a time like this."

Shep nudged her. "There's no need to talk like that," he said quietly.

"Leave me alone," she snarled.

"We should be thankful your father is going to be fine," Abbie said.

"And why weren't we told there was something wrong with him in the first place?" Tori demanded.

"Some people would be thankful not to have had that burden placed on them prematurely."

The alcohol had swelled Tori's anger. "I am not 'some people.' I'm your daughter, in case you've forgotten. I think we should have been told that Dad wasn't well."

"Tori's right," Margaret said quietly. "Why do we have to live with so many secrets?"

Abbie drew herself up. "Who ever said you weren't allowed to speak your mind?"

"God knows, Margaret, you're not exactly a font of information when you're in one of your moods," BJ interjected.

Margaret turned on him. "What's that supposed to mean?"

"Relax. Forget about it!" BJ snapped, retreating into his drink.

Margaret's face was a portrait of someone slightly deranged. "There are lots of things I'd like to forget about! Like the fact that you don't come home till nearly 4 A.M. some nights, or that we can't pay the mortgage yet again because you don't have a real job and I'm stuck raising three kids who all act more mature than you!"

BJ stared, thrown momentarily on finding himself the centre of attack.

"Great, Margaret. Thanks for being candid, but if you really want to talk about things that matter to this family, I don't think our private life is one of them. You don't hear Tim or Angela whining about theirs, do you?"

"Hey!" Tim protested. "Don't drag us into this …"

"I am not whining!" Margaret exploded. "I'm tired of being stuck at home playing nursemaid. When are you going to grow up?"

"Yeah, BJ," Tori chimed in. "Why don't you grow up?"

BJ glanced around the table. "What is this? Pick-on-BJ night? I don't care what you talk about. Talk about anything you like. Tear yourselves to bits!"

Abbie's fingers gripped the tablecloth. A fist came down like a decree dropped among the cutlery. "Stop this! All of you." She looked around the table accusingly. "At a time like this, you could at least try to get along!" She was shaking. "I have never known such selfish, ungrateful children!"

No one spoke. Abbie stood and went out to the kitchen. Tori pushed her chair back and headed for the porch. The others sat, unmoving.

IN THE KITCHEN, ABBIE SCRAPED leftovers into the garbage. Tim came through the door with an offering of plates. Abbie looked up.

"I thought I'd give you a hand," he said.

"Thank you, Tim, but I can manage."

He set the plates on the counter. "I'm sorry," he said. "I'm sorry if I complicated things by coming here."

"I understand. You've got problems of your own to deal with."

He hesitated, wondering whether to speak. He thought better of it and turned back to the dining room.

"You might as well say what's on your mind," Abbie said to his back. "Nothing you can say could possibly make matters worse than they are at this moment."

He stood in the doorway, half in the light, and half out. To Abbie, he seemed part-ghost and part-human — a creature with earthly desires, but lacking physical form.

"I was thinking ... I was thinking that you were right when you told Angela not to marry me. I always thought I'd be good for her. I see now why you said that. You knew I couldn't give her what she needed." He hesitated. "How did you know?"

She wanted to ask him to forgive her, but for what? For speaking the truth? For fearing for her daughter's happiness? For revealing the worm that lay in her heart? "Angela is a hard person to love," she said. "You've seen it yourself. All I've ever tried to do is help her see past herself so that she might be happy."

He waited, hoping for more, but she'd already said what he knew to be true: his wife couldn't or wouldn't allow herself to be loved.

"How do you know when you really love someone?" he'd asked his friend Paul, not long after meeting Angela. "Do you feel so excited you can't stand it, twenty-four-seven?"

"Nah," said his more-experienced friend. "You'd die of exhaustion if that were the case. You know you love a woman by how much of you remains after she's gone. If there's a lot, you're only a little bit in love. If there's a little, you're a lot in love. And if there's nothing left of you when she leaves, you're lost, my friend."

There was nothing left of him now.

"I'm sorry, Tim," Abbie said. "I never wanted to be the thorn in your marriage."

He nodded and turned away. She watched him retreat through the dining-room door before turning dejectedly back to the sink.

SHEP STOOD AT THE PORCH door watching Tori blow smoke into the air. It hung there like a small cloud, a wistful statement against the night's vastness. He needed to get his cue right before he approached. He was attuned to the complexities of human behaviour. His family life had been rife with posturing, unresolved dramas. He thought he had it figured out, but when he put his arm around her, Tori pushed it aside.

"Leave me alone."

"What's wrong? What did I do?"

"I don't need you defending my mother."

It was himself he'd misjudged, he realized, feeling the urgency of his love for her. He recalled the helplessness that tore through him whenever his parents fought. The after-effects of an argument could linger for weeks — the resentment and not-speaking that went on for days like a stale odour in the room. It spread to include inanimate objects: dirty dishes heaped on counters, ashtrays unemptied on a table beside the ingredients for a half-forgotten meal that might never get made. In the morning, he'd pour a bowl of cereal. If there was no milk, he ate it dry with his fingers. Then he'd check the clock and go off to school. Sometimes a can of macaroni would be left out for his supper when he returned.

He feared Tori's silence now. It was a wall between them. There were so many things she didn't talk about. Clearly, this was one of them.

He found his voice.

"Look," he said. "I don't mean to be insulting, but your family's really fucked up. The way nobody talks about anything? All this silverware and matching napkin-ring shit, and those stories about how your family's been coming here every summer since the ice age? That isn't togetherness. It's just a fable you've invented to make yourself feel good."

"Tell me about it," she said. "Like you don't come from the

most dysfunctional family of all time. You don't even know where they are."

Her words stung, but he kept talking, needing her to hear him. The odour was identifiable: the silence that consumed, the suspicions and unspoken resentments that spread until they enveloped everything.

"I made a choice. I cut my losses. But this repression that goes on here — it's not healthy. It kills you. If not now, then later."

"Don't lecture me about my family."

"I'm not lecturing you. I'm trying to communicate something. Isn't that what we agreed relationships are based on — communication? Trust?"

Tori made a face. "Stop right there. You said when we got together we'd be free from all those phoney relationship issues. You sound just like my sisters, going on about trusting and communicating. Don't tie me down with your bullshit rules!"

His anger flared, but he kept his voice calm. "Is that what you think this is about? No rules? No consequences? Because there are always consequences, Tori. You can't just walk away from things and people because you don't want to deal with them."

"Don't tell me what I can't do," she said, stubbing her cigarette on the railing. Sparks fell to the porch. She went back inside, leaving him alone in the dark.

BJ SAT IN FRONT OF the fire, one foot crossed over his knee, a slipper dangling from his toes. He looked up. Tim stood in the doorway.

"Do you think Conrad will make it?" Tim asked.

BJ made the sign of the cross in the air. "*Ora pro nobis peca-toribus.* Let's hope so," he said. "Otherwise, I'll be saying adios to the butter on my bread."

Tim sat and stared into the fire. "Man," he said. "I wish I knew the answer."

"It might help if you told me the question."

Tim looked over. "What?"

"Nothing."

Tim turned back to the fire. "The harder I try, the less I understand life. This misery is not what I signed up for."

"You want my advice? Stop trying. Let everything fall to the floor. Someone will always be there to pick up the pieces."

Tim looked over. "Where does that get you?"

"Out of the frying pan and into the fire. Only when you land, it's not your fault." BJ downed the remainder of his drink and wondered whether he could manage to get up just yet for another.

Tim stared at him. "What are you talking about?"

BJ forgot about the drink. He leaned closer, his voice confidential. "What do you think about guys who cheat on their wives?" he asked. "Though I have to warn you, anything you say may be used against you in a comedy sketch. I mean, how do you feel about having sex with women other than your wife?"

"I'd rather not talk about this."

"Why not? It's just casual conversation." The slipper swung from the end of his foot.

"Because it's a sore spot with me right now, is why."

"Gotcha!" BJ said. "So you're having an affair. I won't say a word."

"BJ, I never know if you're just incredibly naive or completely insensitive."

"I resemble that remark," BJ said. "At least I think I would if I knew what it meant." He tried to regroup his thoughts. The alcohol and the heat from the fire were making him sluggish. "Okay, let's not say 'cheating' in quotation marks. What I want to know is, why do men choose to spend their lives with one woman and still try to grab a good piece of ass once in a while?"

"Beats me," Tim said.

"Or even if we don't — let's say we just look and never touch until it becomes a kind of compulsion, even though we can't help ourselves when we're doing it."

"I'd say your problem is immaturity," Tim remarked.

"I'd say it's hormones."

"I'm not talking about the urge," Tim said. "We all have that. I'm talking about the inability to control it."

"What if you don't want to control it?"

"Self-willed immaturity."

"Isn't that just pressure to conform?"

Tim was annoyed by BJ's persistence. He was like a precocious child who said outrageous things simply for attention.

"I'm serious," BJ said. "I'm asking because I want to know what you think, my friend."

"You can call it whatever you like, but it doesn't change what it is."

"And what is it?"

"You need to grow up."

"Bingo! There's the rub-a-dub-dub. I don't want to grow up."

BJ slouched into his seat as though to entrench his refusal. He'd heard it before. They were all fools, he thought. Hadn't they looked around and seen the mid-life desolation? The frustration and anger. The boredom. More than anything, he thought, they were scared to death that things would just go on like that till the end of time, because none of them had the guts to change anything.

"Someday you have to face the fact that you can't have everything," Tim said.

"But I want everything. Why shouldn't I?" BJ shrugged. It was his hunger for life, the way it just streamed out of him. It left him restless, wanting more. "I know I can be childish and selfish and, hey — guess what! — I'm a misanthrope, too. What great comic isn't? But some people have everything."

Tim's annoyance grew, but he couldn't help being drawn in. "Like who?"

"Movie stars. Politicians. They have everything — money, fame, promiscuity, STDs ..."

"Movie stars and politicians? That's nobody I know. Besides, I don't even think those are real people."

BJ nudged him with his elbow. "Look at Margaret — beautiful babe, huh? Gorgeous breasts, terrific legs, a wonderful personality — when she isn't nuts, I mean. Okay, she's a little kooky, but mostly, she's a knockout."

He paused, arms wide as if to incorporate all that his wife was. Tim was staring at him.

"So why do I do it? Why do the old gonads start acting like a couple of teenage boys when they see some cutie-patootie walking down the street, her breasts bouncing like a couple of ripe melons I just want to catch for her before they fall?"

"That's so kind of you, BJ."

"Can I trust you?"

"About as much as you can trust yourself."

BJ grimaced. "Okay, but you still can't tell anybody what I'm going to say."

"I don't want your confession."

"Just listen to me. Please!"

"This better not be one of your stories ..."

"I swear!"

BJ made a quick check of the doorway. He leaned closer, speaking in whispers. "Last spring, Margaret and I had Tori over to babysit the kids one night. Well, to make a long story short, she made a grab for me in the car when I drove her home afterwards. My wife's fucking kid sister, for God's sakes!"

Tim continued to stare at him.

"I didn't want it to happen. I swear! But she ... she ...!"

"She dropped her melons and you picked them up for her."

BJ sighed. "Yeah. Something like that."

"If you want me to tell you I think you're despicable ..."

"I don't want you to tell me anything ..."

"Good, because I'm not interested in punishing you. You'll have to pay your shrink to do that."

BJ held his head in his hands. He looked up and sighed. "Why? Why do I do it?"

"I told you — it's immaturity. You're an adolescent jerk."

A minute passed accompanied by the hissing flames, sap bursting through the wood and burning off.

"Thank you," BJ said at last.

For a moment, Tim felt he should apologize. Instead, he said, "Don't worry — your secret's safe with me."

BJ stood shakily. He found himself experiencing an unchar-acteristic and uncomfortable moment of self-recognition, the Marquis de Sade regretting a lifetime of moral laxity.

BJ raised his glass. "I salute you, my stalwart friend, for your honesty, your integrity, and your insight." He brought the glass to his mouth, realized it was empty and lowered it with a frown. He looked back at Tim. "But it doesn't help me one fucking bit."

He turned and went out, leaving Tim alone to stare at the fire.

TWENTY

UPSTAIRS, ANGELA PASSED HER MOTHER carrying an armload
of sheets and blankets. They stopped in the hallway, outlined by
the light from a doorway. The bedding shifted in Abbie's arms.

"I thought I would bring these down to Tim," Abbie said at
last.

"I'll take them," Angela said, opening her arms.

Their eyes met. Abbie saw the unspoken accusations. What
a terrible creature I must be in your head, she thought. She turned
back along the hall without another word.

Halfway down the stairs, Angela stopped to look out the
window. Shep's silhouette rested in a deck chair. His cigarette
flashed, an arm crossed over his chest as he rocked back and
forth.

She continued down to the family room where Tim sat staring
at the fire. She held the bedding out like something between a
barrier and a peace offering. She was embarrassed to be handing
over these sheets and blankets as if he was a friend come for a
sleepover.

"I guess you found your bed," she said.

He reached past the bedding to his wife, as though the gesture could overcome the divide between them. The linen spilled onto the floor. For a second Angela felt frightened, but she relented and let him hold her. He'd always taken people's love for granted — not in a bad way, but just that it would always be there. It must have been a shock for him to discover that love had an ebb and flow, and that it could go out a long way and sometimes never return.

"It's so hard without you," he said simply.

Angela pushed back her feelings before they could overwhelm her. During wartime, when people were dying around her, emotions had been easy. Hope was just another four-letter word, like *shit*, or *hate*, or *dead*. Here, she found it harder to face this man who was her husband and who was suffering, but who wasn't a casualty of war. He wasn't asking her for food or antibiotics, or a map to help him escape. He was asking for something she couldn't give.

"I wish we could get back to where we were," he sobbed into her shoulder.

The words reached her from far away. He was talking about another world, another life. She hadn't lived there for years. Fate had sent them in different directions, despite their best intentions. Wasn't that how it always happened? Bridges fell, buildings collapsed, people disappeared.

"What do you want? Please tell me!" His voice was a whisper. "Whatever you want, I'll give it to you. I can't stand not being able to reach you anymore."

His need terrified her. She tried to free herself from his grip, but he held her.

"Do you know how much I love you?"

The guilt stung her. "Yes."

He released her on the word, a rope dropped down a well. Someone had fallen in. As he'd fallen into her the night they met one August evening at the birthday party of a 'mutual friend. The wind was warm on the rooftop of a downtown high-rise. He'd arrived late and the roof thronged with people. He hadn't seen Victor, but he had seen Angela standing apart from the others, watching the sky for a sign of the fireworks that were about to take place over the harbour.

He waited until he saw his chance. He walked over to the bar and stood in line behind her till she got her drink and started to turn away. It was now or never.

"Upper Canada," he said, looking at the bottle in her hand. "Are you recommending the ale or the lager?"

"That depends," she said, "on whether you're flirting or just being neighbourly."

It had been easy to chat with her. Thoughts like *I've never met anyone like you before* kept passing through his mind. It was true.

"You're kidding," she blurted, when he told her what he did. "Somebody my age actually sells life insurance?" She was surprised by his genuine enthusiasm for the business, his whole-hearted belief in it. She was charmed rather than put off by the ordinariness of him. She couldn't imagine anyone so pro-foundly normal.

He was unlike anyone she'd met too — unlike the men who risked their lives for their jobs. She laughed a lot that evening. He couldn't tell if she was laughing at him or not, but he knew she hadn't intended to be mean. He'd just asked her out the following weekend when the fireworks started. They seemed comically timed, like a staged effect.

"Can't," she said. "I'll be in Nairobi."

A month later, on her return, he was waiting for her at the airport.

That was how it began. For a while, Angela thought she'd found what she wanted. Pressed together at night their bodies seemed a consolation for all she'd endured. She felt she should appreciate him for all those who couldn't have what she had — refuge, safety, peace.

It lasted two years. She might have floated safely on the raft of him forever, but eventually she came to see it was made of neither strength nor wisdom. His life was just ordinary, an accretion of non-events. His thinking wasn't courageous, but small. It was something he couldn't help being, rather than something he'd achieved.

She tried to explain how she'd grown to resent the peaceful insularity of their home life. It was an escape, she said. He didn't understand. Soon they could barely speak without an eruption, Angela arguing over faraway events and Tim pleading for what was, by comparison, their own inconsequential existence.

In the end, she realized his river wasn't endless. It hadn't taken her where she needed to go — back into the world. Her own river flowed on, endlessly replenishing itself. He'd always said she was too self-sufficient, that her flaw was in never needing anyone.

"I've loved you all this time," he told her now. "But I think you only needed me for a while." He waited for her to return his look. "What went wrong? What happened to us?"

He still wanted answers, reasons for things that might remain unknowable. She couldn't explain her fevered need to be at the centre of whatever was about to happen — bombs falling, bullets flying — a code that exploded apart moments in time and signalled out a meaning for her alone. What she wanted had no shape or logic. Or rather, it had a logic all its own, regardless of anything else.

"We grew apart, Tim. It's time to stop holding on to one another."

"Why? Why do we need to let go? I thought life was about growing together, making connections. Not letting go of each other because you say it's time to move on."

Her eyes refused him. She wouldn't let him catch her with his need. "That's your life, Tim. Not mine."

"Does nothing hold for you? Is it always about chasing the next horizon, the next armed confrontation?"

"It's my career, Tim. You can't hold me back." Even as she said it, she knew she was on dangerous ground.

His features contorted. "That is such crap! I'm not talking about your career — I'm talking about our marriage!"

"It's over."

"Why? Because you're bored with me, or because you're in love with danger? I think the truth is you're scared to death of letting anyone get near you, so you just keep running ..."

She turned back to the stairs.

"What are you looking for, Angela?"

Her hand reached for the banister, but she didn't move. The little girl in the white dress beside the tricycle in her mother's photograph album turned to watch. She, too, was waiting for an answer.

"Angela?"

"I don't know."

It was an admission of something — fear, guilt, desperation. Whatever it was burned the air around her. It was the invisible enemy. She couldn't fight it because she couldn't see it, didn't even know what it was. Tim saw he'd been a failure to her.

"I wish I could have made you happy," he said. "But I can't compete with your ghosts. And unlike you, I can't just turn off my emotions and walk away from everything."

"I'm sorry," she said. "I can't help you."

He watched her disappear up the stairs into the darkness above, which contained the ruins of Angkor Wat, a labyrinth of war torn streets, the Lacandón rainforests, rivers rising, planes splitting the sky.

MARGARET LAY AWAKE IN BED, her back to the door. She heard BJ enter and begin to undress. A night light threw his shadow across the wall, a child's image of a monster or a giant clown. He removed his shirt and sat on the bed. His wife didn't move. He could feel the distance between them and knew something was dying. He sensed the approaching loss without being able to see its shape.

He extended an arm so its shadow hovered over Margaret's hip. He moved it in the air above her, letting it caress her out-line. He wondered what it would feel like to let go and just … touch. He lowered the arm and moved his hand across her shoulder, down her side, pushing the covers around her waist.

"Please, don't." It was more a question than a command.

He left his hand on her skin like a flag marking a boundary:

This is how far I have come. "I'm sorry," he said. "I'm sorry I got upset with you at supper."

"I just don't want to be touched."

The hand retreated, removing the flag.

"Okay."

He retrieved his shirt, throwing it over his shoulders. Margaret heard the door open and turned to watch him leave, wanting both to call him back and not call him back. Wanting to be the stronger, in either case. Now it was she who felt the loss, the tide withdrawing. She could follow it out as far as it went, but she couldn't make it return.

IN THE HALLWAY, BJ RAN into Tori coming from the bathroom. She'd wrapped herself in a red towel, a Renaissance Madonna.

"Well, if it isn't the stud himself," she crowed, tipsy. She tried to grab him, but he dodged her. "Where're you off to, stud?"

"Downstairs to sleep. Stop calling me that," he demanded, trying to keep his voice to a whisper.

"What would you prefer I called you?"

Look away, he told himself. Don't watch her! But he couldn't help being drawn to the roll of her breasts, the way her hair fell across her eyes when she looked down. She glanced at his bare chest. He pulled his shirttails together.

"I prefer BJ, since you're asking."

"We all know what that stands for, don't we?" She loosened her grip on the towel; it threatened to unravel before his eyes. They were two people clutching at things, barely keeping themselves intact.

"Why are you going downstairs to sleep?"

"Because your big sister is a little bit upset right now, so why don't we get out of the hallway and stop making noise while people are trying to sleep?"

"I'd rather stay here and cause a scene," she taunted. "Wouldn't you like that? I know how much you love an audience."

She lurched toward him, almost tumbling down the stairs as he moved to avoid her. He caught her and she clung to him, the towel entwining them both.

"Maybe my sister doesn't deserve you."

His knees were weak. Not here, for God's sakes! Please, not here.

"I think Margaret's just a little confused right now," he said.

"I'm not," Tori told him, clinging to his shoulder.

"Not confused?"

"Uh-uh." She shook her head. "I know what I want."

"Why am I afraid to ask what that is?"

"And I know what you want, too." She reached down and grabbed him. She felt his erection coming on. "See? I told you I knew what you wanted."

She lifted her face as though expecting a kiss for her cleverness. Their lips met, slid over one another. Moist, soft, warm.

Save yourself, he told himself. It's now or never. Somehow he found the strength. He held her upright for a moment and then pushed her away.

"Tori, hon, you're beautiful, but you're pathetic. Go find your snake-charming boyfriend."

He stumbled down the stairs, terrified by what his life had become.

ANGELA WOKE AND WENT TO the window. She stood looking out. It was past 3 A.M. The rain had come and gone already. Lion's Head Point had disappeared, the massive limestone cliffs cloaked in darkness. She pushed open the window, struck by the roar of waves racing onto the beach at Whippoorwill Bay. They crashed in the shallows, followed by a long dreadful sucking noise as the water withdrew again, like something huge and mournful scraping its giant hands against the rocks. She recognized the sound. It spoke to her again and again, wherever she went. It was the voice of the earth, the never-ending chaos of history.

She'd been dreaming of tanks. She saw them again in her mind's eye. She imagined the tanks heading into the suburbs — where her mother and father and millions of people like them lived — rolling over parked cars and iron fences, uprooting trees and overturning tool sheds, crashing through people's living rooms, and crushing bodies beneath their relentless treads, leaving only the smashed and broken remnants of whatever had been there, and, once everything had been destroyed, slowly turning and moving on toward the next town, the next settlement, until there was nothing left.

BOOK IX
A THIN SMELL OF ROT

TWENTY-ONE

THE FORMER YUGOSLAVIA, MAY–JUNE 1995.

When his lone guest failed to come downstairs the following morning, the concierge used his passkey to check on her. He found her in bed, feverish, the bedclothes twisted around her as though she'd been dancing with someone in her dreams. The woman, Jasna, came in the afternoon. She put a thermometer in the girl's mouth and made her swallow three tablets. Jasna and her husband, Stjepan, ran an *apoteka* in the basement of a house outfitted with beds and medical equipment scrounged from wherever it could be found. That was where they brought her.

It took the better part of a week before the patient's strength started to return and she could walk by herself. She tolerated small amounts of the tinned kasha they served her every morning and night. Its blandness was agreeable. Sometimes they fed it to her cold with milk, sometimes warm with butter and bits of chicken she would hold under her tongue.

She'd come at a good time, Jasna told her, as though there were better and worse times to arrive in a mountain town under siege. With the aid shipments halted, their supplies had nearly run out. Fortunately, they'd just received a delivery of drugs from an evacuating medical team and were able to give her a tetanus shot and antibiotics to prevent the septicemia from spreading. Otherwise, her death would have been painful.

Jasna was surprised to learn Angela had come from an MSF camp. Why had they let her go without treating her? She'd refused to let them examine her, she said, too worried about André and needing to find a place for the night. In any case they, too, had had few supplies.

"Ah!" Jasna's eyes widened like a schoolteacher used to speaking with very young children.

Her short dark hair suited her pixie-like face, quick speech and movements. She spoke surprisingly good English. She had relatives in England and at one time thought she might like to live there. Her story came out in bits and pieces — how she'd grown up in Sarajevo and been a nurse before the war in the same hospital where Stjepan had been an orderly. They'd married and had a daughter, Daniella. It hadn't mattered that Jasna was a Croat and Stjepan a Serb. Then the war came. They'd had to choose quickly between staying and leaving, but decided they could do more good by staying, though Jasna still struggled with her decision to keep Daniella with them.

The *apoteka* had come about naturally as people turned to them for help. Patients arrived infrequently, knocking at any hour on their door, some with serious injuries, others with lesser ailments. Most stayed only for bandaging and antibiotics. Many regarded Jasna with suspicion as she examined them. After treating them, she gave them what medicine she could spare, and saw it stuffed quickly into pockets and bags. The *apoteka*'s operations were illegal and covert, intended for the minorities who lacked access to the hospitals, but none were turned away. Most patients were brought in by families, but convalesced elsewhere to avoid the possibility of discovery. The more serious cases were transferred to the UN or the Red Cross when an opportunity arose, but that hadn't happened since the shellings. When they could, most of the wounded simply returned home. Jasna seldom heard from them again. It was safer for everyone.

The morning they'd come for her at the hotel, Angela asked about a patient medevacked by the UN, possibly to a nearby hospital. Unable to speak, she wrote *André Riel, Canadian Journalist* on a piece of paper, and gave Jasna the picture of André at the well of sacrifice.

Jasna smiled at the photo. "Handsome. I bet he's a handful," she said.

She promised to give them to her husband to inquire when he could. The hotel keeper had offered the use of his telephone, but there were no telephones in any of the hospitals. For now, they would have to wait. The pocket was undergoing an all-out siege; no one could get in or out.

Restlessness soon caught up with Angela. In the afternoons, she sought out the corners of a courtyard where the stone walls caught the afternoon light and shielded her from the street. A crumbling statue of a woman bearing a sheaf of wheat watched over her from the centre of the yard. There were a few shrubs in bloom, and weeds that grew everywhere. She recognized mint and lemon thyme reaching up from beneath the flat paving stones. Her mother had grown both at the cottage. She pulled at the leaves with her fingers and breathed in the scent caught on her skin.

Whenever Angela left the *apoteka*, Jasna made her wear a heavy pleated skirt, like the other women, and cover her head with a scarf to avoid attracting attention. Once, as she sat in the courtyard, a woman called out to her from the road. Startled, Angela waved. The woman waved back as though she knew her.

Angela helped with the cooking and cleaning. The house was modest, but clean and comfortable, despite the sandbags piled at every door. Family photos adorned the walls and china sat on shelves, as they might anywhere else in the world. She befriended Daniella, the couple's five-year-old, a shy dark-haired girl with luminous eyes, and taught her English when her mother was occupied. Despite the lack of news, André was never far from her mind, especially when she lay in bed at night or sat at the kitchen table with a teacup.

By day, the fighting was a distant rumour. Twilight was the worst, the undecided time between light and dark, as they waited to hear whether there would be more shelling or how close it might come. At night the missiles lit up the sky, zigzagging like fireflies as they listened for what followed, no telling where they would land. The terror was all in the waiting. If there was rain, the chance of fighting was less.

Watching them together, Angela saw Stjepan was Jasna's match in every way — cool, resilient, and determined to see them through the war. When the fighting began, the shelling had disrupted the water supply so he built a huge rain gutter to catch the runoff. It siphoned off the side of the roof and into a tank stoppered with a cork and a rag. There was enough water to wash dishes, and sometimes for a quick shower. By the end of the summer, however, the water tasted rank and smelled fetid. They began to think they were being poisoned. During a break in the fighting, he went up on the roof to look into the reservoir and discovered two dead rats floating in the tank. He related this with a laugh. Since then, he'd kept the tank covered with mesh.

Most days, Stjepan went out to look for people in need of help. Jasna busied herself with the patients, waiting for him to return from the dangerous work that no one was supposed to know about. She never appeared worried. Her trust in life was supreme.

She spoke optimistically of a future after the war. "My sister and her husband moved to Holland last July," she told Angela. "She has a job in a chocolate factory. Stjepan and Daniella and I are going to join them when this is over."

Some days there were simple miracles. A flower bloomed yellow through the basement floor. Another day Stjepan returned with a case of wine abandoned at the side of the road. They often stayed up talking till nearly dawn before one of them reminded the other they needed to be ready to work in a few hours. They seemed indefatigable. Occasionally the conversation drifted to politics and their sheer incomprehension that former friends and neighbours were bent on annihilating one another while the country unravelled.

They all might have been good friends under other circumstances, Angela thought. It had taken a war to bring them together.

"Why do you do all this?" she asked Jasna one day at breakfast.

Jasna's hand deftly sterilized needles in a bowl of boiling water. She shrugged without looking up. "Because we have to."

"But why?"

What she meant was, why risk your lives to help others? Why not just leave it all behind — the house, the village, the entire suicidal country?

Jasna looked up and shifted her glasses. "Why do you risk *your* life coming here?" she replied, as though that were the real question.

In the afternoon, an old couple arrived with their granddaughter who had burned her leg on a kerosene stove. While Jasna attended the girl, Angela took Daniella to a neighbour's house. On her return, she stopped at a courtyard. Sitting there alone, she felt André — his breath on her skin, his hand on her shoulder — as though he'd come back for her. Just that. It took her breath away. She rose unsteadily, then stumbled and fell. She lay there, trying to catch her breath. When she stood again, she no longer felt him. For a long time afterwards, she was afraid to return to the *apoteka*.

She was sitting in the kitchen with Jasna when Stjepan walked in. She knew by his face, by the way he entered. He came in slowly, without his usual smile. She told herself she was prepared for it, the absence where there should have been something. The empty word Stjepan brought her — *dead*. A farewell instead of a greeting. He'd hardly stopped talking while he was alive, but now he'd left her with no words.

"He died in the helicopter," Stjepan explained.

He had died in the air, his body too restless even in its dying to remain on the ground. There was no place where she could reach out and touch him, taste him, feel him. How could she comfort him now? She thought suddenly of the father who hadn't understood his son, and how their reconciliation could never happen now. She recalled the mother who had held him in her arms then vanished, leaving him to watch a blinking light on a church steeple as he waited for her to return. The *apoteka* suddenly felt like an island in an ocean of death.

Jasna touched her shoulder in a way she reserved for the more desperate cases, the ones who often died under her hands as she treated them. Angela remembered the words he'd given her, the question he'd left her with.

"How do you make God laugh?" she said.

Jasna looked at her. "I don't know. How?"

"I don't know either."

She knelt and buried her face in Jasna's dirndl, sobbing against the coarse wool. She wanted an alternate ending, something more for him. A foxtrot across the beach in Mexico.

These foolish things ...

FOR ANOTHER WEEK ANGELA SIMPLY waited, going through the motions of the work she'd taken on with Jasna. She was tired — more tired than she'd ever been in her life. She'd been carrying him — the weight on her shoulders, the heaviness in her head and stomach — all through that long month. Now there was nothing left to carry.

She dared death to take her. Come and get me if you want me, she thought. I won't come to you. It was almost a disappointment when it didn't. Going out farther into the country with her camera, she'd witnessed a town burning along the banks of a quiet river. Red crosses painted in circles told which houses belonged to the enemy, which to the friend. History was being emptied, but the memory of what once stood there could never be completely erased. As long as one of its inhabitants lived, Jasna told her not long after they met, then a village still lived on after it was gone.

The courtyard was her only consolation, as though that was where they'd said goodbye, the last time she'd felt his hand on her. When the weather was clear, she sat there among the stones with the weeds growing up between them. She was there when she heard the rumbling of the tanks.

She stood and walked quickly back to the *apoteka*. She rounded a corner only to stop short and turn aside. A few doors away, Daniella stood talking to two soldiers, a tiny pillar in a white dress standing before them. She didn't look alarmed or fearful. She was simply chatting with the men who'd stopped by her home.

Angela pulled the scarf over her face and kept walking. At the next block, she turned and saw one of the soldiers pat Daniella on the head. They walked away. Angela watched her enter an abandoned house across the street from where she lived. Good girl, Angela thought. You've been trained well.

Before Angela could get there, Jasna rushed across the street.

ANGELA SAT IN THE KITCHEN, listening as Jasna and Daniella spoke in subdued voices. Something Daniella said startled Jasna. Her face tightened. She brought her fingers to her mouth in a gesture of fear. Jasna kissed her daughter's forehead and sent her downstairs to read. When she looked up, her eyes glistened.

"The soldiers asked where her family was. She said, 'My father went crazy and drank battery acid to kill himself. I'm waiting for my mother to come and take me away.' Thank God they believed her."

Angela shook her head. "Where did she learn that story about battery acid?"

Jasna looked away. "It's what happened to my father last year," she said. "She overheard us talking about it."

Jasna leaned back and looked around at the walls. "I don't think there can ever be joy in this place again," she said. "I will never come back here once I leave."

That evening when Stjepan returned, Jasna told him about the soldiers. He spoke tersely then went downstairs to find Daniella. Jasna turned to Angela.

"He says we must leave."

"How?"

"Someone is coming to bring you information tomorrow. When she comes, we'll ask her what we are to do."

THE TEA READER ARRIVED WITH her gnarly cane and her careful words that would lead Angela out of the country. After that, Angela simply waited. In a day or two she would leave this pocket of land for the coast, where a boat would ferry her across to Italy.

One afternoon, she returned to the hotel to ask about the Jeep. The old man smiled when he saw her. He had moved the vehicle to his barn for safekeeping. They walked around the back of the hotel where he gave her the keys with a pat on the hand. Everything was still in it, he assured her. She removed her camera bag. She would come for the Jeep at night.

On the way back, she passed a church that had been hit by a mortar shell. Light poured through a gaping hole in the ceiling. Inside, everything gleamed. It was empty. Beside the altar, like a lost toy, lay a human foot. Blue and curled inward amid the debris, it looked as if someone had been trying to crawl beneath the chancel.

A thin smell of rot hung in the air. Flies buzzed over the appendage. They landed on it, crawling across the toes before flying off again. Out of habit, Angela snapped a photo.

An old woman selling vegetables at the side of the road hailed her. Angela picked up some onions and beets. Jasna had said how much she missed beet salad. It would brighten her day. An armoured car passed as she walked along. No one noticed the woman in the heavy skirt, kerchief drawn over her head.

The *apoteka* was silent when she returned. She left the vegetables on the table beside the makings of a stew. No one answered her calls.

In the basement, the rows of empty beds had been stripped and overturned, the mattresses shredded. The medicine cabinets were emptied on the floor. Vials of drugs lay smashed, needles scattered on stone.

Angela stopped and listened, tuning her ears to the pitch of the house. She climbed back up slowly. Down the deserted hallway, a second flight of steps ascended into shadows. Her feet carried her past the jagged glass of a broken window. Outside, distant gunfire. A grey sky. The steps creaked, terrible with voices, till she stood on the landing. She reached out to grasp the door handle, a polished whorl with her image imprinted on it. Absurdly, it reminded her of those Christmas ornaments where you shook the globe and snow whirled into the air before settling on the sleeping village. A sound inside the room stopped her from flinging the snow upward.

Her fingers lay white on the unturned knob. She heard it again: catlike, high-pitched. It might have been a kitten. It might have been the sound of death. What was that story about the lady or the tiger? There were two doors, she remembered. Either way, the hero lost. No alternate endings.

She turned the knob.

Light bled through and outlined the form of a girl crouched on the floor. Beside her, a woman's body lay twisted at a disagreeable angle. A sweetly metallic smell hung in the air, sweat mingled with gunmetal. Angela pushed the door wider. Daniella's hands clutched her mother's dirndl, fingers entwined in the red-and-green leaf print. A whimper emerged from the girl's throat. The only other sound was Angela's heartbeat.

BOOK X
TREES

TWENTY-TWO

She rounded the bend and slowed the car, following the curve of Whippoorwill Bay. The Bosnian War lay behind her: nearly two million displaced and more than a hundred thousand dead, André and Jasna both completely unnecessary losses. Her photographs, the ones she'd taken on that terrible last day with André, were in the hands of men and women whose job it was to secure justice for those who had suffered. It might never happen. In Mexico, the indigenous people of Chiapas continued their struggle, no better off now than before. They still died of curable diseases, remained isolated and uneducated, and lost their land to wealthy cattle ranchers feeding fast-food empires in other countries. There'd been no justice for any of them.

She turned up the gravel drive, passing the white-and-red realtor sign posted at the entrance. She parked and stood looking into the forest and beyond. The sun barely touched the tops of the trees. The wind was a moan in the throat of budding branches, a sign spring had finally come into its own. Although she enjoyed it here any time of year, this was the season she loved most. Not the somnolent days of summer, with their verdant cheer, nor the ripeness of fall with its hint of incipient doom, the fullness that was nature's apology for also being the end of everything. But here, simply, was the beginning of everything — bright, fresh, and buoyantly springing up once again.

She turned the key and stepped inside.

The wind died as she entered what felt like an underwater chapel, solemn with expectancy, as though it had been waiting for her, the bride, to appear and so begin the ceremony. Everything was exactly as they'd left it. There was the rocker and the carefully arranged furniture, there the vase where her mother placed it, emptied now of the roses she'd cut that September morning.

The stone fireplace and lace curtains still lent the room its defining characteristics, as though the room would somehow not be the room without them here. Shep's pile of firewood rested carefully on the floor beside the hearth. Everything was in its place, perfect, and drowned.

In the foyer, Angela's footprints showed in the dust, the first astronaut on the moon. It was possible the moon would feel as still and hushed as this cottage on the tip of the Bruce Peninsula, just as otherworldly as it did right then.

She checked her watch — just past eleven. The real-estate agent would be arriving at two. She removed her jacket and began readying the rooms, sweeping the floor, and straightening the shelves. Upstairs, the bedrooms were made up, the linen changed. Someone had left a photograph album on the floor of her parents' room, the single misstep in all this immaculate housekeeping. She brought it downstairs and returned it to the family room.

In the kitchen, she paused. There was the calendar, stopped at September. If she held fast and let nothing in the room, not a shaft of light or a single thought from outside, it seemed as though everything would stay exactly as it had been when they were all last here.

That day was etched clearly in her mind. She'd got up early and sat at the table, having barely slept. Her dressing gown slid open each time she reached for her mug. Tori stumbled through, looking hungover. Angela watched as she filled a cup with coffee, smiled weakly, and went out to the porch without a word. A moment later Margaret entered, fully dressed. She drained the last of the coffee from the pot and turned off the burner.

"Any word on Dad?" Margaret said.

"Not yet. Mom and BJ drove in to see him about an hour ago."

Margaret put down her cup and rubbed her forehead, remembering to ask, "How did it go with you and Tim last night?"

"Oh, fine ..."

"Really?"

Angela smiled ruefully. "No — not really."

"Are you all right?"

She hesitated. "I'm okay."

She was spared further questioning by Tim's arrival. Margaret slipped out as he appeared in the doorway. He was dressed for travel and looked as though he hadn't slept either.

"How's your dad?" His voice sounded hopeful, but subdued.

"He's going to be okay."

"Good." He'd spent the better part of a sleepless night deciding not to beg for a final reconciliation. "Well, I guess I'm ready," he said, trying to make light of it. It was farewell, not goodbye, as though he were leaving her for a week or two rather than forever.

Angela felt pity welling up, an echo of guilt. "Are you hungry?" she asked, absurdly drawing out the moment.

He shook his head. "No, but thanks. I don't suppose you need a ride to the airport?" The words were feeble, almost as absurd as her offer of a meal. They wouldn't fix anything between them.

"Thanks. I should stay. It'll be the last time I see them all before I leave for Sarajevo."

He put a hand to his temple, prompting himself like an actor forgetting a line. "I guess this is it, then. I thought endings were supposed to be dramatic. But I guess it's really been over for a while." Angela heard her mother saying those awful words: *You never really loved him.* It was true. She would never forgive herself for what she'd done to him.

Tim waited, hoping for some reaction to let him know he still mattered. Nothing came. The moment passed. "I just wish I'd known earlier," he said. "I might've been able to do something about it."

"There's no need for regret, Tim. We can't change the past."

Her mother's words. That was as much as she gave him. She'd already closed him outside of her circle.

"Right," he said. "I'd better go."

Angela took a step toward him. He hoped she didn't expect him to do anything as ludicrous as shake hands.

"I'll be in touch," he said.

Angela could hardly bear to look at him. She was consumed by his expression, the hungry-eyed loss as their world slipped through his hands. They both knew she could change it; she could make it different. This is the moment, Tim thought. Everything changes now. A shutter clicked and froze everything in time. Joy, grief, pain — the future blown up in a flash.

There was nothing left of him.

He turned, shattered by the colossal failure of his leave-taking. The door slipped shut, relinquishing any hold he had over her.

Angela fought to dislodge that final image of him. It held as if it had been burned in her mind. She tried to pull herself together. She knew she would have to find a way to get through that moment before entering the next one and the one after that.

Now, a year and a half later, she tidied the cottage room by room, wondering what it would be like for the people who bought this place, arriving summer after summer from that moment forward. They would have no idea of the lives lived here, no memory of meals eaten, or of what was said by those who sat in this kitchen drinking coffee. The life her family had shared would be no more obvious to anyone who came after them than the people who lived on the top floor of an apartment complex were aware of the lives being lived beneath them: birthday parties, wedding showers, graduations, illnesses survived, plans for the future that may or may not ever arrive, struggles and births, griefs and deaths.

She was just finishing when she heard the car. A maroon suv eased up the drive and came to a stop. Her mother, trim and fresh as ever, stepped from the passenger door and looked around. She was followed by a figure on the driver's side, a busty woman in a purple mid-length skirt, lilac blouse, and green jacket. Her hair was the colour of butter and she wore what looked like a string of fluorescent orange beads around her neck. Her mother's pale pastel outfit looked comically prim beside this vibrant rainbow. Angela couldn't imagine what these two women might have talked about on the drive up.

The agent's voice was bright and upbeat, full of contradictory plans and febrile emotions, quick to reverse them at any hint of her client's displeasure, attuned to the moment when Abbie might change her mind about the sale. She was an orange-throated, emerald-jacketed hummingbird catching currents of air and swerving with each fluttering turn.

Angela came down to greet them. The beads really were fluorescent, she saw. Despite the woman's extreme femininity, Angela sensed she was a lesbian, though there'd be no talk of that here — her private life would be off-bounds. This woman was business first; there'd be nothing to scare off the children and drive the clients away.

"Hello, Angela," her mother said, leaning to kiss her cheek. "This is my eldest daughter, Angela," Abbie said to the real-estate agent. "She's come to give me a hand. This is Marion Baker from Bruce Realty."

Marion offered Angela her hand; their eyes connected and held. "I'm so sorry about your father," she said simply. "From the way your mother describes him, he was irreplaceable."

Angela was surprised by how sincere she sounded. "Thank you. He was."

Marion turned to look over the property. The moment had

been genuine, but the pleasantries were over and it was time to get down to business. But then she paused and turned back to Abbie.

"You know, I always have contradictory feelings about selling places like this, places that have been in families for years. I always want to say, 'Are you sure you won't change your mind next year and regret it?' I know I would." Marion shrugged, as if this shedding of history made no sense to her. "But no one ever does — or at least I don't hear about it if they do."

"I don't think I'll change my mind," Abbie said.

Marion turned to Angela again.

"It's just gorgeous here. You must love it. My partner and I live in Dyer's Bay, about ten minutes up the road," she said. "Sarah just adores this area. She had to drag me out of Toronto, but now she can't drag me back."

Angela was amazed to hear her speak of her partner with total nonchalance, not the slightest sign of hesitation or unease. Suddenly she liked Marion — even admired her — more than she could possibly say.

"You should see their place," her mother said. "They have a beautiful view of the bay from the hill. It's unbelievable."

What was unbelievable, Angela thought, was this conversation and her own mother, cavorting with stylish lesbians — it was too much.

Angela found herself studying her mother. While she hadn't expected her to be a dysfunctional lump, she wasn't anticipating this solid, almost cheery personality.

At the funeral Angela had watched her mother standing by the casket accepting the expressions of sympathy. Angela was looking for signs of what Abbie was going through, and worrying she might fall apart at any moment. But she'd held herself together; she'd functioned admirably. What it must have cost to keep her bearing, her demeanour, Angela had thought. Now she wondered if it might have been something else all together.

"You should come for tea sometime," Marion told Angela. "We're always at home on Sundays."

"I'd like that," Angela said. And maybe, she thought, you can tell me who this woman is pretending to be my mother.

How could her mother not have been destroyed by her father's death? Conrad had been the sun at the centre of their universe; his extinction signalled the end of their line. It threatened ruin, depletion, loss. What could be left after the sun died? Gravity would falter, orbits fail.

Still, here was her mother, examining the tightly fisted buds on a rose bush about to explode into leaf, leading a woman dressed in purple around the cottage grounds. It was as if nothing had happened, nothing had changed.

ANGELA WAITED DOWNSTAIRS WHILE MARION and her mother continued their tour. Every few minutes she heard Marion exclaiming over the selling points — the bedrooms with their original trim, a mahogany stair railing, the tiled bath on the second floor, the incomparable view of Whippoorwill Bay and the cliffs at Lion's Head Point. It was a seller's dream come true.

The family album lay on the coffee table. Angela flipped it open to the Polaroid Shep had taken on that final morning before they'd scattered — the sisters to town in the small blue car, her father to the hospital in Lion's Head. She'd forgotten it.

"My apologies to Angela," he'd said, as he lined them up with his hands. "I know she's the photographer here, but I'm doing her job for her just this once."

He would have been good for Tori — grounded, sensible — but others had taken his place. Angela remembered how she'd snapped at his curiosity about her work, and felt badly for it now. He'd simply wanted to belong. Still, here was the photograph, a small miracle amid all the loss.

Her father stands upright behind her mother. His smile is the final goodbye from a man who never stopped smiling. It seemed not so much a portrait as the end of a story, shockingly human and vulnerable in all it revealed. It was a door to a life — his life — but it led only backward in time.

And there was her mother, clutching the roses they'd picked together. Angela's arm lay across her shoulder. Despite her fears, the arm looked natural, the moment genuine. Here, too, were BJ and Margaret, Tori, and Markus, sitting at their feet like the family dog. Shep's face gleamed expectantly at the centre of the photo. He'd found hope, joy, love — if only for a moment. He'd believed there would be more. Perhaps he thought he'd permeated the veneer of the Thomas family's complex makeup. Perhaps he'd even mistaken it for something else — something brighter, easier to live with. Families could do that.

Upstairs, Angela heard the shower's soft whoosh. It was Marion checking the water pressure. It wouldn't be long before they were gone from this place forever, like a line dividing the past from the present. She thought of her collection of photographs of men who once occupied foreign shores and flew planes that no longer existed. The spaces people left behind were holes in time. Those men had vanished completely, as if they'd flown into the sun, erasing even the memories held by the ones they'd left.

She stopped at a picture of her parents' wedding. She was struck by the unbounded optimism in her father's face. He was the abashed young man at the fair who has just won the grand prize. Beside him, his bride appeared fearful, her eyes downcast, as if she didn't even dare to hope. What, Angela wondered, had kept her mother walled up inside herself? Or had her father's unfailing kindness walled her in, a hothouse flower blooming for him alone?

"Good morning, eldest daughter," he would say. "It's another beautiful day."

How could she say what had once mattered to them or what they had needed from one another? Secrets and mysteries.

She heard her mother coming down the stairs, followed by Marion. Her mother was describing a recent confrontation with Markus. "His language was unbelievable," she said. "Everything was 'effing' this, 'effing' that. So I said to him, 'You're effing right. It's effing terrible that you to have to do your effing homework every effing day.' I actually said it."

Angela stifled a smile. She couldn't imagine her mother using the F-word.

"I think he was shocked," Abbie continued. "He stopped and said, 'Grandma, it's not nice to talk like that.' I pretended to think about it for a moment, and then I said, 'All right. I won't say it anymore if you won't.'"

Marion laughed.

How was it, Angela wondered, that her mother could be so upbeat and easygoing for this lesbian real-estate agent, but not for her? It was tragic, but they would never know one another.

How many times had they simply missed the chance to forgive and forget, instead of wasting all that time and effort fighting and distancing themselves from one another?

The sun coming over the sill distracted her. The album shifted, the loose photographs cascading onto the floor at her feet. These were the forbidden pictures, banished by her mother's hands to the back of the book. They were unsorted, unloved. She scooped them up. The single snapshot of her father and his brother lay on top. Why were there no others of Alex? He hadn't been in the wedding photographs either, she realized. Had he already abandoned his family to go off chasing foreign sunsets?

Here was another picture of her mother as a young woman. Angela couldn't recall it. The date scribbled hastily at the bottom had faded, the day itself lost in time. From the style of her hair and clothes, it would have been taken around the time she'd met Conrad. The expression on her mother's face gripped her. It was so despairing she couldn't meet it without a feeling of hopelessness. It was the expression of someone who had lost her way in life, someone who desperately wanted something, but knew she would never have it. It was a look of almost unendurable sorrow.

For a moment, Angela didn't understand. Then she recognized it. She'd seen the same expression on Tim's face as he slipped out the door that last day, knowing she had the power to crush his dreams or let them live. But she'd asked him to let her go, and he'd had no other choice.

For a moment, she saw the world through her mother's eyes. She saw the camera pointing at her, saw who was there, and it was not who she expected to see. The moment seemed to go on and on, and for that moment she became her mother. She saw the separation, the gulf that had lain between them all these years. The one person missing at the wedding. *A someone who had never really loved her.* She knew the awful mistake her mother had never forgiven herself for.

She dropped the photograph and stood upright. If she didn't get some air she would drown in this underwater chapel where her father was the absent bridegroom. If he were here now she would have wanted to ask him, though she would never have dared speak the words aloud, *You aren't my real father, are you?* For there had been no other in her whole life. And even if she could have said the words, he still would not have answered, *No, I am not your father. You are not my daughter.*

It would have denied her thirty-two years of life.

"I've got the form in the car. I'll just go get it," she heard Marion say.

"Thank you," her mother called out brightly. "It'll give me a few minutes with my garden. I need to say goodbye."

Angela walked out to the porch. Marion passed her on the way to her car and smiled. "Your mother's wonderful — she's so much fun to work with."

"Yes, isn't she?" Angela said, in a voice she didn't recognize.

The garden at that moment was suffused with light, pristine, like a Pre-Raphaelite painting. She watched her mother moving about in it. Yet here was not the chaste goddess of the painting, perfected and unattainable. Here was the artist's model — mortal, ordinary, and fallen. Here, very simply, was her mother.

Abbie looked up. Her smile vanished. "I spoke with Margaret this morning," she said. "I think there's still a chance that she and BJ may get back together, but I don't really expect it, to tell the truth."

This was the mother Angela had always known: mournful, critical, peevish — everyone else's life an inconvenience to her.

"I thought of keeping the cottage for a while, even planting a fourth locust tree for your father, but it didn't seem to make sense without him. Nothing makes much sense anymore."

Angela felt unexpectedly sorry. She wanted to say something to make up for her mother's loss. "You might keep it. There's no need to sell."

"Yes," Abbie said. Then, "No — I don't think I could bear to come back here again."

Abbie looked around at the garden. The lilies would soon be out, splendid in their majesty. Then they would die and next year, miraculously, return again, all without her. They didn't need her to happen.

"On the way to the hospital your father told me I had to stay strong. 'Stay strong for me,' he said. He knew me so well. He knew I wouldn't have been able to go on without him. And I have stayed strong. But I'm doing it for him, not myself."

Angela saw now that her mother wasn't bearing up; she wasn't rising above it all. She was simply being this strong person for Marion, for show, as she had done for the others at the funeral. And if she didn't do it for Angela, it was because Angela did not need hiding from, except for the one thing. It wasn't an insult, this rawness, this harshly featured honesty. It was her gift.

"There were so many times I wanted to tell you," Abbie said quietly. "But you weren't here, or were always just running through, and there never seemed to be an appropriate time."

For a second, Angela wondered if she was talking about her

father's illness or the other thing. They were both awkward with the moment.

Abbie tried to find the nurturing forces inside her, the voice that would tell her how to speak to this child. Her child. It always failed her when she needed it most. It was failing her now.

"I'm sorry," Angela said. "It hasn't been easy for you."

The shadow of leaves swept across her mother's face, darkness followed by light.

"It's funny," Abbie said. "I never wanted a mother's responsibility of having power over my daughters' lives. But every time I look at you I see myself looking back."

This, Abbie thought, is what it comes down to. We give birth to children without knowing who they will grow up to be, and we do our best to make life easier for them. We try to protect them, and they resent us because they think they know better. And maybe they're right. There is such an awful feeling of inadequacy around them, wanting to give more than we have to give, if only because there is a part of us in each of them, and we see it every time they look back at us.

"I don't think the way my life turned out is your fault," Angela said. "But I hope you don't think your life is my fault."

Abbie laughed softly. "What do you mean you hope my life isn't your fault? Of course it isn't. I've never thought it was."

Angela waited. The pause felt like forever. "Why wasn't Uncle Alex at your wedding?"

A look of terror overtook Abbie. The sands shifted beneath her feet. "I'm so sorry ..." Abbie saw her life stretched out behind her, a desert with a few solid oases of green. It had been nobody's fault. Who could be blamed for any of it? A fist of emotion clenched and unclenched inside her. A mistake, really. That's all it was. She'd fallen in love with a man who worshipped horizons. Love could be so devouring. First it held you in its terrible embrace, then it swallowed you whole. Must she pay for it her entire life?

"Mom?"

"Because it wouldn't have been ... appropriate."

"Appropriate?"

Angela stood on a precipice. Here it was, the door to the unknown country she'd been waiting to enter for as long as she could remember. She couldn't bring herself to open it.

"Please — I need to know."

Abbie's gaze retreated. Safety, caution — the words sprang to mind. This road led down. But, no. She could be strong. Conrad had taught her that.

"Because I was pregnant with his child — with you."

Angela saw the fear in her mother's eyes. She reached out and saw a little girl's hands clutching at the world of her mother's dirndl, clinging to it like a lifeline.

"Please — could you just ..."

"What?"

"Please don't freeze me out now. I just need to hear you say you love me ..."

It was all tumbling out, the words, the fears she'd held inside her. I'm thirty-two years old, Angela thought. I'm thirty-two years old and asking my mother to tell me she loves me.

"Of course I love you ..." Abbie protested, her eyes brimming over. "But I don't know how to take care of you anymore. I don't know what to do."

"You don't have to do anything!"

Abbie reached out, the smallest gesture across space, touching the cheek of her eldest daughter. "I was in a hospital ..."

"I know ..."

"They said I tried to kill myself but ... I don't know if I would have done that."

Angela felt the moment seizing up. "Did Uncle Alex ...?"

"No — he didn't force me." Abbie hesitated, words on her lips that had never been spoken.

"It's all right, you don't have to ..."

"I let him. I thought I could hold onto him that way. If it hadn't been for your father ..."

"You don't have to ..."

Abbie shook her head, unable to believe it had come to this. "We brought you here right after you were born. We sat on this porch and I pointed things out for you. I said, 'This is a lily; that's a pond; those are stars.'"

Behind them, a figure reached down and touched the flowers. It was Mrs. Grey, Abbie knew. It was the lady of the gardens.

"After everything I'd been through, I was so grateful ... I planted that tree to remind myself. All I wanted was to know that you would grow up to dangle your toes in a river, or climb a tree and whistle in the moonlight one day."

Angela let go her grip on her mother's skirt, taking her into her embrace and rocking her like a baby.

"I'm sorry ... so sorry," Abbie repeated.

Marion returned. She saw them standing there together and waited silently.

"You have to go ..." Angela said, finally.

"Yes," Abbie said, releasing her. A hand reached up and wiped a tear before patting her hair in place. "Yes. Thank you. Thank you for everything."

Angela watched her mother enter the cottage with Marion Baker. She saw her mother smile and put on her best face, the practised one of mother, widow, survivor. The smile dissolved as she turned to look one last time at her garden. She waved to the daughter who had always been so troubled and so troublesome.

Maybe, Angela thought, that was as much as she would ever know — that her mother had once been a young woman full of hope, a young woman who fell in love with the wrong man, and let herself be used and betrayed. She might never understand the enigma of her mother any better than she did right now.

EPILOGUE

LION'S HEAD, BRUCE PENINSULA, APRIL 1996.

She sits on the porch beneath the locust trees. Her mother has gone. The sky turns overhead. She holds a book of photographs that have taken on an infinite richness in her hands. Lives that were given up, destroyed, absorbed into the infinity that is time. Even those who'd survived the war all those years ago will have dwindled and withered by now. But somehow they remain here, within her.

Angela thinks she'll put the photographs away, along with her pictures of André. She wants to put them somewhere they'll be safe, but where she won't see them again until she decides it's time. For now, she has work to do.

She closes her eyes and imagines herself back in the courtyard in Bihać. She's wearing the dirndl and the kerchief Jasna forced her to wear whenever she went out. A small child approaches. It's Daniella, followed at a distance by her mother.

"The war is over!" Jasna cries. "It's unbelievable, but it's true! We're going down to the market. We'll be back for dinner — a celebration!"

Angela watches them go. Time passes, and she waits. The sun has already started to set when she hears footsteps, senses his approach. A hand touches her shoulder from behind. She turns and finds him smiling. There are scars on his face, but the wounds have healed.

"Here I am," he says. "I brought you something."

He pulls out the tape recorder. It's playing a piece she recognizes. *These foolish things* ...

They dance until they tire and fall to the ground together, his face pressed against hers. She wishes she could hold him there forever, keeping him with her. It's the alternate ending she promised him. There's nothing more she can give him. At last, she lets him go again.

She leans back and tries now to imagine herself from a distance. Behind her stands the forest and across the bay the limestone cliffs. Beyond these lies one of the largest freshwater lakes in the world. Eventually it connects with the St. Lawrence, that great river the Natives believed was the start of all life, flowing past them to the ocean.

It's going on early evening. The sun has begun to fade, leaving traces of pink on the underside of the clouds. In the top boughs of a locust tree, a squirrel chucks angrily; somewhere a bird calls out. Angela wanders over to the pond. Dead leaves cover the bottom where aquatic *hyphomycetes*, the tiny archangels of decomposition, attempt to take them down to their level, just another year's residue in the great reach of time. Before the wind ripples it, Angela thinks she catches the expression of a little girl in white, standing beside a tricycle and staring up at her from the invisible, alternate world that lies hidden just beneath the surface of this visible one.

All of a sudden — or maybe it's been coming on gradually for some time without her realizing it — Angela is aware of an unearthly sensation, something joyous and alive, stealing over her. This isn't me, she thinks. It isn't her, and yet it's inside of her. It seems to go on and on, as if she could stay like this forever, so long as she doesn't move. And suddenly it strikes her it's always been there, at every moment, and if she could only sit beneath the locust trees and stop and listen, she'll hear a heartbeat, a silent pulse running through the world. And in this silence, in this empty space, is a world where she can dangle her toes in a river, or climb a tree or whistle in the moonlight, if she wants to. In this world of great terror and irredeemable horror — and, sometimes, unsurpassable beauty — it's a kind of peace she feels. There's no other word for it. She has lived her entire life just to know it.

ACKNOWLEDGEMENTS

IN WRITING THIS BOOK, I have not attempted to explain the war in Bosnia. I have merely tried to imagine the conflict, for my own purposes, as an event that captured and held the world's attention from March 1992 through November 1995.

Although my brother Mark has suggested that the three sisters in this book are aspects of him, our brother Brian, and me, I cling to the irrational belief that the book's characters and experiences are largely fictional. Fictional inspiration notwithstanding, three texts were crucial to my understanding of the Former Yugoslavia, its history, and recent conflicts: *The Serbs* by Tim Judah, *Sarajevo Days, Sarajevo Nights* by Elma Softić as translated by Nada Conić, and the chapter on Bosnia in Leanne Olson's *A Cruel Paradise*. These authors experienced the war firsthand; I salute them for their insight and their bravery.

The writing of this particular book has been a tortuous process. I owe much to several diligent and obliging readers along the way: most recently, D. M. Thomas and Marc Côté, who helped me see the story with fresh eyes at crucial stages in its development; Shane McConnell and Margaret Hart, whose encouragement and support kept me on track in the interim;

and my most demanding critic, Dawn Rae Downton, who urged me to do better at every step. I can only hope I have kept that pledge. This book would be very different without each of them. I am honoured by their contributions.

Early readers John Davison and Scott Hall were helpful, as were B. Haagensen, with his explanations of chemical munitions; the late Joanne Kellock, who believed in this book; Enrique García Pereña, who lent his expert knowledge of Mexico; Elizabeth Ruth, who urged me to go deeper; Bill Hurley, who gave me Elma Softić's book; Richard Beurling, who generously shared tales of his brother George's achievements; Bill MacAdam, who sparked my interest in Malta; and Norah Toth, Natural Heritage Education Specialist with MacGregor Point Provincial Park, whose eloquent explanation of rock formations in the Bruce Peninsula was enlightening.

I also extend my gratitude to the crew at Cormorant Books. You've been a joy to work with. Special thanks to Angel Guerra for the beautiful cover art.

Financial assistance during the final stages was provided in the form of an Ontario Arts Council Works-in-Progress Grant, a scholarship from the Humber School for Writers, as well as grants offered through the Writers' Reserve Program, each of which allowed me the necessary time to write and research my subject, while giving me an invaluable opportunity to explore.

For all of the above, I am deeply grateful.

ENVIRONMENTAL BENEFITS STATEMENT

Cormorant Books saved the following resources by printing the pages of this book on chlorine free paper made with 100% post-consumer waste.

TREES	WATER	SOLID WASTE	GREENHOUSE GASES
19	8,755	532	1,818
FULLY GROWN	GALLONS	POUNDS	POUNDS

Calculations based on research by Environmental Defense and the Paper Task Force.
Manufactured at Friesens Corporation